Praise for *Hings* & Chris M

WINNER: Best Short Story C

'Scotland's next great writing talent…Chris McQueer is the next big hing.' – *Daily Record*

'True original…McQueer's tales offer a surreal, sometimes grotesque vision of the Glasgow schemes.' – *The Herald*

'Scotland's favourite short story revolutionary.' – *The Skinny*

'Chris McQueer will be a firm fixture in Scottish literature's top tier for years to come. Believe the hype.' – *Glasgow Live*

'Hilariously surreal snapshots of working class Scotland. Limmy meets Irvine Welsh.' – Ewan Denny, Link & Lorne

'It's clever, funny, irreverent and Scottish as fuck. I'm loving it!' – Joanna Bolouri, author of *The List*

"Properly, laugh-out-loud, funny…McQueer's voice is irrepressible and undeniable.…[He] is writing about people and places which are at the best marginalised, more often ignored. Chris McQueer may claim he's only having a laugh, but there's more going on here. Funny that." – *Scots Whay Hae*

'*Hings* more than lived up to the hype. Absolute belter of a book! Utterly hilarious and brilliantly mental.' – Martin Compston

'He gets it from me.' – Tracy McQueer

HINGS

SHORT STORIES 'N THAT

CHRIS
MCQUEER

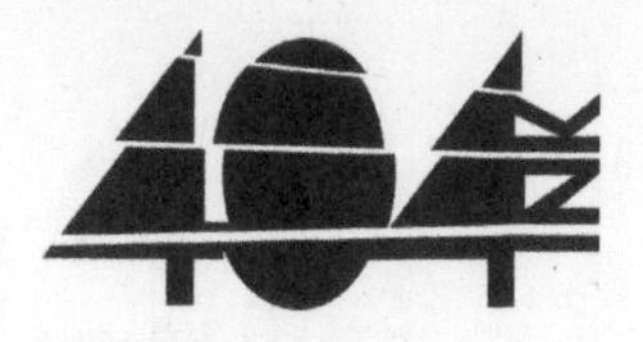

Published by 404 Ink
www.404ink.com
@404Ink

ISBN: 978-0-9956238-6-6
ebook: 978-0-9956238-7-3

Editor: Robbie Guillory
Cover: ELEMdesign

Printed and bound in Great Britain
by Clays Ltd, Elcograf S.p.A.

CONTENTS

Sammy's Bag of Whelks.. 1
Is it Art?.. 5
Top Boy.. 11
Pish the Bed 25
Alan's Shed... 31
Knees.. 41
Korma Police 47
Lads... 51
Offshore 59
Night Bus 69
Sammy's Da's Funeral.. 75
Shiftswap.. 79
Fitbaw 85
Bowls 93
A Fistful of Coppers 131
Scudbook 135
Posh Cunt... 147
Pat 153
The Dug... 165
Sammy's Mental Christmas............................... 171
Tourists.. 177
The Universe Factory...................................... 187
Davie 193
The Void.. 195
The Budgie 201

For Henry.

Miss you, Big Man.

SAMMY'S BAG OF WHELKS

Saturday efternin. 'Whelks... Mussels... Caaaandy aaaap-ppullls,' this cunt's shouting as ah watch him stoat through the scheme fae mah room windae, swinging his blue poly bag full ae goodies. Fuckin weird combo ae hings the cunt's sellin but who um ah tae question it? Anyway, ah check how much money ah've goat in mah poakit – a pound – an ah rush oot the door an chase efter him.

'Here, mate,' ah shout.

The cunt spins roon. 'Awrite, pal? Wit ye efter?'

'Wit cin ah get fur a pound?'

'Well,' he goes intae his bag, 'ye cin get a candy apple urr a bag ae whelks. Mussels are two pound ahm afraid.'

Candy apple or a bag ae whelks. Ah dae like candy apples but ah've never tried whelks.

'Wit dae whelks taste like?'

'They're nice. Salty.'

'Mah da likes whelks. He says they're nice anaw.'

'Well dae ye want a bag or no?'

'Aye, fuck it. Gies the whelks. Ah want tae try thum.' Ah gie the cunt a pound an he hawns me this wee bag ae the hings. The bag feels dead hoat. Ah open it an huv a look in. Hunners ae wee shells.

'Here, how dae ye eat thum?'

'Aw fuck, sorry pal. Ye'll need this,' the cunt hawns me a needle. 'Ye use the needle tae pick aff the wee eye at the opening, right? Then stab it intae the meat, twist an pull it oot.' Then he pats me oan the back an off he goes.

'Da, ah've bought us some whelks,' ah say, walking intae the living room.

'Aw, magic, Sammy,' he says. 'Ah've no hud whelks in years.' Ah hawn the bag tae mah da an he starts wiring right intae thum like he's no ate fur weeks. He's like a man possessed. He hawns me the bag back. Ahm curious as tae wit these hings taste like. They must be good if mah da likes thum – the cunt disnae like anyhin. Aw he eats normally is chips. He's never even hud a Chinese before an here he is getting tore intae a bag ae sea creatures. Fuckin weirdo. Anyway, time tae try wan ae these bastards. Ah take the needle aff mah da an pick aff the wee eye, just like the guy said tae me tae dae. Ah jab the needle intae the soft flesh an pull. The hing comes oot nae bother an it's jist sittin there oan the end ae the needle. It's a weird sortae beige colour, which ah wisnae expectin. It really disnae look too appealin. But, ah eat it anyway an FUCK ME, it's a taste sensation! Salty but no too salty, if ye get me. Jist nice. Tasty as fuck. Mah da finds another needle fae somewhere in the kitchen an the two ae us power through the bag while we watch the scores come in oan Sportscene. It's nice tae sit like this wi mah da, we never really spend much time thegither.

Ah wake up during the night. Ah check the time oan mah wee alarm cloak – 2 in the fuckin mornin. Mah belly's killin me an mah mooth's waterin like fuck. Ahm gonnae spew, ah cin tell. Ah get up ootae bed an double err in agony. The sick's comin oot soon an ahm wonderin if ah cin ah make it tae the toilet in time or no. Ah open mah room door an as soon as ah step fit err the threshold ah fuckin projectile vomit aw err the tap landin man, it even goes up the fuckin walls. But there's mare tae come – ah cin feel it. Ah take the stairs two at a time then when ah get tae the boattum ahm sick some mare. But ah've still goat mare jist fuckin waitin come pourin oot mah gub. Some sick comes up but ah manage tae contain in mah cheeks like a squirrel. Well, until jist before ah get tae the toilet an a wee bit leaps oot oantae mah maw's nice white tiled flair. Ah get the pan lid open joost in time as another wave comes. It hits the water wi some force man an ah even get a bit ae splashback. It's fuckin rotten. Pure fishy smellin. Efter a few dry boaks tae make sure ah've nuhin left ah head back tae bed. Troddin up the stair ah furget that ah wis sick oan the landin an ah step right fuckin in it. The vomit seeps through mah soak an ah feel like ahm gonnae be sick again man. Ah should've probably chapped mah maw an da's room door tae tell thum aboot the flood ae vomit awaiting thum jist ootside thur room incase they get up fur a pish an stawn in it like ah jist did but ah hink 'Fuck it,' an go back tae bed. Ah've no been sick like that before in mah life man, must've been they fuckin whelks. That's wit ah get fur tryin ae be nice an buy mah da a wee present – fuckin food poisoning. Ah get aw cosy back in bed an try tae resume mah dream where ah wis captain ae Celtic an jist aboot tae rifle a volley intae the tap coarner in the Champion's League final.

Jist as ahm startin tae drift aff, ah hear mah da getting oot ae bed an boakin like fuck. Weird how ye cin tell who it is dain wit in yer hoose int it? How ye cin even tell who it wis that farted jist by the tone an aw that. Anyway, ah get up tae warn mah da aboot the puddle ae sick at the tap ae the stair. As ah open mah room door he flies past me.

'Da, be careful ah wis-' **BANG BANG BANG**

Too late. Mah da slips in mah sick an goes heid over heels right doon the stairs an cracks his nut aff the skirtin board at the boattum, landin wi a splash in the other puddle ae vomit.

'FUCK SAKE, SAMMY!' he shouts up at me, getting tae his feet an running doon the hall intae toilet.

'Ahm sorry,' ah say, gawn doon the stair efter tae make sure he's awrite. An ah wis sorry, ah meant it. Ah watch mah da run intae the toilet an he slips in a wee bit ae sick and goes heid first intae the side ae the toilet pan. Wit a fuckin noise it made man. The pan pure smashed. Hink he died straight away.

When the ambulance came, the paramedic cunt asked me wit happened. Ah said tae um ah hink it wis food poisoning fae some dodgy whelks an if ah ever see the cunt that sold me thum again ahm gonnae kick his heid in fur making me sick an basically killin mah da.

Cannae believe it wis a bag ae whelks that killed mah da in the end an no the forty fags a day. Poor cunt. Wit a way tae go.

IS IT ART?

Crawford stood alone in the art gallery. It was a rainy Tuesday afternoon and he had the entire place to himself. Studying the scene in front of him, he stroked his beard. He allowed his mind to wander as he considered what the artist behind this piece could have been trying to convey. In front of him stood a concrete bollard. Resting on top of the bollard was a ball of multi-coloured wool. Crawford postulated that the wool perhaps represented the creatives of the world while the concrete stood as the uncultured proletariat. Perhaps, he thought, the whole thing was a scathing attack on the capitalist system. Or maybe it was…

Crawford's contemplation was disturbed by the presence of someone standing directly behind him, chewing loudly. The sound of lip smacking and heavy breathing filled the empty gallery. Crawford sighed, turning round to see who had ruined the ambience. He was met with the scornful gaze of a teenage boy, maybe about 15, holding a box of chicken nuggets.

'Wit's this aw aboot, mate?' the teenager asked him.

'Um, um, I'm sorry?' Crawford said. He always felt intimidated by the working class.

'That,' the teenager nodded at the concrete and wool exhibit in front of Crawford. 'Wit's it aw aboot?'

'Well, um, I think, in my opinion, it's ummmm…' Crawford stumbled over his words, he hadn't expected to be put on the spot like this. He didn't really know much about art. He just liked to kid on he did. It made him feel clever. Like when his pals spoke about Eastern European politics or something, he knew no one really had a clue what they were saying, they were just regurgitating facts they'd memorised from the paper in order to feel smart. 'I think what the artist is trying to portray here is the, um, class struggle as viewed by –'

Crawford was cut off as the box of mechanically-reclaimed chicken was thrust into his face. 'Ahm Deek, by the way,' announced the teenager, 'want a nugget?'

Crawford struggled to process what was going on. Sizing Deek up, he noted he looked like a caricature of a ned. He had a standard short back and sides haircut with the rest of his hair gelled forward. He was wearing a bright blue tracksuit, the joggies tucked into yellowy-white sports socks. Topping off the look was a pair of chunky red trainers.

Crawford declined Deek's offer of a nugget. 'Um, no thanks,' he said. 'I try not to eat junk food,'

'Suit yerself,' Deek said and ate the last one, dropping the empty box and wiping his hands on his tracksuit top. 'Wit is this meant tae be exactly, mate? You look smart. Wit is it? And wit's the deal wi your accent? Where ye fae?'

'Well, I suppose, technically, it's a sculpture or maybe it would be classed as an installation. And I'm from Hillhead, Byres Road actually.'

'Hmmm,' Deek mused, stroking his own bum bluff covered chin. 'Is it art though?'

Crawford snorted. 'Of course it's art.'

Deek walked around the concrete bollard, rubbing his greasy hands on his tracksuit top. 'Is it though? Ah mean, don't get me wrang, ah don't know much aboot art. Ahm just here incase anycunt catches me doggin school, but it disnae look like art tae me.'

'Just because it doesn't conform to normal artistic styles it doesn't mean it's not art.'

'Dunno man. Bein honest, ah hink it's a bit shite.'

Deek shrugged and turned his back on Crawford and made his way to another gallery. Crawford shook his head. He went to join Deek in the other gallery, leaving the empty chicken nugget box behind, he decided he was going to try and educate this lad.

In the next gallery, Deek stood watching a video on a giant screen. One by one, glass bottles of juice were dropped from a great height and onto a pristine white surface while a woman's voice recited the names of the different kinds of juice as the bottles smashed.

'Pineappleade. *Smash.* Limeade. *Smash.* Cream Soda. *Smash.* Lemonade. *Smash,*' and on she went.

'Here,' Deek motioned for Crawford to join him in front of the screen. 'Ye cannae say this is art, surely? That's just makin a fuckin mess.'

Crawford sneered at Deek's ignorance once again. 'The artist is obviously trying to get a point across,' he said. 'Maybe it's about the fragility of man's ego?'

Crawford turned to see Deek's bewildered face.

'Maybe the burd joost disnae like gless boattils ae ginger? This isnae art either.'

'Well what exactly would you class as art then, Deek?'

Deek looked deep in thought for a moment. 'Ah want tae see what else there is in here. Then ah'll show you wit art is, mate.'

'Okay,' Crawford said. 'It's a deal.'

Upstairs, they explored a gallery displaying a range of rubber fetish-wear. Gas masks, gimp suits and all manner of imposing black instruments adorned the walls. Crawford felt a bit uneasy about seen with a minor in this room so he tried to make this viewing a quick one.

'OOFT,' Deek announced, touching a shiny black gimp suit. 'Is this wit goths wear cutting aboot the hoose?'

Crawford rubbed the back of his head. Deek clocked his uneasiness straight away.

'You no intae this kind ae hing then, big man?'

'No, I can't say I've ever tried it.'

'Wit? Shagging?' Deek laughed, examining a huge double-ended dildo.

'No, I mean, just not, um, this kind of, um,' Deek burst into laughter.

'Ahm pullin yer pisser,' he said breezing past Crawford and out of the gallery. 'Moan, big man. This place is fuckin weird.'

Crawford found himself following Deek through the streets of Glasgow. 'Where are we going exactly?' He asked his new pal.

'We're gawn tae see some REAL art, mate.'

Deek took Crawford on the bus to Easterhouse. The furthest east Crawford had ventured before this trip was to the gentrified area of Dennistoun. This was an entirely different world to the one Crawford inhabited despite only being 20 minutes away from where he lived.

Hopping off at the shopping centre, Deek motioned for Crawford to follow him. They made their way to a pub where Deek stopped to talk to one of the many grim faces huddled outside.

'Da,' Deek said to a man who looked like a smaller, dehydrated version of himself. 'This is Crawford. Ahm gonnae show him mah art.'

'Fucking art,' Deek's da snorted. 'Should you no be in school?'

'It's an, eh, in-service day. Tell mah maw ah'll be in fur dinner, awrite?'

Deek's da blew smoke in Crawford's face. 'Nae bother.'

'Moan,' Deek motioned for Crawford to follow him again.

'What do you mean *your* art? You said to your dad you were going to show me *your* art.'

'Aye,' Deek said, 'exactly. Mah art. Ahm something of an artist maself.'

'No way? Really?'

'Aw aye. Ah'll show ye. Ah've goat a wee 'installation' as you might say roon fae mah hoose.'

Crawford and Deek stood in front of a dilapidated garage covered in graffiti. In amongst the various FUCK THE POLIS and hash leaf daubings, some more wholesome things were sprayed in pink paint on the wall.

LIVE, LAUGH AND LOVE said one, nestled beneath a crudely drawn dick. FOLLOW YOUR DREAMS said another. Crawford stood open-mouthed.

'Was this you?' he said, stunned.

'Aye,' Deek replied proudly, puffing out his chest. 'Ah like tae think ae maself as, like, a mare positive version ae that cunt Banksy.'

'This is beautiful, Deek. I mean the juxtaposition of the positivity of your messages and the language of the streets is just staggering. I love it. And this mural,' Crawford ran his hands over a painting of a young couple, both clad in Kappa gear from head to toe, 'is just stunning.' Crawford couldn't wait to tell his friends about Deek's work. 'Outisder art' he was sure they called this kind of thing. He imagined himself hosting an exhibition of Deek's work and being hailed as a hero for discovering this incredible new artist from the fringes of society. He wasn't usually one for thinking about money, but he could see himself now as Deek's agent, making them both an absolute fortune. Deek also had visions of making some money as watched Crawford bend over to inspect his work more closely; Deek noticed Crawford's wallet peeking out of his back pocket. It was too good an opportunity to resist. Deek grabbed the wallet out of Crawford's chino pocket and bolted away down the street. Crawford felt himself go red in the face and felt his now-empty back pocket with a shaking hand.

'Cheers, mate. You're the only person that likes it though. Everycunt else just hinks ahm weird. Especially mah da. He fucking *hates* it.'

'You're right ah fuckin hate it,' said a gravelly voice from behind Deek and Crawford. It was Deek's da.

'Your son has a real talent,' said Crawford, his voice quivering as he tried to defend Deek. 'And it's a shame you won't encourage him.'

Deek stood in silence.

'Know where he gets that talent fae, eh?' Deek's da pointed a finger at his own chest. 'Me – that's who. Ye know who ah um, mate?'

Crawford shook his head. He felt his mouth go dry as Deek's da took a step towards him. Even though he was a small man, he looked like he could fight like fuck.

'Ahm Banksy.'

At this, Crawford breathed a sigh of relief. This guy was obviously at the wind up.

'*You* are Banksy?'

'Ye fuckin deef as well as stupit? That's wit ah said.'

'Prove it,' Crawford said smugly.

'Just look right there,' Deek's da pointed to the mural. 'There's a wee signature ah added. It's in aw mah work. Just look, mate.'

Crawford went up to the wall and studied the mural.

'I can't see anything,' he said, squinting hard with his hands on his hips.

'Look closer,' Deek said, 'he's right.'

As Crawford bent over, inspecting the mural, Deek looked at his da. His da replied with a wink. Deek pulled Crawford's wallet quickly out of the back pocket of his chinos and sprinted down the street, laughing.

Crawford felt himself go red in the face and felt his now-empty back pocket with a shaking hand. He felt sick. Deek and his da had had made him look like a right tit.

'Fuck you and yer daft accent!' Deek's da shouted back at Crawford. He high-fived his son and they both headed back to the pub.

TOP BOY

Stevie sat alone in his BMW, staring at his house through the windscreen. Maybe tonight he would stay home and spend time with his family for a change. Then his phone buzzed. When he saw who it was from, he instantly decided he was going out again tonight. He picked it up and read the text from McGregor.

Come over pronto. Need to talk aboot plans fur bonny night.

He smiled. He was sure the gang had big plans. He got out the car and pulled his tie off from round his neck as he walked up the gravel driveway. He couldn't wait to get out of his suit.

'Awrite, hen,' he said, kissing his wife on the cheek. 'Need to run back out after dinner. Need to, eh, pick something up from the office.'

Heather eyed him suspiciously and then went back to leafing through her copy of *The Digger* magazine. She loved reading about all the petty criminal goings on in the east end; fights between rival scheme families, shoplifters and the odd person being falsely accused of being a paedo. She fucking loved it. But she couldn't focus on the words on the last page. She couldn't help wondering what Stevie was up to. He was acting very weird. Sneaking out of the house at night or coming home late from work, reeking of smoke. She knew he was up to no good. She didn't know what exactly and she wasn't sure she wanted to know. Not yet anyway.

'Aye, okay,' Heather said, trying not to sound disheartened. She hadn't seen much of Stevie recently. He was a pain in the arse when he was around but she missed him. Stevie went upstairs to change while Heather finished making the dinner.

He came back down wearing a pristine white Lacoste tracksuit. The fabric of the top stretching to accommodate his pot belly. Heather looked him up and down and burst out laughing. Stevie sat down at the dining table.

'What's with the trackie?' Heather laughed, setting down his plate in front of him.

'Aw, I'm, eh… going to the gym later,' Stevie spluttered.

'Thought you said you were heading to the office?'

'Aw aye, fuck. Eh, I'm going to the gym *after* the office. Aye that's it.'

'Well wherever you're going, you should probably get changed. A man of your age and,' she looked at Stevie's belly, '…build, shouldn't be wearing things like that.'

'Och what's the matter with it? My pals wear trackies like this.'

'Pals? As in plural? Your only pal is Brian and he only wears hillwalking gear?'

'Eh, aye, I know. I meant folk at the gym.'

They ate their dinner in silence while their three young kids nattered away to each other. Stevie realised he should have tried to sneakily change into his trackie before heading out. Or at least he could have told Heather he was going to the gym in the first place.

Looking at her husband in his ill-fitting, all-white tracksuit, Heather realised there was no chance he was cheating on her. This made her all the more intrigued as to what he was up to. Stevie made his excuses and left.

Half an hour later, Stevie pulled up in front of a grubby block of flats. He reached into his glovebox and pulled out an Aquascutum cap. He pulled it down on to his head as far as he could. Then he felt around blindly in the back seat for his matching scarf. He tied the scarf round his neck and pulled it up so it covered his mouth. Now he just looked like any other Glasgow ned and not Stevie Dunn, 42 year-old sales manager and father-of-three from Bothwell. It felt good to be out of his suit and into his trackie. This was who he really was. He got out of the car and walked up the path and pressed the buzzer.

Stevie walked up the stairs in the close. He ran his hand over the graffiti covered walls. He chapped three times on the door when he got to the top landing. Inside, Stevie collapsed on to a manky old cream couch. Detritus was strewn across the threadbare carpet—crisp packets, fag ends, empty bottles of cider and Mad Dog and crumbs of unknown origin. Stevie was immediately handed a bucket.

'Naw, I better not,' he said passing it back to wee Ronny sitting next to him, 'I'm driving.'

'Shitebag,' chirped McGregor, the de facto leader of the YSF— the Young Springboig Fleeto.

'Hawl, I'm no a shitebag. Don't call me that. I've got trainers aulder than you ya wee wank,' Stevie fired back. The rest of the gang laughed. McGregor smiled and mumbled something under his breath. Stevie was sure he'd just called him a dick. Stevie had a wee chuckle to himself.

This was where Stevie felt most comfortable. Here in this dark flat surrounded by teenage neds. He'd missed out on this kind of camaraderie growing up. He'd stayed away from gang fighting and despised neds as a boy. He'd eventually found the company he was after when he started working in sales. Every day he'd be around like-minded people, sharing jokes and swapping stories. Competing with each other. Stevie loved it. He'd eventually outgrown his first job however and moved on in search of more money. He got the money he craved but it came at a price. Stevie had described the new office he worked in as a 'patter vacuum' to the gang. After he'd taken his new job, Stevie lost contact with his old colleagues and his new ones weren't exactly welcoming. Stevie had been outperforming them all from the day he arrived and now, just four months later, he had been promoted to head of sales. They fucking hated him.

Stevie met the gang two months ago when they asked him

to buy drink for them. After a hard day's work in the land of no joy, Stevie stopped off at an off licence to buy a bottle of wine. McGregor and the rest of the Fleeto had approached him as he got out of his car and begged him to get them a couple of bottles of Bucky. He said no at first but then he remembered his own struggle to buy drink when he was underage. After some pleading from McGregor he reluctantly agreed. When he came back out of the shop with four bottles of Buckfast for the gang, he was heralded as a hero. Jokingly, they invited Stevie back to McGregor's maw's flat (McGregor had an empty as his maw was in jail) for a drink. Stevie thought, *Fuck it–why not?*

That night changed his life. He laughed, smoked hash and drank Buckfast for the first time in his life. He felt right at home. His only pal, Brian, just wanted to play golf or drink in old man's pubs. This was the life for him. If only Heather would understand.

'Right,' McGregor stood up and everyone looked his way. He had the aura of a true leader. Even Stevie found himself in awe at his charisma. 'Noo that the auld dick's finally decided to join us,' McGregor nodded at Stevie and everyone laughed once again, 'we can talk aboot wit wur dain fur bonny night.'

'Ma da can get us fireworks,' said Emma, McGregor's on again off again girlfriend. Just now they were very much 'on again'.

'Naw, naw, naw,' McGregor shook his head, 'nae fireworks. We should dae somethin bigger.'

'Like what?' Stevie ventured.

'Like a huge big fuck-off bonfire.'

'We've left it a bit late have we no? It's bonfire night on Saturday. How we gonnae get enough wid in two days?' said Ronny, the youngest of the gang. At just fourteen and painfully awkward, he was constantly the object of ridicule. He squirmed inside the humungous tracksuit his older brother had given him. He hated speaking up in front of people.

‘We’re no gonnae be traipsing aboot looking fur wid. We’re just gonnae steal somecunt else’s bonfire.’ McGregor looked around the living room at the adoring faces of the fleeto.

‘You’re aff yer nut,’ John said. The quiet man of the gang. Often the voice of reason.

‘Listen,’ McGregor sat back down and started rolling a joint. ‘This will be a piece a piss. Ma big cousin stays in the flats on Old Shettleston Road, right? Just down fae Tesco. He says the Shettleston Tigers are hiding their bonny wid round his back. He’s sent me a picture, look,’ McGregor held up his phone screen. Dozens of wooden pallets lay piled up against a row of wheely bins. Bits of plywood and MDF were scattered around as well. An impressive haul for a young team full of out and out morons, thought Stevie. He was very familiar with the Shettleston Tigers. He’d grown up in Shettleston and often found himself being chased by a group of neds after his football.

‘We’re gonnae steal this wid oan Friday night. Meet here at 8 o’clock and we’ll all dive doon. Maybe have a half bottle a tonic each to get us aw fired up. We’ll fire aw the wid intae wheely bins and drag them back along here.’ McGregor had it all figured out.

In work the next day, the raid was all Stevie could think about. He sat at his desk and stared into space. This was the most exciting thing he’d ever been a part of.

‘Stevie!’ barked Ian, Stevie’s boss, from across the office. He’d been watching him for the last twenty minutes. ‘Are you actually going to phone some clients today or just stare out the window?’

‘Aw, sorry, Ian. Sorry,’ Stevie fumbled for his phone handset and knocked it off his desk.

‘Mate, are you okay?’ Ian came striding over and placed a sympathetic hand on Stevie’s shoulder. Stevie shuddered at the man’s touch. He had huge, fat, pink hands which reminded Stevie of big chunks of ham. He imagined ham juice seeping through his white shirt. The rest of the office cast jealous glances Stevie's way. Getting that fabled touch on the shoulder from Ian was the sign that he liked you. The rest of them yearned for such approval. For Stevie, it was an invasion of his personal space. He hastily jerked his shoulder away.

'I'm fine, Ian. Sorry. I'll get back to work.'

'Aye, make sure you do. You haven't made any sales today and it's almost three o'clock,' Ian snapped his fingers, 'Let's make some money eh, mate?'

Later that night, Stevie once again changed into his trackie and slipped out of the house. This time he told Heather he was going to Brian's.

Heather text Brian just after Stevie left. Just to see what he'd say. She was positive he wasn't going to Brian's. *Can you ask Stevie if he has a key when he gets to yours? He's not answering his phone. Must still be driving,* she said. Brian replied instantly. *Nae bother*. Thick as thieves those two, Heather thought. Always covering for each other.

Stevie pulled up outside the flat at eight o'clock on the dot. The rain pelted down on the roof of the car. He looked through the passenger side window. McGregor and the rest of the gang spilled out of the close, bottles of Bucky in hand. Stevie got out of the car, turning up the collar of his trackie as if it would it somehow protect him from the downpour. The rest of the fleeto had on North Face and Berghaus jackets.

'Here, big man,' McGregor said, advancing on Stevie, 'this is fur you.' He screwed the lid off his dark green half bottle and went to pour it into Stevie's mouth. Stevie ducked and weaved out of the way. He brandished his car keys.

'I'm driving,' he announced.

'Shitebag,' was McGregor's response, the same as it was every time Stevie refused a drink, smoke or a line. John and

Ronnie huddled together, they were freezing despite their big jackets. McGregor put an arm around Emma.

The five of them walked to McGregor's cousin's house in Shettleston, hardly seeing a soul along the way. The rain made Stevie's trackie cling tight to his skin. Skulking through the close, McGregor text his cousin to get him to open the door to the back court. He came down and after exchanging a few quick pleasantries with McGregor, he unlocked the heavy door and pulled it open.

'Right, go. Quick,' he said. The gang immediately set to work. Ronny and John emptied out a couple of wheely bins, stuffing the black bags within them into other bins or flinging them over the fence and into the next close's midden. With five bins empty now, one for each of them, they all started to fire the wood into the bins. Stevie was significantly larger than everyone else so he was tasked with jumping on the pallets and breaking them into smaller chunks. With the bins filled they started to wheel them through the close.

Stevie had a quick scan round the back court before pushing his own bin through and joining the rest of the gang. He had the sense he was being watched. He was sure he could see curtains twitching. Maybe even the flash of a phone camera. He had a bad feeling about this raid. It was the single most daring thing he'd ever been a part of; stealing an entire bonfire from a young team. The adrenaline rush had worn off now, however, to be replaced by paranoia and dread. McGregor's cousin looked him up and down as Stevie walked by him in the close.

'Bit auld to be hanging about wi wee guys, are you no?' he sneered. Stevie ignored him.

Racing ahead of the rest of the gang, Stevie pulled his scarf up over his face.

'Stevie, slow down, eh?' Emma shouted after him, giggling. The rain was still battering down hard. Stevie ignored Emma and looked down at his feet. His brand new, all-white Air Max trainers were ruined. Covered in grass stains and scuffed from breaking the pallets apart. He stopped suddenly and turned to face the gang.

'What if someone sees us?' he asked, panicking. 'The noise from these bins will be drawing all sorts of attention.'

'It's awrite,' McGregor said, 'no cunt knows who we are or where we're fae. It's dark. It's hawf nine an it's pishing doon, naebody's aboot. We're nearly hame anyway.'

Stevie felt calmer after hearing McGregor's words. *That boy could go far in business,* he thought to himself. This was why McGregor was the so-called 'Top Boy'—calm and collected at all times. A leader of neds. The schemie Mussolini.

John patted Stevie on the back. 'We're nearly there, big man,' he said, 'we'll dump aw this round the park then head back to Danny's for a few cans and maybe a game a FIFA or something. Then we'll set the bonny up the morra night. It's all good.'

'Aye, you're right,' Stevie conceded, 'just me being my usual shitebag self, eh?'

The gang laughed.

'I need to be hame for midnight though. No later. Awrite?'

The next thing Stevie knew it was 6am and he was hoovering up lines of coke off a sleeping Ronny's freshly shaved head. He flopped back onto the grubby couch and checked his Breitling watch.

'FUCK,' he shouted, jumping back on to his feet. Stevie had to work every second Saturday. He tried to work whether or not that meant he was working today. He was. He started work in two hours and he was very much off his tits on gear and Bucky. The tinny, techno beat of DJ Badboy's classic *Friday Nite* pounded at his eardrums; it had been playing on a loop for three hours now. The nasal whine of the rapper made his eyeballs feel like they were vibrating. The rest of the gang had passed out long ago, Stevie was only now noticing.

DJ fuckin Badboy here, steamin as shite. Ahm boot ti tell you a story boot mah Friday night.

Stevie reckoned that must've been the millionth time he'd heard that lyric this evening. Time to leave. He grabbed his car keys from the coffee table and made his way out of the flat. The cold wind shocked him as he stepped out into the morning air. He got into his car and navigated his way out of the scheme. To get home he would have to cut through Shettleston. The very thought of this filled him with the fear. He wasn't afraid of the police stopping him—he was just scared of being seen by the Shettleston Tigers out looking for whoever stole their bonfire. DJ Badboy continued to provide words of encouragement as *Friday Nite* echoed through his mind.

Ahm a lightweight and I am stickin, bottle a beer and ahm oot ma chicken. DJ Badboy's got the baws a steel, off a bottle a Bucky and a fiver deal.

His heart raced. He started sweating despite the bitter cold. He rubbed his nose as the last of the coke slid down into the back of his mouth leaving a horrible, chemical taste.

Home, shower, get to work, head down, get out. Easy, he said over and over in his head. Trying to reassure himself the way McGregor would.

He stopped at a set of traffic lights. He tapped the steering wheel with his fingers, willing them to change to green. A group of three young guys, no older than 17, staggered out of a flat directly across from where Stevie was sitting in his car.

FUCKFUCKFUCKFUCKFUCKFUCKFUCKFUCKFUCK

In Stevie's drug and drink-addled mind, they were obviously looking for who stole the bonfire wood. They knew it was him and there would be a price on his head. They looked in his direction then, much to his relief, started walking down the street, away from Stevie. He put his foot down as the lights changed to green. He was home in record time.

He had an hour to get himself together before he left for work. He tried to calm down. He realised he could hardly remember the drive home; he was absolutely steaming. He looked down at his trackie top. A dark green stain covered most of the left side of his chest while a few holes that looked like burns had appeared around his belly. The cuffs were black with dirt. His joggies were covered in grass and other substances Stevie assumed had been picked up from the bogging couch in McGregor's flat. His trainers were ruined.

He opened the car door and had a quick look around for any rogue Shettleston Tigers on the prowl. The coast was clear. He sprinted up the drive, the gravel crunching loudly under his feet.

He unlocked the front door as quietly as he could. He'd noticed from outside that the bedroom light was off which meant Heather was still asleep. He skulked through the house, looking for his suit, tie and smart shoes for work. He pulled on his suit jacket on top of his trackie top. Stevie slid off his now stinking Air Max trainers and replaced them with his brown brogues. In his hurry to get back out of the house before Heather woke up, he didn't realise he still had on his white joggie bottoms.

On the drive to work, still drunk and feeling the effects of his excessive cocaine consumption, Stevie kept his head down low. He was convinced there was a hit out on him. He felt like Ray Liotta at the end of *Goodfellas.* It was a rush. He felt alive for the first time in decades. But he decided, after the bonfire that night, he would cut his ties with the Young Springboig Fleeto.

Heather woke up just after Stevie left for work. She felt around the empty space in the bed where Stevie should have been. She expected him to have snuck home during the night. She got up and went downstairs. She noticed Stevie's manky Air Max trainers sitting by the front door. Caked in mud, grass clinging to them and absolutely humming. She deduced that there was no way he was cheating on her, there was no way he was going to the gym and he definitely wasn't at Brian's. She shook her head and went through to the kitchen, wondering what the fuck her husband was up to. She pulled out her phone from the pocket of her housecoat. She had text Brian last night about 10pm to see if he would still be covering for Stevie. He said Stevie was there and just about to leave. She had then text Stevie who had said he would be leaving Brian's at 12am. Caught out a belter, she thought. She then did her usual morning check of The Digger's Facebook page:

Late night bonfire raid in Shettleston

A gang of youths rumoured to be from the notorious Young Springboig Fleeto last night completed a daring raid to steal the equally notorious Young Shettleston Tiger's bonfire wood. The five youths stole five wheely bin's worth of wood. These pictures were taken by a relative of one of the YSF gang members who said he was "ashamed to be related to a thief".

Heather stifled a laugh. She couldn't believe how different the world these people lived in was compared to hers. Her face fell when she zoomed in on one of the pictures.

One of the more chunky members of the gang, pictured here in the white Lacoste tracksuit is rumoured to be the leader or 'Top Boy'.

There was no denying who the big fat 'Top Boy' in the picture was—it was Stevie. He could try and hide his face with that ridiculous scarf all he wanted but there was no covering up that belly. It was unmistakably him. So this was what her husband had been sneaking out at night to do; hang around with a bunch of wee neds collecting bonfire wood. She burst into hysterical laughter, waking up the kids in the process, as she looked at her pathetic bastard of a husband in his sodden trackie. She saved the picture of him and decided she'd show him it later when he inevitably tried to lie about his whereabouts when he got in from work.

Stevie's car screeched to a halt in his designated parking space. He took a deep breath and opened the car door. He bolted from the car park and into the office, dodging his dour-faced colleagues. He felt they were all staring at him. Like they knew exactly what he had been up to. *Maybe they all hang about with young teams in their spare time too,* he thought. *Oh god, what if they're all secretly Young Shettleston Tigers.* Stevie started hyperventilating as he sat down at his desk. His phone rang immediately, causing his heart to almost burst through his chest. He let it ring. He was in no fit state to speak to anyone today. He checked the time. It was only 8:30am. The boss usually didn't turn up until after 12 so maybe he could make his excuses and leave early before the bastard appeared.

Stevie kept his head down until half eleven then left the office under the guise of a migraine. He text Heather apologising for not coming home the night before and saying he'd explain everything when he got in.

'Heather,' he said walking forlornly into the living room, 'I'm so sorry.'

Heather looked up from her phone, a wry smile spreading across her face.

'It's awrite,' she said, 'I know what you've been up to.'

'Listen, I'm no cheating on you if that's what you think.'

She shook her head and laughed.

'Obviously not. Look at you,' she nodded at Stevie's attire. Brown brogues, grass stained white joggies and navy blue suit jacket.

'Aw, fuck,' Stevie said looking down, noticing his white trackie bottoms for the first time.

Heather tapped on her phone a few times then flashed it in Stevie's face.

There he was. Dragging a wheely bin full of stolen bonfire wood with a group of neds.

Stevie's heart sank. He was so preoccupied with the thought of being caught by another gang that he forgot what would happen if anyone else found out he was hanging about with a group of neds.

'So,' Heather laughed, 'when and where is this bonfire?'

That night Heather and Stevie stood holding hands, looking into the flames of the stolen bonfire. The crackling of the wood as it split and burned was almost drowned out by the infernal squawking of ned laughter. Heather looked at her husband as he stood nodding in approval at the fire.

'I built that, you know,' he said, adjusting his tie.

'I can tell,' Heather laughed, 'It's fucking pathetic. Is that all the wood you could find?'

'Och, give me peace,' Stevie retorted, 'It's the best we could do.'

McGregor shouted over.

'Here, check wit a got yer weans tae dae.'

They looked over as their three kids waved their sparklers around, spelling out 'YSF'.

PISH THE BED

The four managing directors sat around the table in the boardroom. They exchanged nervous glances with each other. The CEO had called them into the meeting and hardly a word had been uttered since he'd broken the bad news. He paced around the room, sweat pissing out of him. The company was in a bad way. A very fucking bad way. They were about to go under unless they could come up with a plan.

'How about,' Sonia ventured, 'we do that marketing campaign from last year again? You know, the one where we told people you should buy a new mattress every eight years? We do it again. We say "Ground-breaking new research has shown you should replace your mattress every *four* years" or something.' She looked around the room. Her fellow directors were chewing on their pens, their nails or just staring into space. That plan wasn't going to work.

'What would happen then,' Arnold McVey, CEO of *Arnold's Mattress Emporiums,* said, 'would be that all the folk who bought a mattress last year would come back four years from now. That's no bloody good is it? We need punters through the door NOW.' He slammed a fist on the table. Everyone flinched.

The room fell silent. Just as everyone's heart rate returned to normal, the intercom buzzed loudly.

'Jesus Christ, Anne,' Arnold said down the line to the receptionist, 'You very near gave me a heart attack there. What is it?'

'There's someone here to see you,' Anne said. 'He says he has something you all need to see. Will I send him up?'

Arnold rolled his eyes and puffed out his cheeks. 'Why not, eh?' He put the phone down.

Thirty seconds later there was a knock at the door.

'Come in,' Arnold said, looking out the window forlornly. He didn't even turn round when he heard the door open.

In walked a skinny, spotty, teenage boy in a short sleeve shirt. The thin end of his tie hung well below the fat bit and was tucked in behind his Batman logo belt buckle. Under his arm was a flipchart and under the other was the stand for it. He pushed a blue poly bag full of bottles of juice along the carpet with his feet. Arnold turned round, looked him up and down then back out the window. He turned his gaze to the sky and muttered, 'Give me strength.'

'Hi everyone, I'm Evan.' He gave a meek wave. The directors looked at one another, trying to suppress their laughter.

'Evan,' Arnold boomed, 'We're in the middle of a very important meeting here, son. So if you wouldn't mind cutting to the chase, eh pal?'

'Eh, right,' Evan shuffled. It was obvious how nervous he was. 'Well, I'm told yous aren't doing too well as a company, am I right?'

The directors nodded.

'Well, I'm here to help,' he knelt down and produced a bottle from his poly bag, the Irn-Bru logo still visible beneath the hand drawn label Evan had applied to it. 'I present to you – *Mellow Yellow.*'

The directors all turned to look at Arnold. He was notoriously hard on people who he believed were wasting his time. Arnold took off his glasses and rubbed the bridge of his nose.

'This is all well and good, pal,' Arnold said, 'but we're a fucking mattress company. Why are you here? Is this a wind up?'

'Naw, naw, naw. I'm well aware this is a mattress company. It used to be the biggest and best in Scotland, I'm told. And I'm here to make a deal with you, Mr. McVey.' Evan set up his stand and flipchart proudly in front of the table of directors.

'Oh are you now?'

'Aye. You give me the two hundred grand I need to get this off the ground, plus ten percent from the sale of every mattress and your company will be back on top. I can guarantee it.'

Arnold was incensed with rage now at the young boy's cheek.

'How the fuck,' Arnold roared, 'are bottles of bloody juice, which looks like PISH by the way, going to save my company?!'

'Because this juice makes you pish the bed,' Evan said with a smile. He was growing in confidence now.

'I've never heard so much bloody nonsense in all of my life. Get out!' Arnold started to walk towards Evan but Sonia got up and pulled him back by the arm.

'This could work,' she said, 'let him finish. Sit down for a minute, Arnold. Calm down.' Arnold was blue in the face. Getting as angry as he was now often got him into a state. He was grossly overweight.

'Right, as I was saying' Evan put a bottle of Mellow Yellow in front of each person sitting round the table, 'this juice helps put you to sleep. It's essentially the opposite of an energy drink. Eh, I wouldn't drink that just now, mate,' he nodded at one of the directors who had just screwed the lid off a bottle and was holding it to his lips.

Arnold looked around at his directors. They were hanging on Evan's every word.

'Have you all lost your fucking minds? Look, pal, you're no getting two hundred grand off me and that's that.' Arnold was shaking with rage. He was practically vibrating as he tried to control himself.

'Let me explain,' Evan said, opening up his flipchart. 'You pump money into Mellow Yellow. We market it as a sleeping aid. Fucking everybody struggles to sleep at night nowadays, right?'

'Oh my god. *I* struggle to sleep at night!' said Sonia.

'Exactly. People will go daft for it. Imagine a drink that helps you get a good night's sleep that isn't that bogging Horlicks shite? We'll sell millions of litres of the stuff every week!' Evan turned the page over again.

'And this is where you come in. The drink is full of Valerian root extract. It's a natural sedative. It's used to treat insomniacs and people with anxiety. But it has one major side effect,' Evan turned the page once again.

'It's a diuretic,' Evan looked around the room. Blank faces. 'Basically, it makes you pee,' he said. They all nodded. Evan's flipchart showed a crude drawing of a stick figure lying on a bed. Surrounded by a big yellow stain. There was a price tag attached to the mattress saying £300. Evan flipped the page again. The stick figure was in a mattress shop now. He was handing over another £300 for a new mattress. Then on the next page he had pished that one as well.

'Customers buy a new mattress. Your salespeople recommend they buy some Mellow Yellow on the way home. The poor bastards do as they're told. They go home expecting the best sleep ever. They get it. But when they wake up they're lying in a pool of their own pish. Mattress ruined. They need a new one. Boom. There's another three hundred quid in your tills,' Evan stood with his chest puffed out.

Arnold nodded at him.

'This is all well and good. In theory,' Arnold said, 'but what happens when people start realising that drinking Mellow Yellow makes you pish yerself? People talk, Evan.'

'Let me put it this way,' Evan replied, 'would anyone here tell another living soul if you pished the bed?'

Everyone in the room shook their heads.

'You, my boy,' Arnold said, getting to his feet, 'have just saved this company.' He shook Evan's hand.

'Two hundred grand? I'm going to write you a cheque for three. You make sure this stuff becomes the most potent bed-wetting formula ever and we'll take care of the marketing and everything else.'

In the months that followed, Arnold's mattress Emporium

recorded their best sales figures ever. Arnold bought the rights to Mellow Yellow from Evan for several million pounds and started selling it all over the world. He almost became a billionaire.

Almost.

He got greedy. He upped the dosage of Valerian in the drink and soon people were pishing themselves constantly. After a government inquiry into what was dubbed 'Peegate', Arnold was fined hundreds of millions of pounds and jailed for fifteen years.

A year down the line and Evan was floating on a lilo in his pool, the water lapping gently at his toes. He'd paid for it to be dyed yellow as an homage to how he had made his fortune.

ALAN'S SHED

Alan took a step back and admired his work. His new shed was a thing of beauty. It was the entire width of his garden and eight-foot-tall. He was particularly chuffed with the bar he'd installed. Plenty of room for a pool table as well, he thought. He wanted to spend some time in his new shed, get to know it a bit better—run his hands along the wooden slats of the walls. God, the very thought of it made him giddy. He had the rest of the week off work and he planned to spend the majority of it in his shed. But for now, it was time for bed—Alan was gubbed.

He stood at his bedroom window and stared at his creation. He'd built it himself with materials he had 'acquired' from his work.

'It's a belter, eh, hen?' Alan said to his wife, Mary.

'Mmm-hmmm,' Mary said, glancing out the window. She didn't seem impressed. The sound of Alan hammering and sawing and fucking drilling all day long had nearly driven her to murder. The two of them climbed into bed, shattered from the day's events; Alan from building his dream shed and Mary from listening to him.

Around 2:00am, Alan woke up to the sound of old guys singing. He sat up in bed and listened intently. He heard laughter and shuffling footsteps. There was a bowling club just round the corner. Aye, that's where the noise is coming from, he thought. The auld boys must be having a late wan, good on them. Alan fell back asleep with a smile on his face.

The next morning, Alan couldn't wait to get out to his shed. He stood with one hand leaning on the kitchen worktop with the other shoveling Weetabix into his mouth, staring out at his masterpiece. He noticed something on the ground around the shed. Fag ends? And… was that a pint glass he could see inside? Surely not. He flung the bowl in the sink, fired on his crocs and bolted down the garden to the shed.

There was a pile of fag ends sitting in the grass. Alan opened the shed door. There was indeed a pint glass inside the shed. Many pint glasses. A deck of cards lay on the wee table and a puggy machine now stood in the corner. Alan made his way over to the alcove where he kept his tools. He poked his head round to check they were still there since the shed had clearly been broken into. They were all there – lying behind a sleeping old guy in a bunnet. Alan hauled the old guy up to his feet by the collar of his jacket.

'Awrite, awrite, awrite. Ahm leavin the noo,' the old guy said.

'Aye, too fucking right ye ur,' Alan said, marching his geriatric lodger up the garden. Alan steered him into the house, through the kitchen and out into the hall. As he fumbled to find the key for the front door, Mary came downstairs to see her husband grappling with an old man.

'Who the fuck's that?' she said.

'Mah name's Fergus,' he said to Mary, 'an ah wis just leavin.' He finally pulled free of Alan. 'Ye don't have tae man-handle me, son.'

Alan was raging. 'Wit were ye dain in mah shed, eh? This is private property ya daft auld bastard.'

'It wis pensioner's night. It was quiet, seeing as it was the first time it's been oan in there, ye know? But we had a rare wee night.'

Mary and Alan looked at each other and agreed, without a word being spoken, that auld Fergus was doolally. Alan finally found the front door key and sent Fergus on his way. They watched as he stoated along the path, bouncing off the hedges and then away down the street.

Alan spent the rest of the day cleaning the shed, he brushed up the fag ends and mopped the floor. Behind Alan's bar, beer pumps had appeared and the mini fridge was fully stocked with cans of lager. Dozens of pint glasses were lined up under the bar, ready for use. Alan wondered what the fuck was happening. There was even a till. He quite liked the puggy machine though – that could stay.

That evening, Alan fished around in the cupboard under the sink in the kitchen and found a big belter of a padlock. He secured it on the shed door, locked it and went to bed. *That'll keep that daft auld bastard oot,* he thought.

2:00am. Alan awoke to the sound of laughter and pop music floating in through his window.

'Mary,' he said, gently rousing his wife from her slumber.

'Wit is it?' she said, rubbing her eyes.

'You hear that?'

'Aye, sounds like somebody's oot the back. It's no that old guy again, is it?'

Alan peeked out from behind the curtains. Four teenagers milled around outside the shed, smoking. A man, almost the same height as the shed and dressed in black, stood in front of the door with a clipboard. The four teenagers stubbed out their cigarettes and went into the shed. The man with the clipboard gave them a curt nod. Alan fumbled around in the dark for his slippers and housecoat.

'Wit's happenin?' Mary asked him.

'There's people in the shed again, look,' Alan told her. Mary rubbed the sleep out of her eyes, got up and looked out the window.

'Is that a… is that a bouncer?'

Alan raced down the stair and out into the garden, his housecoat billowing behind him.

'HAWL,' he shouted to the bouncer, 'WIT YE DAIN IN MAH SHED?'

The bouncer didn't even glance up from his clipboard. Alan was incensed. He advanced towards the bouncer, shaking with rage. 'How dare these cunts use mah shed,' he muttered to himself. Alan was toe-to-toe with the clipboard-wielding bouncer. He looked at Alan and rolled his eyes.

'Sorry mate. Thursday night is student night,' his eyes returned to his clipboard.

'This is private property, and this,' Alan gestured wildly with his hands, 'IS MAH BASTARDIN SHED.'

'Look pal, yer no gettin in—yer too auld, beat it.'

Alan looked in the shed window. Lights flashed and students danced around. They spilled their drinks all over Alan's freshly mopped floor.

'Ahm phonin the polis. You're trespassing.'

'Ah'll be phonin the polis oan you if ye don't fuck off, mate,' the bouncer took a step towards Alan. He shat it and ran in the house.

Alan phoned the police and ten minutes later the doorbell rang. He opened the door and ushered the two officers through to the kitchen. He pointed out the window, 'Look,' he said, 'they're using mah shed as a nightclub or somethin.'

'I'm assuming you have planning permission for that shed, sir?' the male police officer asked as the female officer went out to investigate. She conversed with the bouncer who disappeared inside the shed and returned with a piece of paper. She took it from him, smiled and re-joined Alan and her colleague in the kitchen. 'Aye, course ah've got plannin permission. They bastards on the other hand,' Alan pointed out the window, 'don't have mah permission to be in mah bloody shed.'

'Well, according to this, it's a fully licensed premise. They've more right to be there than you do, actually,' the female police officer said. She put the piece of paper on the kitchen worktop for Alan to read. 'Well, if that's all, we'll be on our way then,' the two officers left the kitchen and let themselves out. Alan picked up the piece of paper and read through it. His shed was officially a nightclub imaginatively named *Alan's Shed.* Alan went back to bed and fell asleep to the sound of gimpy teenagers chanting the Yaya/Kolo Toure song.

Alan and Mary woke up late the next morning. Footsteps and banging noises came from down the stair. They went down to find a fleet of guys hauling DJ equipment, lights, speakers and crates of alcohol through their house and out into the shed.

'Wit is gawn oan noo?' Alan groaned. One of the workers explained to Alan that Friday night was techno night in *Alan's Shed*. 'Fur the love ae god, this is mah hoose, mah shed, how can this be allowed?'

'Look, mate, don't be a dick. We're just doing our job,' the worker said.

Alan thought, *fuck this for a carry oan*, and decided to go for a walk. Having old guys, arsehole bouncers and obnoxious students making his nice new shed into a nightclub was no way to be spending his week off work. And now this, a fucking techno night. When was this nightmare going to end? A poster was stuck to his front door:

Hullabaloo @ Alan's Shed.
This Friday
Filthy Techno Beats
£5

He went to the shop to get a carry out. Alan's plan was to get steaming and pass out so he wouldn't have to listen to said 'filthy techno beats'. Twenty-four cans of Stella—that should be enough, he thought.

He was woken at 1am by a pounding bassline. He had somehow managed to drag himself up to bed in his drunken stupor, he was impressed with himself. He looked out the bedroom window; strobe lights flashed inside the shed, smokers stood in a wee roped off area and there was a queue of people waiting to get in, snaking all the way up the garden to the back door of the house.

'Have you seen this, Mary? Wit a bloody nuisance,' Alan

turned round to see if Mary was awake. She wasn't in bed. He looked out at the shed again. He could swear he could see her curly hair bouncing about through the shed window. He found himself nodding along to the beat of the music. He looked at what the trendy young techno crowd was wearing; it was a sea of vintage Adidas and Tommy Hilfiger gear. The same kind of thing he had worn in the late 80s when he would sit in grubby flats with his pals, listening to The Stone Roses, smoking hash and gubbing valium. Those were the days.

Alan pulled on his good sannies and decided he was going out. He went out the back door and started queueing to get into his own shed.

'That's such a cool vintage Slazenger polo, man,' a guy in tartan trousers and Doc Martens said to Alan.

'This?' he replied, looking down at his polo shirt as it stretched over his belly, 'Wis only four quid or somethin.'

The bouncer from the night before eyeballed Alan as he got closer and closer to the front of the queue. Alan wondered just how many people could fit in the shed.

'Think your missus is in here, auld yin,' the bouncer said, taking a crumpled fiver off Alan and putting it in his jacket pocket. The heat hit Alan as he entered the shed. Then came the bass. He could feel it thumping at his chest so hard he thought his ribs were going to crack. The shed was unrecognisable now; the bar had been extended to run the entire width of the rear wall with four staff serving drinks behind it, a DJ booth sat to the right-hand side with two guys providing the tunes and two portaloos stood to Alan's left. He found himself nodding in approval. The shed was packed and the crowd were going mental. Alan couldn't help but start to dance.

A hand clasped Alan's shoulder, he spun round to see Mary. Her jaw was swinging.

'You awrite, hen?' Alan said to her

'Fuckin magic,' she took Alan's hand and placed something

into it. She clasped his hand closed into a fist, 'get that doon ye.'

Alan opened his hand up, it was an ecstasy pill, pressed into the shape of a gorilla's head. 'Mary, we've no took these fur twenty year!' he shouted into her ear. 'Wit's it meant to be? A gorilla?'

'Some lassie sold me two ae them, it's that gorilla that got shot apparently. Harambe or somethin...'

Alan shrugged and swallowed the bitter pill.

'Tenner each, they were! Can ye believe the price ae drugs these days?' Mary laughed in his ear.

Alan felt the effects of the Harambe eccie after only a minute or so. It started with a tingle in his feet and blossomed into a furnace of love and happiness that coursed through his entire body. For the first time in years, Alan felt fucking fantastic.

Mary and Alan raved their pan in until shutting time. As the music cut off and the lights came on, the two of them were nowhere near ready for the party to end. They listened to the chatter of the rest of the revellers.

'Any cunt managed to find a gaff?'

'Naw, nae joy.'

'I've tried phoning my pal but she's no answering.'

'I can't have people back to mine. If I get another complaint off my neighbours, my maw says she'll take me to court. Again.'

Alan and Mary looked at each other and smiled.

'Everybody,' Alan shouted as they filed out of the shed, 'back tae oors.'

As if everyone was linked telepathically, a shout of YAAAAASSSSS went up and Alan and Mary were hailed as heroes. People poured into their house. There must have been at least twenty people in the living room alone with more in the hall and up the stairs. Alan plugged in his old hi-fi for the first time in years and fired on some Iggy Pop. Him and Mary raided their cupboards for any drink they could find. Bottles of whisky and half-bottles of vodka were distributed among their guests. Mary sat on the couch between two lassies who told her they were studying at Glasgow School of Art.

'Ah wis gonnae be an artist, ye know,' Mary told them, draining the last of a bottle of whisky, 'and Alan wis gonnae be a singer, can ye believe that? We were gonnae fuck off tae America...'

'What happened then? How come you two are still here in Glasgow?'

'Life, hen. Life happened. An it'll happen tae you as well if yer no careful.' After plunging them both deep into existential crises, Mary fell asleep.

Alan was with the two DJs, showing off his CD collection.

'Tell me yeez have heard ae this wan,' Alan said holding up a copy of *Right on!* by Silicone Soul, 'It only came oot a couple ae year ago.' One of the DJs took it from Alan.

'Couple of years ago? This came out in the year 2000,' The peroxide blonde DJ laughed.

'Aye, exactly. That's why ah said "a couple a year ago".'

'Mate, that was seventeen year ago. I was seven,' said the taller, lankier DJ.

'Fuckin hell, boys. Ah never realised how auld ah actually wis til ah started talkin tae yous...'

Dealing with an existential crisis of his own now, Alan went and sat out the back. The sun was just coming up now and there was a pleasant warmth to the late summer air but Alan felt cold. 'The eccies might be better than they were twenty year ago, but the comedowns certainly urnae,' he said to a dread-locked lassie as she silently puffed on the last of her fag. She stubbed it out on the ground and went back inside, ignoring Alan. He walked down the garden, drinking in the sight of his masterpiece as first light washed over it. He opened the door and went inside. He pulled a stool over from the corner and sat at the bar. He ran his hands along it and wondered just who the fuck decided to turn his shed into a nightclub anyway. He wanted to thank them. He leaned forward, put his head down on the sticky wooden surface, closed his eyes and fell asleep.

THUD

Alan woke up on the floor of his shed. Sunlight was streaming in the windows now. It hurt his eyes. He squinted and looked around. The place was empty. No bar. No DJ booth. No portaloos. No strobe lights. Nothing. The shed was empty. He got up and rubbed his forehead. He'd skelped it a belter. Must have fell aff the bar stool, he thought. He looked around for it—it was gone as well. Alan went outside and recoiled from the midday sun. He turned round to close the shed door and found a note nailed to it:

The management and staff would like to thank every single punter who came to Alan's Shed over the last three nights.

Here for a good time, no a long time.

Until next time x

KNEES

Glasgow, Scotland–8:28am, GMT
Ryan, eyes half shut, checked the time on his phone. *Slept in for uni again, aw well.* He lifted one leg out from under the covers, he was feeling quite hot. But upon moving his leg he noticed something didn't feel right. It wasn't an unpleasant feeling but still a rather strange one. His legs were moving differently somehow. His knees felt odd. He reached a hand down to feel around, trying to figure out what was happening. *Cramp, probably. Naw, wait, it's no that.* He flexed his knees. They were bending the wrong way. *Wit the actual fuck?* Ryan flung the covers off the bed and looked at his legs. Everything was where it should be. No signs of injury – no cuts, bruises and no pain either. His legs were fine – his knees just bent backwards.

Ryan screamed. He screamed until his face turned blue. His maw came running in to his room.

'Has it happened to you tae, son?' she said with a smile on her face. Ryan looked at her in horror. She turned to the side.

'Look at this.' she said, bending her legs down as far she could. Laughing as she caught sight of herself in the mirror. 'This is mental.'

'This isnae funny, Ma. Wit we gonnae dae?' said Ryan.

'It's happened tae everybody apparently. Mon doon and watch the news. It's funny walking doon the stairs, try it.'

Ryan looked at his maw. He looked at her backwards facing knees. She looked like an ostrich, he thought. He looked down at his own misshapen legs. 'Am gawn back tae sleep, this is fucked up.'

London, England–10:51am, GMT

The Prime Minister paced up and down the lobby, he was finally getting the hang of walking in this new fashion and was starting to enjoy it. *Seems more efficient if you ask me.* He checked his watch – nine minutes until he addressed the nation. He read over the speech that had been handed to him by one of the few staff that had turned up for work that day. *Everyone please stay calm...we are investigating what has happened...why this has happened...similar reports coming in from across the globe...this is NOT the result of a terrorist attack...the finest minds in the world are working on a way to fix this...* He was to simply tell the public what they needed to hear.

People naturally migrated towards hospitals despite pleas from Prime Ministers, Presidents and various spokespeople not to. A&E wards in hospitals everywhere were queued out the door as people congregated outside demanding their knees be fixed. Fights broke out and even turned into riots in some places. Nobody had any idea why or how this had happened. Conspiracy websites popped up within hours blaming everything from chemtrails and genetically modified foods to terrorist groups and even aliens. The only thing people knew for certain was that it had happened to everyone at exactly the same time. At 7:00am GMT, a high pitched noise rang out across the globe and everyone's knees bent backwards. Nobody could drive, they simply couldn't fit into their vehicles. Emergency services were suspended, public transport ground to a halt. People couldn't even sit in chairs properly anymore. The world was in chaos

Texas, United States of America–6:09am (12:09pm GMT)

The floor of the trailer creaked and groaned under the weight of her considerable bulk as she rolled around in bed. Alma was the biggest and fattest woman in the trailer park and had been wheelchair bound, on account of her size, for the last three years. When she woke up that morning, at 6:00am like she always did, and hoisted her legs round into her wheelchair at the side of her bed, she found she could move a lot more easily. Her legs felt stronger, more powerful. Alma was confused by this feeling and tried to stand up. No problem. Her new knees bent backwards and her feet stuck out further forward, spreading her weight more evenly. 'Hot dang!' she exclaimed. Alma didn't care about this deformity she had woken up with – she had always been a freak. She padded through to her bathroom. Alma stood in the doorway, staring at the toilet, ready to perform her morning ablutions. 'Huh,' she said. Sitting on a toilet designed for people whose knees bent forward was going to be difficult. She regretted eating so much of that chilli last night. Alma hitched up her nightdress and tried squatting over the bowl and lowering herself down. No good – her massive legs couldn't fit in the gap between the toilet and the wall. She tried standing. The aim was all wrong. Shit would go everywhere. The noises coming from her stomach grew more ferocious. She was going to have to go outside. She waddled back out into the hallway and opened the door of the trailer. The smell of faeces filled the air.

'Morning, Alma!' shouted Mr. Grenville from across the yard, squatting like a dog as he shat on the ground.

Glasgow, Scotland–4:00pm GMT

Ryan, still in bed, flicked through Twitter –

@BannedAccount–You guys, with these new knees I'm even better at skateboarding

@DooferTheDragon–i pass my driving test then just 3 days later i am rendered physically unable to drive

*@CelticBhoy1888–Still can't believe R*ngers signed Joey Barton who suports Celtic lol*

@FudWedding–I KNEED to know how this has happened. Haha!

@Buzzfeed–As the rest of the world panics, Scottish people are having the time of their lives with their new backwards knees...

That's plenty.

Ryan looked under the duvet and flexed his knees. Still backwards. *Fuck sake man.* He hadn't tried walking yet but the sound of laughter from outside his room window made him curious. He flung the covers off once again and jumped out of bed. His knees crumpled backwards instantly as he landed and he hit his head on the floor. *Bastard.* He put his hands on the bed and pulled himself to his feet. He bounced on the spot a couple of times. He felt a strain on his abdominal muscles but apart from that felt lighter and more agile. *Gonnae have a six pack nae bother if ah stay like this.* He tried to jump as high as he could.

BANG

'AHHHHH FUCK, MAH HEID!'

He crawled back into bed. *Back tae sleep until aw this goes away.*

'Aaahhhhh ya daft bastard!' laughed his maw from downstairs.

London, England–6:59pm GMT

The Prime Minister was ready to go live on air and address the nation once again. The British public had, largely, refrained from the rioting and looting that had plagued many other nations and, despite a few isolated reports of fighting, the country was set to go back to business as usual the next day. He poured over his notes for his final speech of the day. *No answers as to why and how this has happened as yet...I'd like to commend you all for your exemplary behaviour during this strange time...emergency services will be up and running first thing in the morning...I urge you all to go to work as usual tomorrow...many doctors and scientists believe our new legs may well be more efficient than our old ones...new seating is being developed as we speak to adapt to our new knees...* He approached the podium.

'3... 2... 1...' said the cameraman.

'Good evening,' said the Prime Minister 'First of all, I would–'

The same high pitched noise that had been reported twelve hours ago rang out across the Earth. People dropped to the ground, their hands covering their ears. Instantly, everyone's knees went back to normal.

The Prime Minister flopped on the floor like a fish out of water. Realising the camera was still on him and still broadcasting to the world, and that the noise had stopped, he stood up and composed himself. He smoothed his hair back down and looked at his legs.

'Um… well… it appears that everything is now back to normal. I am looking around the room and, well, as you can all see and I'm sure have noticed that our knees have been… uh… fixed…'

Texas, United States of America–1:02pm (7:02pm GMT)
As the ringing noise died away, Alma tried to get back on her feet after collapsing in the dirt outside her trailer. She tried to stand up, as she had done earlier that morning, but she wasn't able to. She looked down at her legs. Back to normal. She called out to Mr. Grenville, as he stood up across from her.

'Could you fetch my wheelchair from my trailer please, mister?' said Alma.

She was heartbroken. Mr. Grenville wheeled her up the ramp and into her trailer. Alma went to bed and hoped when she woke up her knees would once again bend backwards.

Mr. Grenville looked at the toilet in his bathroom. He would continue to shit outside regardless.

Glasgow, Scotland–8:30pm GMT
Ryan was still in bed. He had slept right through the noise which had signalled the end of the backwards knees fiasco. His phone vibrated under his pillow, waking him up. He opened the message from his maw:

U back 2 normal as well?

He pulled his knees up to his chest then kicked off the

covers. *Thank fuck for that.* He clicked on the Twitter icon on his phone and refreshed his timeline.

@JadenSmith–How Can Our Knees Be Real If Our Eyes Aren't Real?

KORMA POLICE

Paul was choking for one last hit. He'd nearly been caught so many times before that he'd had to come off them completely. His hands shaking, he picked up the phone. His daughter, Hayley, knew exactly what he was doing.

'Da,' she begged, tears welling up in her eyes. 'No again. Please. You said you were aff them.'

'I know, hen, am sorry,' he replied, putting an arm around her. 'Just one last time. Then that'll be me. Nae mare kormas after this. I promise.'

Paul dialled the number for the Spice of Life Indian takeaway – the only place still willing to sell kormas to desperate punters.

'Home delivery please,' Paul said flatly. 'Thomson. 14 Kilnside Road. Vindaloo, extra hot please. Boiled rice and a plain naan. Aye am sure. It'll be awrite. I know, I didn't get it from yous if anyone asks. Cheers. Bye.'

Extra hot vindaloo with boiled rice and a plain naan was the code name for a chicken korma. You couldn't even say the word korma these days. It was dirty. Taboo. It started off with people just being laughed at but soon escalated into something more serious. Korma lovers were ostracised. Bullied for their love of the creamy curry. Then they became illegal. People were imprisoned under the so-called 'Spice Act 2018'. Bootleg kormas started doing the rounds. Passed about in secret between those who liked the milder things in life.

There was a chap at the door. Paul got up and looked through the spy hole. A tiny, frail looking Indian man in a baseball cap shuffled nervously on the doorstep. Paul opened the door slightly.

'Twenty pounds please, sir,' the man said.

'Wit? It was only a tenner last month?' Paul said indignantly.

'This is risky business my friend. We have to make it worth our while.'

Paul passed a twenty pound note to the man. The man looked at the money in his hand as if Paul had just deposited a humungous shite into his palm.

'Sorry,' Paul shrugged, 'I've nae change for a tip.'

The man handed Paul the blue poly bag and shook his head at Paul.

'Cheeky bastard,' Paul muttered as he closed the door.

Back in his car, the delivery driver dialled a number into his phone and held it to his ear.

'Yes, hello. I'd like to report a suspected korma eater. 14 Kilnside Road. Thank you. Bye.'

He hung up and drove off.

Paul poured the pale gold sauce on to the bed of rice. Steam wafted up his nose.

'Oh fucking YES,' he said. Hayley sat on the couch biting her nails as she watched him.

Paul could feel himself salivating as raised that first forkful to his gaping mouth.

BANG BANG BANG

Three loud chaps at the door.

Paul dropped the fork. He and Hayley looked at each other.

'KORMA POLICE. OPEN THE DOOR!' boomed a voice.

'Shit. Right, you open the door,' Paul said to Hayley, 'and I'll get rid of this.'

Before either them had even lifted their arses from their seats, the front door flew off its hinges and a team of police had their guns trained on Hayley and Paul.

'Don't move,' said one of the Korma Police, raising the visor on his helmet.

Paul looked at Hayley. Then to the policeman in front of him. Then down at his curry. Paul's eyes darted back to the policeman as he advanced on him, gun poised and ready to fire.

'Step away from the foul substance,' the Korma Police said.

Paul looked back down at his korma.

'It is NOT a foul substance!' he sobbed. 'It's the most delicious, perfect thing in the world. Try it and you'll see. You'll all see.'

'I will not be polluting my body with that FILTH,' barked the policeman, firing a round into Paul's plate. Korma sauce splattered everywhere. Paul licked some from his hands and the corners of his mouth.

'Is your sense of masculinity so fragile that you'd sit and burn the mouth off yourself with a vindaloo to prove you're some kind of hard man rather than enjoy this delicious taste sensation?' he asked.

The Korma Police all looked at each other. The leader nodded and advanced on Paul. Paul picked up his fork. The leader halted. Paul scraped some korma sauce up off the carpet with the fork.

'Sir, put down the fork,' the leader said, raising his gun to Paul once again.

Paul smiled at him. He raised the fork to his mouth, keeping eye contact with the leader of the Korma police the whole time.

'Sir, if you do not put down the fork we will be within our rights to use lethal force against you.'

Paul's tongue had barely made contact with the sauce when a bullet flew into his forehead, killing him instantly.

Hayley wailed in anguish.

'That's my da! You shot my da,' she sobbed. Two of the Korma Police ushered her away from the scene.

'Cover up this cunt's face,' the leader said with disdain to one of his subordinates. 'I don't want to look at him anymore.'

'Yes sir!' a young officer said, covering Paul's face with the now cold naan bread.

LADS

It was 9:00am. The lads had fallen asleep huddled between two bins behind Burger King after staggering out of a club, drunk and under the influence of several class A drugs. They had woken up in each other's arms. Aldo looked into Daryl's crusty eyes as he opened them slowly, his pupils constricted to pinholes compared to the giant dinner plates they had been just hours before.

'Wit the fuck, mate?' said Daryl as Aldo's face came into focus.

'We just feel asleep, man. Ah've been watchin ye. Makin sure yer awrite an that.' Aldo said, feeling a bit hurt by the tone of Daryl's voice. Daryl pushed Aldo off him and got to his feet.

'Think anycunt seen us?' asked Daryl.

'Naw, man,' Aldo replied. 'We're awrite, ah think.'

'Thank fuck, we're lyin here like a couple ae benders.'

The two of them made their way down the Ayia Napa strip back to their hotel in silence. Last night was the lads' first night out and they had overindulged big time. In between coke and ecstasy pills, which they had procured from a Cypriot man moments after stepping foot on the strip, they had downed shot after shot of sambuca and, as well as being hungover, they were coming down hard and fast.

'We really need to calm it doon a bit, mate. We've got four days left here and we're gonnae end up running oot ae money,' said Aldo. 'Or end up deid. Ah feel like ahm dyin after last night.'

'Fuck up,' said Daryl. 'We're here for a mad wan. It's the whole point ae comin. Don't pussy oot now, ya gimp.'

'Ahm no pussyin oot, mate. Ahm just sayin maybe we should ease aff oan the gear an the eccies an that. Ahm no used tae takin hunners ae stuff.'

'Well ye looked like ye were enjoyin yerself last night so we'll dae the same again the night.'

Back at the hotel the lads collapsed onto their respective single beds. The soft hum of the air conditioning soon lulled Daryl into a deep sleep while Aldo lay freezing as the drugs wore off. Even under the covers with his clothes on, Aldo couldn't get a heat into his body. He thought about turning off the air conditioning but that would cause Daryl to fly into one of his notorious temper tantrums. Aldo was shivering like a neurotic Chihuahua as his body fought to restore some internal order.

'Daryl,' Aldo whispered through chittering teeth. 'Daryl, mate, ahm freezing, ahm gonnae turn aff the air con.'

No reply.

'Daryl,' he tried a wee bit louder.

Daryl's light snoring continued, undisturbed by Aldo's attempts to rouse him.

He probably won't even notice if ah turn the air con aff, Aldo thought. The air conditioning switch was next to Daryl's bed. Aldo tip-toed around his sleeping pal, desperately hoping he wouldn't wake up. He moved the switch down to off as quietly as he could. As he crept by, Aldo could feel the warmth radiating out from under Daryl's sheets. The lure of it was too much to resist. Enough alcohol remained in Aldo's system for him to think that what he was about to do was a good idea. He slid a hand under the covers and let out a gasp at the heat within. He climbed in beside the catatonic Daryl. Instantly, Aldo felt his temperature start to return to normal. He put one arm around Daryl and brought his knees up to fit into the back of his friend's legs, spooning him. Clutching Daryl like a human hot water bottle, Aldo closed his eyes and drifted off with a smile on his face.

Not for long though. Daryl woke up after Aldo began snoring directly into his ear.

'GET FUCKING AFF ME!' Daryl screamed as he realised his mate had crawled into bed with him and was cradling him in his arms. Aldo woke up in a panic as Daryl hurled a size eleven flip flop at him.

'Mate, ah wis freezin. Ahm sorry,' said Aldo, deflecting the other flip flop away before it could hit his sunburnt forehead.

'WIT YE PLAYIN AT? GETTIN INTAE BED WI ME?' Daryl shouted, the veins in his neck bulging, signalling that he was in full-on tantrum mode. 'THAT'S TWICE IN A COUPLE AE OORS I'VE WOKE UP TAE YOU FUCKIN CUDDLIN ME. YE FANCY ME OR SOMETHIN? IS THAT IT?'

'Ah wis freezin, ah wis fucking shiverin. Ah had nae choice.'

'GET FUCKIN OOT YA FREAK!' Daryl grabbed Aldo by the collar of his '*Ayia, Ayia, Ayia fuckin Napa*' t-shirt and flung him out into the hall, slamming the door shut in his face.

No money. No phone. No room key. No reasoning with his raging pal, Aldo walked dejectedly along the strip in the midday sun. He made his way down to the beach. *Ah'll leave psycho alone for a couple of hours to calm down*, he thought. He sat in the sand and stared out into the water. He pulled his t-shirt up over his face and lay back. The soothing sound of the waves, the soft rabble of conversations in many languages and the early July heat enveloped Aldo and he fell asleep.

A soft kick to the ribs woke Aldo up several hours later. He pulled his t-shirt down from his face to see what was happening and found, occupying his entire field of vision, the chubby, smiling face of a sallow-skinned middle-aged man.

'Hello,' said the man.

'Eh… awrite, mate?' Replied Aldo.

The man produced an enormous bouquet of roses from behind his back.

'You want to buy rose?' The man asked.

Aldo stood up. The man looked him up and down and smiled. Intrigued by the intense friendliness emanating from the man, Aldo took a step back and sized him up.

'My name is Nicolae. How are you?' said the man.

He was the most beautiful thing Aldo had ever seen. His trepidation towards Nicolae melted away as he drank in the sight of him. The receeding hairline, the moustache, the brown leather jacket, the grey joggie bottoms, the Jesus sandals. Nicolae was everything Aldo never realised he was looking for.

'Ahm Aldo an ahm a lot better for seein you, big man,' Aldo extended a hand for Nicolae to shake.

It was love at first sight for them both.

Aldo and Nicolae spent hours drinking together in a quiet open-air cocktail bar. Nicolae's English wasn't brilliant, but they managed. Aldo spoke slowly and Nicolae listened intently.

'Excuse me, please. I have to use the bathroom,' said Nicolae.

'Aye, nae bother,' replied Aldo. Aldo sat alone and played with the miniature umbrella in his glass.

'There he is!' Came a jovial voice from across the road. It was Daryl. *Shit,* thought Aldo. Daryl swaggered in and stood at the table.

'Listen mate, ahm sorry aboot earlier. Ah've been lookin fur ye. Ah shouldnae have shouted at ye like that,' said Daryl. Aldo looked at Daryl's eyes. His pupils were canyons of blackness surrounded by a tiny rim of blue. He'd taken another pill.

'It's awrite, man. Listen, eh, ahm a bit busy the noo. Ah'll catch up wi ye later, right?'

'Wit? Moan oot wi me, ahm no kicking aboot Ayia Napa by maself.' His jaw was all over the place. Teeth clenched tight together between sentences.

'It's just, ahm, eh, kinda wi somebody the noo.'

Daryl clocked Nicolae's bouquet of unsold roses. 'Aaaah, ah see. Met a wee burd, eh? Tidy?'

'Somethin like that,' Aldo looked over his shoulder towards the toilet. No sign of Nicolae. If Daryl saw them together he wouldn't understand. Or would he? Daryl had clearly taken a pill after all and seemed to be in a good mood. *Fuck it,* Aldo thought.

'Mate, ahm, eh, wi a guy. His name's Nicolae,' said Aldo.

'HAHA! Fuck off. Ye oan a date wi this guy then?'

'Well… aye. Ah suppose ah um.'

'Wit? Since when were you gay? In fact, it disnae matter. You're mah boy. Mah mate. Ah don't care if ye like guys.' The serotonin flooding Daryl's brain was suppressing his usual homophobic nature.

'Wit? That's it? You don't care that ahm intae guys noo?'

'Course no! Who's the unlucky cunt then?'

'Here he comes the noo.'

Nicolae strolled over. His gut peeked out from underneath his washed-out polo shirt, jiggling as he walked. He caressed Aldo's face as he sat down.

'Who is your friend?' Nicolae asked Aldo.

'Nicolae, this is mah best mate Daryl. Daryl, this is Nicolae.'

Nicolae held out a hand for Daryl to shake. Daryl stood in silence. Rooted to the spot. He looked at Aldo. Then he looked at the sweating man sitting across from him. He looked at Aldo again and burst into laughter.

'He is a happy man,' said Nicolae.

'Mate!' Daryl said, doubling over and still howling with laughter. 'Mate, this cannae be real. You at the wind up?'

Aldo smiled and looked at Nicolae.

'Wit's so funny?' asked Aldo.

'Look at him!' said Daryl.

'Wit? He's stunning.'

'Mate, that's an actual auld guy!' After another five minutes of laughing, Daryl calmed down. Not quite sure if what he was seeing was real or just a hallucination caused by one of the pills he had taken. 'Right, anyway ahm fuckin droothin here,

wit you two loveburds wantin tae drink?'
A glorious night was had by the two Glaswegian teenagers and the middle-aged Romanian rose salesman. They downed lurid coloured shots, drank vodka that clawed their throats to shreds as it slid down and Daryl kept swallowing just enough eccies to keep his anti-gay vitriol submerged under a sea of good vibes. The three of them entered a Scottish-themed karaoke bar.

'This cunt botherin you two?' asked a man who Aldo assumed was the owner of the establishment. 'Cause if he is just let me know and he'll be oot oan his arse, awrite?'

'Dis it look like he's botherin us?' said Aldo, giving Nicolae's arse a cheeky squeeze. The owner gave them a disgusted look and returned to his spot behind the bar. Nicolae blushed.

'Know wit,' Aldo said, screwing his face up as he finished the last of his warm, flat pint. 'We should aw go up an sing.'

'Ahm gonnae rap Lose Yerself by Eminem,' said Daryl.

'Bit intense if ye ask me, but batter in,' said Aldo. 'Ahm gonnae sing a duet wi handsome face here.'

Nicolae smiled vacantly. He was having difficulty tuning in to the lads' accents but was having a great time regardless.

After watching a wild-eyed Daryl rap monotonously about his 'Maw's spaghetti' it was Aldo and Nicolae's turn to sing.

'...ISLANDS IN THE STREAM, THAT IS WIT WE URRR,' screeched Aldo, one arm around Nicolae. His pungent BO invaded Aldo's nostrils but to him it smelled like freshly-cut roses.

'...SAIL AWAY WI ME, TAE ANOTHER WORLD. AND WE RELY OAN EACH OTHER, AH-HAAA. FROM WAN LOVER TAE ANOTHER AH-HAAA.'

Aldo stared into Nicolae's eyes as the interlude faded out. Tears streamed down Nicolae's face. Aldo leaned in and kissed him. Their first kiss.

The bar went silent as the punters watched the incredible scene unfold before them.

'FUCKIN YES, BOAYS!' Daryl shouted, choked with emotion. No-one else shared Daryl's enthusiasm however. The owner stormed over, grabbed the two kissing men and shoved them through the crowd and out onto the bustling strip. Daryl had to be restrained by two baldy men, the colour of lobsters, as he tried to land a punch on the proprietor.

'Leave it, mate. It's awrite,' said Aldo as Daryl was pushed out next to them by the lobster-coloured men.

Emotionally drained after perhaps the most eventful day of their lives, the three lads arrived back at the hotel. Aldo and Daryl had only spent a grand total of six hours in their hotel room since arriving in Ayia Napa but it was already a tip. Even the ever-musky Nicolae was somewhat taken aback by the smell of the room.

'Know wit you two should dae,' slurred Daryl, 'go Facebook official. You got Facebook, big man?'

'Facebook? Yes, I have Facebook. Friend me,' Nicolae replied, winking at Daryl.

'You ready for that, Nicolae?' asked Aldo. 'We'll tell everybody aboot us?'

'Yes, yes, let's do it,' he said, rubbing Aldo's leg.

Aldo pulled out his phone, opened the Facebook app and typed in his new boyfriend's name. 'That you there, Nicolae?' he said, showing Nicolae his phone. On the screen was a picture of Nicolae on a moped. The visor of his helmet pulled down over his eyes and flashing a smile from beneath his moustache. Aldo added him and set about crafting the status which would announce their relationship to the world:

Came to Ayia Napa to get a buzz wi Daryl Maguire and here I am noo wi the love ae ma life Nicolae Popescu.

'In fact, here Daryl. Gonnae take a picture ae us two so I can put that up anaw?' said Aldo. No reply. 'Daryl?'

'Wit? Wit is it?' said a groggy Daryl. 'Ah fell asleep there sorry boays. Here, come we'll…' He drifted off again.

'Moan we'll get a selfie then,' Aldo said to Nicolae. The two of them stood in front of the mirror. Nicolae put a hairy arm around Aldo and planted a kiss on his cheek while Aldo took the picture.

'Very nice,' Nicolae said as Aldo showed him the photo. Aldo uploaded it and posted the status to Facebook.

The two of them climbed into bed. As Aldo turned off the lights, Daryl got out of his own bed and climbed in beside Aldo and Nicolae.

'Ahm, eh, a bit cauld,' said Daryl.

Aldo lay there in bed with his best pal and his new Romanian boyfriend in his arms. Moonlight danced in from the open window. Daryl on one side, Nicolae on the other. Aldo thought this was probably the most perfect moment of his life. He knew he should enjoy it while it lasted. The calm and serenity of this moment would evaporate into thin air when Daryl eventually woke up. Nicolae scratched his arse and let out a rapturous fart.

OFFSHORE

I had only been on the rigs for a wee while, maybe a couple of weeks, when I first saw the thing. I didn't tell any of my new colleagues what I'd seen as I could already tell they either didn't like me or thought I was a bit weird. Me and my pal, Craig, went through the application process together and ended up on the same rig. He got on with the guys straight away. A man's man. He has good opinions about football, he's good at pool, he's funny. He's basically everything I'm not. Not that I'm jealous or anything like that. I like being me. I like being odd. While Craig made new pals among the other workers, they all seemed to take an instant dislike to me and I was left to either hang about by myself or with the other weirdos. I opted to be alone most of the time. I didn't really mind it.

The first time I saw the thing was when I was up on this wee platform. On the opposite side of the rig from the canteen and the sleeping quarters, it was my own wee space. Nobody else ever went up there. I liked to look out towards where Aberdeen was, beyond the horizon, and imagine I was looking directly at my ma and da's house. Other times I would just stare down into the pitch black sea, watching the waves crash around the metal framework. It was hypnotic at times. That first night when I saw the thing, it was foggy and rainy, I remember that. Visibility was poor but I could definitely see something thrashing in the water directly below me. I only saw glimpses of the thing's shiny black skin that night. It seemed to be around the size of a person so my first thought was that it was one of my new colleagues who had somehow fallen overboard. I was panicking but I couldn't move. I continued watching then it stopped thrashing and started gliding through the blackness before disappearing.

I didn't tell anyone what I'd seen because I was afraid they'd think I was mental. Well, when I say I didn't tell *anyone* that's a lie. I told Craig. I had to tell somebody or else I'd have ended up blurting out in front of the entire canteen. It felt good getting it off my chest. Craig said I did the right thing by telling him and nobody else and that I was to keep it that way. It was probably just a big fish, he told me, nothing exciting.

I started going up to my platform every night after that for ten minutes before bed. Everyone else would sit with their faces in their phones, sliding their grimy fingers all around the screens. I didn't have a phone. I think that was one of the reasons they didn't like me; Because I didn't like staring at a device full of bad news for hours on end. A strange thing to dislike someone for, in my opinion. So when they all stopped talking and went into trances playing with their phones I'd nip up to my platform for a bit. I wanted to see the thing again. I had to get a good look at it to see what it was. I could tell I was about to start fixating on it at this point – I'm like that, I tend to get obsessed with things. I saw it for the second time about a week after the first. Not clearly though, just another few glimpses. I saw that its black skin was totally smooth, like a dolphin's, and that it had very human eyes. I can't be sure, but I think it was smiling at me as well.

The next evening, I went to the library we had on the rig and got a book about the fish and other creatures of the North Sea. After flicking through the book, I managed to convince myself that what I'd seen was a "Greenland shark" and I was finally able to relax. I read everything I could about them. They were fascinating.

Me and another roustabout (that was my job title on the rigs. I was really just a labourer) were unloading supplies. It was one of the older guys I was working with that day. John I think his name was. He wasn't saying much and I felt a bit awkward with the quietness so, armed with my new knowledge of Greenland sharks, I tried to strike up a conversation.

'Have you ever heard of Greenland sharks, John?'

'Naw, Mick,' he replied, not looking at me.

'Well,' I said, 'they live right around here and they can live for over five hundred years.'

'I feel like this conversation has lasted for over five hunner year,' he said to me.

Fine, I thought, *if he doesn't want to hear about the most interesting thing out here in the North Sea then it's his loss.*

I managed to stay off my platform for a few weeks until curiosity got the better of me. The clocks had just went forward and the nights seemed a wee bit lighter. I asked Craig to come up with me. He reluctantly agreed.

Up on the platform, we watched the sun set. I remember how red the sky was that night, it was amazing. Like the colour of Tizer. Craig had a pair of sunglasses on. He looked so cool.

'It was down there I seen it,' I said, pointing down into the water. Craig nodded and leaned over the railing. As he did his sunglasses fell off his face and down into the water.

'Bastard,' he shouted after them. 'They were ma good wans.' He stormed away in a huff. I felt a bit guilty that he'd lost his sunglasses. He wouldn't have come up here if I hadn't asked him to. I leaned my elbows on the railing and looked downwards again. The thing appeared after a couple of seconds. I could see now it definitely wasn't a Greenland shark. I don't think it was even a fish. The thing poked its face through the water and stared right at me. Well, I'm assuming it was staring straight at me – I couldn't tell as it was wearing Craig's sunglasses. It had a big bulbous nose which was stopping the sunglasses from slipping off its face. And it was grinning at me. It had these really white teeth that looked as if they could have come straight out of one of the Osmond's mouths. I stared back at the thing for a few moments until it raised a webbed hand at me and waved. I swear it said something in an Australian accent. I fainted on the spot, hitting my head on the metal floor of the platform.

I woke up in my bed with Craig and a nurse looking over me.

'It's awrite,' Craig said holding me down as I tried to sit up. 'You had a wee blackout or something. You're fine but, mate.'

'You've sustained a mild concussion,' the nurse said, writing down some notes. 'I'll speak to your shift manager and get you a couple of days off until you're fit to work again, okay?'

'That thing,' I said to Craig. He placed a finger on my lips.

'What thing?' the nurse asked.

'Aw, eh, he said "it stings", didn't ye, Mick?' he raised his eyebrows at me, I could tell he was begging me not to make a scene.

'Well you've got a wee cut, but nothing more. You'll be fine in a couple of days,' the nurse smiled and left the room.

'I saw the thing again, Craig, it wasn't a Greenland shark.'

'Mate, let it go. Cunts will think you're mental if you keep talking about it. Just pack it in, awrite?'

I chucked working on the rigs after that. For my own sanity more than anything else. Two months I lasted. To be fair, in that time I'd had two decent wages and they were sitting untouched in my bank account when I got home. My ma and da didn't seem surprised when I told them I'd quit. It was my fourth job in two years. I managed to land a job at an amusement park after a few weeks.

Despite being away from the rigs, the thing still occupied my mind. Some days it was all I could think about. I'd worked at this amusement park when I was seventeen and it was a bit weird going back more than ten years later. The park sat right on the beach. On my lunch breaks I'd go for a Burger King then sit on a wee wall looking out at the sea, just beyond the horizon was the rig I used to work on. I remember thinking surely the water here at the coast was too shallow for the thing to appear. Of course, I was wrong. I was sitting on my wall eating my chips one day when I saw it for the fourth time. It bobbed around in the water, lying on its back and still wearing Craig's sunglasses. It saw me, pushed the shades up onto its forehead and waved at me. My jaw almost hit the floor. I raised a hand to wave back and caught a glimpse of my watch. Shit, I thought, I was due back from my break. I looked around to see if anyone else was seeing what I was seeing, but no one was looking. As I walked away I allowed myself another look at the thing. I think I enjoy torturing myself to be honest, I'm very self-destructive. It tipped down its sunglasses and waved at me again.

'Mick,' my boss shouted from across the road, 'you're due back! Hurry up, eh?'

'I'm just coming,' I shouted back, not even turning round to look at my boss. The thing cupped its webbed hands to its mouth and shouted, 'Hooroo.' Even over the sound of the waves I could hear its thick, Australian accent. It disappeared under the water. The last I saw of it was its black tail slipping beneath the waves.

After that, I walked back into work and told my boss I was quitting. He begged me to stay, told me that no one else was as good as I was operating the dodgems. This was nice to hear but I had to get away from the North Sea.

I text Craig to tell him I was moving away from Aberdeen and was going to move to Glasgow. He said he was gutted but that it was a good excuse to have a 'piss up' as he put it, a sort of going away party for me. I'd never had a party in my honour before so this sounded like a good idea. My boss had managed to sort me out with a job in M&Ds theme park just outside Glasgow. I'd be operating the dodgems again and best of all I'd be well away from the North Sea and safely inland so there was no chance of seeing the thing again.

It was around 2:00am during my going away party. Craig had brought some guys I'd worked with on the rigs and had managed to convince the landlady to keep the pub open until after it was supposed to shut by showing her the amount of money in his wallet. I wasn't exactly thrilled to see the guys from the rigs again but it was nice of them to come I suppose. Anyway, they were annoying me. They'd been on their phones all night and I'd had enough of it. I left the pub without saying goodbye and decided to walk home. I'd had at least four pints and was feeling a bit funny. I staggered my way to my front door and was about to put my key in the lock when I felt some overriding urge. I wasn't ready to go home – I had something to do first.

I made my way to the beach. I had to see the thing one last time before I left Aberdeen for good.

I could see it bobbing in the water as soon as I stepped onto the sand, its black skin glistening under the moonlight.

'G'day,' it shouted.

'Hello,' I replied, walking towards it.

'Nice ta see ya again, mate.'

'Eh, you too,' I stood in the water up to my ankles and the thing swam over. It was still wearing Craig's sunglasses. It stood up on its tail, like I'd seen kangaroos do on the telly. It was around the same height as me and had a long, slender body. Totally and perfectly black. It extended a hand and I shook it. It was leathery and warm, if a bit wet.

'Been out for a few beers? Can smell it off ya from ere.'

'Yes, I have. It was my leaving party. Do you have a name?' I asked. I couldn't think of anything else to say.

'Ethan. Well, that's what they called me in the lab y'see. That and 'The Specimen' but I've always preferred Ethan.'

'In the lab? What do you mean?'

'I was created in a lab, mate. I'm a blobfish-human hybrid. First and only one of my kind, I'm told.'

Ethan bounced out of the water and flopped onto his belly. He dragged himself up the beach a few yards before turning onto his back and supporting himself with his elbows. He looked like he was sunbathing.

'I'm Mick,' I sat down next to my new pal. I wondered if I was imagining all this but all I'd had was four beers.

'Good ta finally be formally introduced, mate. That's a few times we've bumped into each other now, ain't it?'

'Aye, it is. What brings you to Aberdeen? Aren't you from Australia?'

'Incredible powers of observation there, mate. You obviously don't miss a trick. Yeah, that's roight. I'm making my way round the world. I've got nothing else ta do with me time, y'see.'

'Wow. That must be amazing. I've never even left Aberdeen. I'm moving to Glasgow though, so that should be good.' I looked out to sea.

'Glasgow? Never been there. Maybe I'll come down and pay ya a visit?'

I laughed. 'Maybe.'

'Listen,' Ethan said to me, in a more serious tone. 'I need some help.'

I nodded, showing him I wanted to help.

'What I need is a wheelchair. I don't have legs, as you can see, and I want to be able to explore land. The seas and oceans get a bit boring after you've seen everything. Mariana Trench? Overrated, mate, let me tell ya that. Been down there twice. Pitch black. Freezing cold. Fucking awful. Don't know what the big deal is with that fucking hole.'

I thought about where I could get a wheelchair. I realised I had no access to one. Well, apart from my mum's. But I couldn't give my mum's wheelchair to a weird sea creature called Ethan I'd just met could I? Course I could. I was drunk; everything seemed like a good idea right now.

'Wait there,' I said, 'I'll be back in a minute.' I ran home and got my mum's wheelchair from the kitchen, along with a panama hat that belonged to my dad and a big throw I could put over Ethan to disguise the fact he was a horrible half-human abomination, and wheeled it through the house. It seemed to bang off every object in the hall, the house phone fell off the wee table and clattered to the floor.

'Mick!?' My da shouted. 'Is that you?'

'Eh, aye. It's alright though. I just, em, fell.'

'FUCKING KEEP THE NOISE DOON, EH?!' my ma screamed.

'You okay, son?' my da said, trying to take the edge off my mum's outburst.

'Aye, I'm fine. I'm heading back out. I'll see you in the morning.' And with that, I left for the the beach, pushing an empty wheelchair through the streets of Aberdeen in the middle of the night.

Back at the beach, I struggled to get the wheelchair through the sand towards the sea.

'Ya beautiful bastard,' Ethan shouted, once again crawling out of the sea and belly-flopping onto the sand. 'Gimme a hand into it.'

This was a struggle.

'You can stay at mine tonight,' I said to Ethan, 'but you'll need to leave early tomorrow morning. My mum will go wild when she sees I've given away her wheelchair and I don't want you to be there when that happens. She might kill you.'

'Not a problem. She sounds like a roight fearsome Shiela, your mum.'

'You're right, she is, mate. Now put these on,' I put my dad's hat on Ethan and covered him up with the throw.

I pushed my half-human half-blobfish pal down the road back to mine. I prayed we wouldn't bump into Craig and the rest of the guys from the rigs but, obviously, with my luck, we did. Ethan saw them first.

'Who's this mob?' he said.

'Ah, fuck,' I replied. How was I going to explain this situation to them?

'Mick?' Craig shouted, approaching us fast. 'Mick, is that you? Who the fuck's this?'

I leaned down and whispered into Ethan's ear, (well, what I assumed was his ear. It was a hole in the side of his head. He told me when we got home it was actually a kind of blowhole.) 'Don't say anything at all. Even if they speak to you, just ignore them.'

Ethan nodded solemnly.

Craig and the rest of the guys surrounded us. Three of them sung some football chants and didn't seem to take any notice of Ethan and I but Craig and a guy I recognised called Clint both stared at what was sitting in the wheelchair. I was starting to sober up now and starting to panic as well.

'Who's this? Jesus Christ, what's *wrong* with him?' Craig asked, his face contorted with disgust.

'This is my uncle,' I said. 'He has a, eh, condition.' Ethan waved meekly. 'I have to get him home. I'll see you later. Thanks for tonight.' I said, then I ran all the way home.

When I woke up the next morning and saw the thing which I'd been seeing in the North Sea for the last few months lying asleep on my bedroom floor I freaked out. I screamed and threw my telly remote at it.

'What the fuck's the problem, you drongo?' Ethan deflected the remote with a flick of his webbed hands.

'WHAT'S THE PROBLEM?' I screamed. 'YOU'RE THE FUCKING PROBLEM. GET OUT OF MY ROOM. GET OUT OF MY FUCKING LIFE AND LEAVE ME ALONE!'

'Well, you'll need ta help me back to the sea. Then I'll be gone. Out of your hair forever. Sorry for bothering ya,' Ethan said, looking despondent. Through the haze of my hangover came the memory of speaking to him on the beach the night before. I felt bad for shouting at him.

'I'm sorry,' I said. 'This is just a very odd situation and one I could do without to be honest.'

'I understand,' Ethan patted me on the back. 'I'm sorry for

the hassle. I just thought we could be mates, y'know?'

He seemed to gather from my silence that wouldn't be the case.

'C'mon, my mum's still asleep.'

I wheeled him back to the beach. It was still early in the morning and we didn't see a single soul. I told Ethan to look after himself. He thanked me for giving him a night away from the sea for a change. We said our goodbyes and he disappeared beneath the waves.

That all happened around two years ago. Since then, I've been working with a group of gypsies who take their amusements all around Europe. They have a big wheel, snack bars and even dodgems. I've been all over the place, Spain, Turkey, Italy, Romania – you name it. It's been amazing. Just now we're in Vienna. The best thing about this is that Austria is landlocked so there's no chance of me seeing Ethan splashing around. In fact, I haven't seen him at all since I bid him farewell on that Sunday morning. It's been good – I have my sanity back. I still wonder if he was real or just a figment of my imagination. Just now I'm sitting in a wee café in Vienna. It's nice and quiet and I'm enjoying a cup of tea. There's a nice ambience in this place, I like it. The soft babble of the people of Vienna speaking whatever language it is they speak is very soothing for an uptight guy like myself. I sip my tea and lean back in my chair. I'm the closest to content I've been for years. Then I hear a very familiar, very Australian voice coming from behind me.

NIGHT BUS

Mel placed a crumpled tenner into the bus driver's hand. The driver just stared at her with zero emotion behind his eyes.

'It's eleven quid, pal,' he said. No emotion in his voice either. He might as well have been a robot.

Mel sighed and rummaged in her purse for a pound coin. She heard a muttered 'fuck sake' coming from one of the other passengers.

Don't look up. Don't aggravate anybody.

'Look, it was only a tenner the last time I got the bus home from Edinburgh,' she pleaded with the driver.

'Well, it's eleven quid noo. If you've no got another pound, get aff.'

She rifled through her bag.

There must be some loose change in here somewhere...

'Here, hen,' came a voice from behind her. The voice of an old Glaswegian guy. His vocal cords ravaged by years of smoking and drinking. The old guy gave her two 50p pieces and Mel dropped them into the driver's cold hand with aplomb.

'There,' she said to the driver, ripping her ticket from the printer as aggressively as she could.

'Ta,' she muttered to the old guy.

'Fucking weird cyborg bastard, eh?' The old guy laughed as he sat in front of Mel.

Mel gave him a smile and exhaled through her nose sharply. The universal sign for 'aye, your humorous remark is spot on but no further comment is required.'

The old guy tipped his bunnet and nodded at Mel. He turned round to face the front of the bus.

Behind Mel, a lassie, who couldn't have been any older than seventeen, tried to drop donner meat into her mouth. Her jaw swung left and right. Mel was sure she could hear her teeth grinding over the noise of the engine. The lassie dropped the questionable meat, aiming for her mouth but it landed back in its tray.

Mel checked her bag for her headphones.

Bastard.

She'd forgot to lift them.

She played with her phone. She considered playing her music out loud to drown out the sounds of the masticating lassie behind her and the wailing of the guy lying across the back seats. Even if she sat and played techno tunes, she still wouldn't be the most annoying person on this bus.

She cycled through her social media apps in the same order she always did – Twitter then Facebook then Instagram until there was nothing new for her to see, which didn't take long. It was the small hours of a Saturday morning; everyone was either asleep or steaming. She kept going through the apps until a wee warning notification popped up on her phone.

OMB of data left.

Fuck.

Now she was going to have to sit and look out the window like some kind of fucking freak.

The old guy turned round to face her, as if he'd been waiting for her to come off her phone.

'Ye intae Flat Earth Theory, pal?' he asked, taking a long draw on an electronic cigarette that Mel thought looked like a futuristic screwdriver. Or a space dildo perhaps.

She exhaled sharply through her nose again. She was very well-versed in Flat Earth Theory. She'd totally destroyed a guy who fervently believed in it at the house party she'd just left.

'Don't laugh, hen. Ye'd be surprised at how wrong yer perception ae hings can be.'

'So you think the Earth is flat?' Mel asked.

'Naw, naw, naw,' he puffed on his fag again and blew out a cloud of fruity-smelling vapour. 'Ah don't just *think* it – ah *know* it.'

'You're a fucking idiot then, mate.'

'Ah only need hawf an oor ae yer time tae prove it tae ye. If ye don't believe me efter that then fair enough. Ah'll no bother ye for the rest ae the journey.' The old guy held up his hands and cocked his head. Mel loved hearing mental bastards ramble on a lot of shite but this guy seemed relatively normal. He looked quite suave in his suit and black bunnet. Crevices criss-crossed his face. She couldn't tell if they were wrinkles or scars or both. He didn't smell of drink either and, after all, he had given her the quid she needed for her journey home. If it wasn't for him, she'd still be stranded in Edinburgh. She decided to give him a chance.

'Right,' she said, putting her phone into her bag, 'give me this theory then.'

The old guy took one last puff of his fag and tucked it into the inside pocket of his suit jacket. When he brought his hand back out, he was holding something else.

'This,' he said, 'is a map of the Earth, the *real* Earth, as seen from space.' He handed the folded-up map to Mel. She looked around to see if anyone else was listening to their conversation. She started to unfold the yellowing map but the old man snapped his fingers and told her to stop. She was sure she could smell something foul. Mel looked at the other travellers and wondered who the source was.

'Ye don't open that until you get aff this bus, awrite?' he said. 'First, ye need tae hear the story of how ah know aboot the true nature ae the Earth an how ah got that map.'

'I'm all ears,' Mel said, putting the map into her bag.

'Right, we're gawn back years here, hen, right? Ahm talkin the 1800s. Ah wis probably the same age as you – twenty-four, twenty-five somethin like that?'

Mel nodded then, after doing some quick calculations, screwed up her face.

'Wait, so you're, like, over a hundred years old then?'

'A hunner and seventy-eight to be precise. No that it matters to the story. Anyway.'

The old guy looked down at his feet. He was deep in thought. Mel thought to herself, *this is going to be good.*

'Aye,' he said, 'so there ah wis; on what was supposed tae be mah first jaunt tae America. Ah wis oan this ship called *Fortitude*. We left fae Ireland, Cork tae be precise, an we were due to land in New York twelve weeks later. But we never made it that far,' the old man looked deep into Mel's eyes to gauge her reaction. He expected eyes full of wonder but instead she gave him one raised brow and folded her arms.

'And?' she said.

'Well, we never got tae America because we actually ran intae the end ae the Earth. We went too far north. Right up into the Arctic until we reached the Great Ice Wall.'

Now he had her attention. Mel realised she was sitting on the edge of the seat, drawn in by the old guy's tale. She sat back and resumed her previous uninterested pose.

The old guy looked around the bus to see if anyone was listening in. The vibrations of the bus as it trundled along over the tarmac of the motorway had lulled most of the passengers to sleep. He carried on.

'The Great Ice Wall is exactly what it sounds like; a big wall made ae ice. It's a good, maybe, seventy-feet-high, it circles the Earth and it stretches oot for infinity – there's nae end tae it. It's basically the floor ae the universe and we're right in the middle ae it.'

Mel pulled her phone out of her bag to check the time. There was that smell again. They were still forty minutes away from the safety, and relative sanity, of Buchanan bus station.

'Aw, ahm sorry!' The old guy said in a sarcastic tone. 'Ahm ah boring ye, hen?'

'Naw, it's just... It's a wee bit hard to believe. I'm sorry.'

'Use yer phone, pal. Google it. Look it up. There's umpteen

videos aboot this oan YouTube.'

'I don't have any internet left or I would.'

'Well then, looks like ye'll just need tae take mah word fur it. Where wis ah again?'

'The Great Ice Wall. How did you end up there instead of America?'

'Aye, that's right. Well see, the captain ae the ship refused tae believe the Earth was round. He wis obsessed wi provin that it was flat, if only tae himself. So he wanted to see the Ice Wall. An he was fuckin right! Everycunt oan the ship wis ragin we never got tae America but ah wisnae. Ah'd seen somethin that normal folk like me an you urnae meant tae see.'

'What about all the other passengers? Did they not see this ice wall as well?'

'Aw they seen it awrite – they just widnae listen as the captain explained wit it wis. They just demanded tae go hame. They thought the guy wis mental. He gave me the map as a thank you for believin him an he told me tae spread the word that the Earth wis really flat. Ah wis too feart to tell anybody what ah'd saw so ah've kept it quiet aw these years. Noo is the time tae pass oan the truth though. See yous young yins? Yeez are a lot mare open minded than aulder folk.'

'So have you got any pictures of this infinite wall of ice kicking about then?'

'Well, obviously no, hen. This wis a time before cameras and recordin equipment and such like.'

'Convenient, eh?' Mel had decided this old bastard was definitely of the daft variety.

The old guy shrugged his shoulders.

'Fine. Believe wit ye want hen. Just don't open up that map until ye get aff the bus, awrite?'

He turned his back on Mel, leaned his head against the window and nodded off to sleep. Mel decided to do the same.

'Wid ye mind moving, pal. Some ae us have hames tae get tae,' the bus driver shouted in Mel's ear. She opened her eyes and looked out the window at the bright lights of the bus station.

Home at last. Thank god.

'Sorry,' she meekly said to the driver, clutching her bag to her chest and shuffling off the now empty bus. The station was deserted. Not a soul lingered about as she made her way towards the taxi rank. A lone taxi sat waiting, its diesel engine ticking over noisily. As she approached it she saw, smiling out at her, from the back seat, was a familiar face.

It was the old guy.

He pointed at her handbag then made a motion with his hands as if he was unfolding something. She could hear him say something to the taxi driver but she couldn't make out what it was.

Mel pulled out the map and held it up to the window. The old guy gave her a thumbs up then made the unfolding motion again.

Mel was quite excited to see this map of what the Earth supposedly really looked like. She smiled and unfolded the tattered map. A smell very much like shite wafted up into her nostrils. It smelled exactly like what she'd smelled earlier on the bus. She wondered if the smell was coming from her. She opened it up until it was the size of a broadsheet newspaper. As the smile disappeared from Mel's face, a broad grin spread across the old guy's. Then it turned into a cackle. Then hysterical laughter from both him and the taxi driver.

Mel held the map up. It was just a normal map of the Earth. Normal except for one thing – the huge smear of shite on it. It ran from South Africa right up to Norway. A big, dirty brown skid mark. It was particularly thick across the middle where it tore across Italy and Mel, for a moment, imagined millions of Italians running around screaming, caked in shite.

She tore her gaze away from the map and back to the old guy's face. He was slapping the window as tears ran down his face. He fell backwards across the seats, roaring with laughter, as the taxi sped away.

SAMMY'S DA'S FUNERAL

Ahm at mah da's funeral, right, an mah uncle plonks his big fat self doon in the pew in front ae me. Ahm no sittin right doon the front man, nae chance. Mah da's funeral or no – sittin doon the front, whether it's oan the bus or at school or whatever, is fur gimps. An ahm no a gimp, right.

Anywey, right, no seen mah uncle in years. No since ah wis a wean, right. Know wit the cunt used tae dae ae me? Naw, nuhin like aht. He's no a beast. He used tae, like, bam me up. The big cunt wid skelp the back ae mah heid, right, then deny aw knowledge ae it. Hings like that. He'd hide toys ah wis playin wi when ah wisnae lookin, right, makin me hink ah wis losin mah mind. Sometimes he'd whisper mah name, pure under his breath, like that, 'Sssssaaaaamy,' right, then ah wid go like that 'Who said mah name?' an he'd be like, 'Ooft, ye hearin voices, pal? That's the first sign ae madness.' Ah wid freak oot, right, start hinkin ah wis gawn schizo or suhin. Ah hink the cunt wis actually tryin ae gaslight me man.

Anywey, that wis years ago. Must be aboot, pfffft, mibbe ten, fifteen year since ah last seen um. It's been bliss – ahm no gonnae lie. Watter under the bridge, though, right. He wis only tryin ae huv a buzz wi his daft wee nephew. Ahm no that bothered aboot it. Ah dae the same hing ae mah wee cousins noo.

But ye know wit. Ah still want tae get ma ain back oan this big basturt – dae suhin tae wind HIM up fur wance. See, the worst hing ae wid dae tae me wis always when we were in mah da's motor, right. He'd tell me ae sit in the front and ahd be like that, 'Yass man.' Noo, ah know ah said sittin doon the front at hings is fur gimps but it's a different story when it comes tae motors. You're a gimp if you're in the back. That's joost how it works. Ah don't make the rules. Anywey, he'd let me sit in the front but it was only so he could terrorise me fae the back seat. He'd wait until we were oan the motorway or suhin, heading ae mah granny's hoose, then, when ah wis least expecting it, he'd lick wan ae his big fat fuckin sausage fingers an stick it right in mah ear. It used tae make me want tae turn inside oot man. It was fuckin rank. Ah'd fucking wriggle aboot in the front seat like a fish an him an mah da wid be fuckin howling. Pair a wanks. At least wan ae thum's deid noo, eh?

Anywey, right, here ah um. We're at mah da's funeral. It's aw quiet apart fae the priest droning oan a power ae shite an ahm bored oot mah nut. Mah uncle's big, crusty, exposed ear hole is right there in front ae me an ah can barely control masel. It's fuckin mental. Mah maw's sittin next tae him. If she catches me dain this she'll be fuckin ragin. It'll be well funny. Mah auntie's sittin next tae me, mah maw's sister, she disnae like mah uncle so she'll probably find it funny. I lick mah finger as sneakily as ah can. I make sure it's fuckin soakin, right, fuckin drippin wet, then ah count tae three.

Wan.

Mah heart's fuckin racing, man. This is gonnae be amazin.

Two.

Aw fuck, ahm gonnae spew wi excitement.

Three.

Ah fuckin go fur it man. Plunge the fucker in. Swear tae god man, nae word ae a lie, ah swear ah felt as if ah touched the cunt's brain.

He lets oot a big scream like a big fuckin lassie. He used to slag me fur screaming when he did it tae me. Well take that ya big fat basturt.

Ma maw turns roon an stares at me. The priest's stoapped talkin. Fuckin everycunt's lookin at me noo. Mah uncle stawns up an spins roon as if he's gonnae crack me. His massive face turns purple cos he's so ragin.

'Wit's the matter wi you, eh?' mah maw says tae me. 'This is yer faither's funeral, Sammy – show some respect.'

Ah joost start fuckin howlin. That was worth the wait man. Well worth the wait.

SHIFTSWAP

Peter felt her staring at him from across the kitchen. He faced the chip fryer, ignoring her, praying she wouldn't ask him. He'd heard her whispering about asking him all night. He reckoned she was probably waiting on him offering. It was Peter's first Saturday night off in months and there was no way he was giving it up so fucking Shelley could go out with her stupid pals. No chance. He was having Saturday off and he was going to enjoy it. He had a cracking game of Football Manager on the go and he loved nothing better than sitting in and commentating on the games to himself.

'Peeeeeturr?' Shelley asked, sidling up next to him. *Aw fuck, here we go*, thought Peter. 'Would you be able to do me a big favour?'

'Eh, depends what it is?' Peter screwed up his face.

'Well, I was wanting to go out tomorrow night… but I'm supposed to be working… and you're off… sooooooo… would you do my shift for me?'

Peter had been dreading this question. He was too busy worrying about being pressured into saying 'aye' that he'd forgotten to think up an excuse he could use to say no.

FUCKFUCKFUCKFUCK. Say something. Anything

'Aww, eh, a would, but… I've got a, eh, party the morra night.'

…and it's cleared off the line by Peter! Incredible save from the big man. He won't be working tomorrow night, that's for sure.

Shelley looked devastated. She was so sure he'd do her shift; he never went out or went to parties or even seemed to have any pals at all.

'Aye, I've got a party. Sorry. Gonnae be a mad wan, so it is.'

Right Peter, that's plenty. You've made the save don't fuck it up now...

'My pals are mental,' he couldn't stop talking. He was sweating. He willed himself to just shut the fuck up. The ice cream machine started beeping along with the chip fryer. He hit the buttons to silence them.

'No bother, Peter,' Shelley said, 'it's not like you to be going out, though.'

She knows you're kidding on, mate, she fucking knows.

'Have a good night anyway. I'll see you on Sunday morning then, and you can tell me all about the party and your "mental pals",' Shelley traipsed away, gutted.

Fuck. He hadn't thought this far ahead; he didn't realise he was going to have to talk about the "party" afterwards. He was going to have to invent some pals.

The nightshift staff came out of the staff room, tying their aprons and adjusting their caps. Time for Peter to head up the road.

Saturday night came. Peter arrived back home from the shops with his carry out – two bottles of orange flavour Mad Dog 20/20. To convince people he really was at a party, he was going to have to be convincingly hungover in work the next morning.

In his room, Peter unscrewed the lid off the first bottle. He lifted it to his nose and recoiled. The only alcohol he'd ever had was a sneaky swig of his da's Tennent's when he was fifteen. The taste of the flat lukewarm lager had been enough to put him off. Peter shut his eyes and downed half the bottle in three long, slow gulps. The liquid burned his throat as it tried to climb back out of his body but he managed to keep it down. He could feel it hitting him already. He finished the first bottle and fell back onto his bed.

Peter opened the Facebook app on his phone; it was time for the second part of his plan. It wasn't enough just to be hungover.

He needed proof, concrete proof, that he was at a party. So Peter created two Facebook accounts – one for a guy named Jamie Woods and one named David Henderson. He opened up Google and looked for display pictures he could use for his new virtual pals. None looked convincing or cool enough. In his drunken state, he decided to just use the profile pictures of two random guys in the 'People you may know' section on Facebook. A genius idea, he thought. He logged in as Jamie Woods and tagged himself and David at a party in David's house.

Right, am I steaming? Aye. Have I been tagged at a party on Facebook? Aye. What else can I do to make this more believable? Aw fuck. I told Shelley my pals were mental. She's gonnae be expecting mad stories...

Peter googled 'what happens at crazy parties' as he'd never actually been to a party before, crazy or otherwise. The first link suggested that party goers shouldn't fall asleep as fellow revellers may shave off one or both of their eyebrows. He shuddered, he was glad David and Jamie weren't real; they looked like the kind of guys that would enjoy taking a razor to their pal's face.

Peter finished the second bottle of Mad Dog. It went down a lot easier than the first. He sat on the edge of his bed and waited for the room to stop spinning.

Peter decided to write down some notes for stories he could tell in work. He pulled a notepad out the drawer of his bedside cabinet. He looked for a pen but could only find a thick, black Sharpie permanent marker. He tried to think of ideas but his mind was as blank as the page in front of him. He looked at his inebriated self in the mirror across the room. He tapped himself on the chin with the pen. He felt something wet.

Aw fuck *sake.*

Peter looked at his chin in the mirror, there was a big black spot on it now. He looked at the pen. He had an idea.

Ha! Quality. They'd definitely believe I was at a party if they see pictures of me on facebook with pen all over my face. I could say I fell asleep and my pals drew on me. Genius... I'm no shaving off an eyebrow though. I'm no going that stupid.

Peter walked over to the mirror, grinning inanely. He lifted the pen to his face. 'My pals are mental,' he laughed. He turned to the side and started drawing a big, bulbous, scrotum on his neck. He connected the testicles to a veiny, triumphant shaft that ran up his right cheek. The penis curved round to the centre of his forehead and then Peter dragged the marker back down his cheek and connected it to the balls of his masterpiece. He added a flurry of pubes and stood back to admire his work in the mirror. It was a belter. He began laughing at himself and fell back on to the bed. He picked up his phone and opened the camera app. He rolled onto his left side and closed his eyes as if he was asleep and snapped a few pictures of himself. He sat up and looked at the photos he had taken. Peter was astounded at how well this plan was turning out. He was having the best night ever. A real party probably wouldn't even be as much fun as this, he thought. Peter uploaded the pictures to Facebook as David Henderson and tagged himself in them.

This daft cunt fell asleep so we drew a big dick oan him hahahahaha, he wrote as the caption.

Peter was bursting for a pish. He went down into the toilet and laughed again as he looked at himself in the mirror. 'Some party, eh lads?' he said. As he washed his hands, he clocked his mum's razor sitting on the window ledge.

Peter picked up the razor. He held it up to his left eyebrow. He didn't want to shave it off, he had no reason to either; he just couldn't help himself.

'My pals are mental,' he repeated. His smile vanished. He dragged the razor through his eyebrow. It hurt Peter as it tugged at and ripped out the wiry hairs. He winced in agony. Spots of blood dropped down into the sink. He rinsed the hairs out of the blades and washed the blood away. He continued until no trace of the eyebrow remained. He went back to his bedroom and passed out.

The next morning Peter woke up with a banging sore head. He remembered drinking a lot of Mad Dog but that was about it. He checked his phone; he had ten minutes to get to work. He had a lot of Facebook notifications as well. This was unusual for Peter. He clicked on the Facebook app but his phone died; he'd forgotten to put it on charge the night before. He jumped out of bed and pulled on his uniform. He didn't even brush his teeth before heading out the door.

He walked through the front doors of his work and into the brightly lit seating area. The lights made his head pound even more. A few customers sniggered at him as he walked past. Shelley stood behind the counter, pouring change into a guy's hand and missing as she couldn't take her eyes off Peter. He walked through the kitchen and everyone went quiet. Peter looked at them all, then put his head down and went into the staff room. He hung up his jacket and looked at himself in the mirror on the back of the door.

FUCK.

The dick was still well and truly there on Peter's face. The same could not be said about his left eyebrow. Shelley pushed the door open from the other side, almost hitting Peter in the process.

'Peter, what the fuck?' she said.

Peter laughed and pointed to the penis on his face.

'Aw, eh, I told you. My pals are mental, eh?

'Everybody knows you did that to yourself. It's all over Facebook.'

Peter laughed nervously. 'Naw. Wit? Naw, it was my pals, eh, David and...'

What the fuck was the other cunt's name?

Shelley raised a hand to stop him. She pulled out her phone.

'Look,' she said, 'there in the mirror.' When Peter uploaded the picture of himself pretending to be asleep, his own reflection was visible in the mirror behind him. Arm raised, taking a photo of himself.

'And these "pals" of yours. I take it you made them up as well? They don't have any friends on Facebook apart from you. And this Jamie guy's profile picture is actually my pal Kenny.' Shelley shook her head. 'If you didn't want to do my shift, you just had to say no. You didn't have to kid on you were at a party. And what the fuck happened to your eyebrow?'

Peter looked down at his feet. He rubbed the space on his forehead once occupied by his eyebrow. All he could mumble was, 'My pals are mental.'

FITBAW

Terry stood with his forehead pressed against the cool glass of his office window. He watched as Graham, once his favourite client, climbed out of a black taxi below him. Only he wasn't a passenger in said taxi – he was driving it. Terry let out a sigh which fogged up the window, clouding his vision for a moment. Terry hoped when the window cleared all his problems would disappear along with the condensation. He had no such luck.

Graham strode across the road, looked up and gave Terry a wee wave. Terry reciprocated, grudgingly. He was finding it harder and harder to contain the rage he felt towards Graham. Terry walked over behind his desk and slumped into his office chair. The phone buzzed.

'Terry,' came Sharon the receptionist's voice from the loudspeaker, 'Graham Reid's here to see you.' The usually gregarious Sharon sounded as if she'd had all the joy sucked out of her. This was a common side effect of speaking to Graham Reid – the world's most boring footballer.

When Terry first met Graham, he had clocked him straight away as the perfect client; quiet, shy, a bit awkward but with an enormous amount of talent. He didn't smoke, drink or even do drugs; Terry thought he was a freak but he knew Graham would make him a fortune and he was right. And now, after nine years of working together, Graham was throwing it all away to drive a taxi.

Fucking cunt taxi, taxi cunt fucking, fucking taxi cunt. Terry sighed again, 'Send him in, the door's open.' A moment later there was a single knock on the door. *My God,* Terry thought, *even the way he knocks on doors is boring*. Graham swung the door open then gently closed it behind him. Terry motioned for him to take a seat.

'Hi, Terry,' Graham said. His voice bored its way into Terry's ears. Terry rubbed the bridge of his nose. He felt a wave of tiredness wash over him. 'Awrite, Graham,' Terry stifled a yawn. 'So, this is it, then? You're actually going through wi this?'

'Aye, just picked up my new brief this morning. She's a belter, eh?' Graham nodded to the window.

'I cannae *believe* you're chucking fitbaw to drive a *fucking* taxi!' Terry slammed an open palm down on the table. 'I had a move to Man United sorted oot fur ye. Five times the wages yer oan the noo and you go and fucking retire? You're twenty-eight year auld!'

'You don't have to be so aggressive, Terry,' said Graham. He didn't see the problem with retiring from football at twenty-eight. He'd captained Partick Thistle to a monumental Scottish Cup final win over Celtic, won a domestic treble after moving to Celtic the following season then single-handedly dragged Scotland to the semi-finals of the World Cup in Russia two years later. He was heralded as the best Scottish player in generations but he'd had enough. He wanted a job that wouldn't make his Da moan about 'how easy he had it.' He bought himself out of his contract with Celtic and officially retired. He didn't want to be in the public eye anymore. He was constantly derided for being boring. The way he dressed – boring. His choice of car – boring. His haircut – boring. The taunts hurt him. Graham couldn't understand what was wrong with driving home after a game on a Saturday afternoon (in his second-hand Citroën Picasso) and doing some work at his allotment (the one luxury he afforded himself). He always felt a sharp pang of guilt course through him whenever he checked his bank balance. His Ma and Da had struggled through a string of low paying jobs while Graham had made millions just from kicking a ball. He didn't have any friends. Graham turned his nose up at the activities of his fellow pros; drug-fuelled orgies, driving supercars, mad parties and reckless gambling. Graham often thought to himself, *how could they be bothered?* It was staying behind at the training ground after everyone else had left, early nights, steam engine documentaries and gardening for our Graham.

'Look, for the love of God, please reconsider this?' said Terry.

'It's too late, I've passed all my tests. I start tomorrow. I'm looking forward to making some good, honest money,' Graham replied with a smile.

An idea popped into Terry's head. Graham was right, there certainly was some good, honest money to be made here – especially by Terry. He could see it now; magazines and papers wanting exclusive interviews, telly appearances, sponsorship deals, the fucking lot. Graham's new career would be big news all over the world.

'Do the papers know yet?' Terry asked, narrowing his eyes.

'Eh, I don't know, mate. Wait, hang on, I'm a taxi driver now, why *would* they be interested in me?'

'Graham, just because you've retired from fitbaw doesn't mean everyone's going to forget about you. If anything, you'll be more famous now. And you'll definitely still be needing me as your agent…'

The next day Graham was on the front and back pages of all the Scottish papers:

REID 'EM AND WEEP! – CELTIC'S STAR MAN RETIRES TO BECOME TAXI DRIVER

TIME YOU ON 'TIL? – GRAHAM REID CLOCKS OUT OF FOOTBALL

And there was, of course, the inevitable, *TAXI FOR REID!*

Graham started work at 7:00am in the city centre. It was a drizzly, grey morning. A man in a suave, navy blue trench coat flagged Graham down.

'Just round to Pitt Street please, mate. I don't fancy getting soaked walking round,' the man said as he got in, rain dripping from him onto the floor of the cab. He looked at Graham in the taxi's rear view mirror. 'Here, you're that footballer, aren't you?'

'Used to be,' said Graham, 'not anymore, though.'

'You're fucking mental giving up that kind of money,'

'Ach, money's not everything.'

As Graham pulled on to Pitt Street, the man said, 'Anywhere here.' Graham obliged and smoothly brought the taxi to halt. 'Just three quid, please,' Graham announced.

'Fuck off!' the man spat the words at the glass separating him from Graham. 'As if *you* need any more money,' he said, jumping out the vehicle and disappearing into a glass-fronted office. Graham was far too timid to chase after him. He hadn't expected that kind of reaction from people. He put the light on top of his taxi back on and drove off.

The rest of Graham's shift was just as eventful. He was threatened by a woman stabbing a needle through the holes in the glass behind him as he drove her through the Gallowgate. An elderly man pished all over his back seat and he was pulled over by the police as he unwittingly helped a shoplifter make his getaway.

Graham's phone rang as soon as he got home. It was Terry.

'Graham, my man! You're no gonnae believe what I've got lined up for you. You'll need to take the morra aff work, you've got photoshoots, interviews, the full whack,' Terry gushed down the line.

'Nah, you're awrite. I was hoping to try a few airport runs tomorrow. Maybe hang about the taxi rank at a shopping centre or a supermarket or-'

Terry butted in. 'Fuck that for a carry on, daft arse. There's money to be made here. We can make a fortune off this without you having to drive some fucking auld biddies hame fae ASDA. Be at my office for nine the morra morning. You can drive us to yer first photoshoot.'

Graham's ma and da fawned over their son as he joined them in the dining room. Mince and totties for dinner, Graham's favourite. No butter through the mash though. No salt either and just a wee bit of gravy with his mince. He liked his food plain and simple, nothing mental for him.

'I'll tell ye something, son,' Graham's da said, 'That fitbaw. That's nae way tae earn a living if ye ask me. Bunch a big jessies, nae offence son, prancing aboot in their wee shorts and getting paid a bloody fortune fur it.'

'I know, Da. It's a nice feeling to be earning some good, honest money for a change,' Graham said. His mouth was dry from shovelling in the arid mashed totties. He thought he might celebrate with a nice glass of fizzy juice for a change. That notion passed quickly though and he opted for a glass of milk as usual. He didn't want to be up all night, after all.

'How much did you make today then, son?' his ma asked, 'hope ye got some nice tips.'

'Mary, fur chrissakes. Ye cannae be asking the boy how much he's earning. Ya cheeky cow,' Graham's da said.

'Wit? Ah need to know how much ahm gonnae be getting for dig money,' his ma retorted.

Graham allowed himself a rare chuckle at his ma and da's wee fight. 'Well, it's early days, I'm still figuring out the best areas after all. But, after paying for diesel, I've walked away with thirty quid,' he smiled.

His da spat a mouthful of mince back on to his plate. 'Fuck sake, son. Yer auld maw would make more than that punting her arse to the lowest bidder!'

At Graham's first photoshoot, he posed awkwardly in front of his taxi. He sat on the bonnet, his arms crossed and flashed his trademark squinty teeth at the camera. Terry stood behind the photographer laughing and shouting encouragement at Graham. After striking a few more poses, it was time for Graham's first interview as a taxi driver.

'So, Graham,' the interviewer said. She got herself comfortable in the chair and opened her notebook on her lap. 'You really are big news just now since you retired from football at such a young age to become a taxi driver. What everyone wants to know is, why?'

'Um, I wanted to quit football so I did and I wanted to become a taxi driver – so I did,' said Graham. His monotonous voice hung heavy in the air. The interviewer couldn't help but let out a yawn. Silence filled the room. She apologised and painted a fake smile across her face as she waited for Graham to continue. He didn't. Terry thought to himself that if they were in some shitty American sitcom there would be the sound of crickets chirping in the background. He had to intervene.

'Hi, I'm Terry. I'm Graham's agent,' he said, pulling a stool over next to Graham. 'I think what Graham would like people to know is that he had become, shall we say, disillusioned with football. Yes, he's had a glittering career, he's won everything, he's earned a good living from the game but that's not what Graham's after. He's after real…' Terry snapped his fingers as he searched for the right word. '*Fulfilment*. Aye, that's it. He's after happiness. He's a grafter at heart, is oor Graham. He needs to be working hard tae be happy. He's just an old-fashioned Glaswegian man. Bit like masel to be honest.'

The interviewer looked Terry up and down. 'I see, I see,' she said, nodding. 'Graham, how was your first day on the job? Did you enjoy it? Did you get any grief off the punters? Any funny stories? Anything interesting?'

Graham thought about the events of the previous day;

almost being stabbed in the neck with a hypodermic needle, cleaning pish off his back seats, assisting a shoplifter…

'It was okay, nothing much to report,' he said with a smile. The interviewer snapped her notebook shut and picked up her phone. She couldn't be around the world's most boring man for another second or she thought she'd end up tanning her wrists.

Over the next few months, the interest in Graham from the press and the public waned. Being a footballer had been the only interesting thing about him and now, with that behind him, he was free. Terry was raging he couldn't cash in on the initial media furore that surrounded him but soon even he almost forgot about Graham's very existence. Graham, however, loved his new life.

A year after Graham's retirement, Terry stood in the queue for a taxi outside Glasgow Central Station after a night out. He swayed as he devoured a black pudding supper. The grease on his fingers glistened under the streetlights. As Terry reached the front of the queue, a marshal guided him gently into a taxi. He flung the remnants of his late-night munch at a seagull in the middle of the road.

'Where ye off to, pal?' the driver asked. Terry concentrated hard on the back of the driver's head. He was sure he had been in this taxi before.

'Bearsssssden,' Terry slurred. He looked in the rear view mirror to get a look at the driver but he couldn't quite focus on the man's face. He thought he recognised him but the memory of who he was or where Terry knew him from faded out of existence. Trying to remember who this unremarkable, almost featureless man was felt like trying to catch smoke.

Graham had clocked Terry immediately. He didn't say anything. He always thought Terry was a bit of a prick.

At a taxi driver's awards ceremony, Graham received the prestigious 'New Driver of the Year' award. Graham's eyes filled with tears as his name was read out. He hadn't expected it; he was thrilled to even just be nominated.

'That's ma boay! That's ma fuckin boay!' Graham's da shouted, punching the air, as his son went up to collect his trophy. At the after party, the other drivers stood around as Graham regaled them with his tales of difficult customers, fights and celebrity passengers. Graham had become the resident patter merchant of the taxi ranks of Glasgow.

Arriving home, Graham went to his room, clutching his trophy; a golden taxi on a plinth. He looked at his shelf full of his football trophies; Man of the Match, Player of the Year, Goal of the Season, a plethora of winner's medals. Graham snorted and with one sweep of his arm he sent them flying. The mementos of his previous life crashed to the floor. He proudly sat his golden taxi in their place.

BOWLS

1

Ahm walkin towards the bowlin club. Mah orange leather-effect bowls bag in wan hawn, a fag in the other. It's Saturday efternin an it's fuckin roastin. Ahm sweatin under mah Rangers joggie bottoms but ahd rather wear these than that flouncy skirt ah need tae wear when ahm playin bowls. Fuckin guys an their poxy rules.

Ahm in the buildin noo, stridin up to the bar.

'Usual, Angie?' the wee guy behind the bar says tae me. He never looks me in the eye this wee cunt. Bag ae nerves, so he is. Maist folk are roon aboot me.

'Aye,' ah say tae him.

'Nae b-b-bother,' he stutters as ah slam a two pound coin doon oan the widden bar. It echoes like fuck and he just aboot draps the pint ae Stella he's pourin me. I hear some auld biddy in the corner tut but when a spin roon tae gie her a dirty look she's lookin doon at her paper. Shat it. Ah take mah change an go an get changed intae ma bowls gear.

It always feels weird wearin this skirt. Ah hate no wearin joggies. Occasionally ah'll stick oan leggings, maybe denims every noo an again, but ye'll never catch me wearin a skirt unless ahm oan that bowlin green. Ah lift mah bowls oot mah bag an put them doon next tae me. That smug bastard Phil is eyein me up. He's always fancied a game against me. Well, today's the day, mate – you're getting humped.

'Phil,' I shout over tae the cunt. Ah know he hates it when ah call him that instead ae Philip. 'Me an you. Right noo.'

He looks right at me. He's started sweatin. His wee tache is drippin wet.

'Okay,' he says, 'why not?'

I gie mah bowls a wee quick polish while he flings the jack doon the green. He won the coin toss but that's aw he's gonnae win. Everycunt's got their eyes oan us noo, patchin their ain games to watch this clash ae the bowlin titans. Ahm the best wummin here an Phil, somehow, is the best guy. He's awrite. Nuthin special though.

He pulls his arm back an his skinny wee wrist looks like it's gonnae snap wi the weight ae the bowl. He really is a pathetic specimen ae a man. Fuck knows wit Dolly sees in him. He rolls the bowl oan the grass and lets it go. He does that thing where he takes a few mad steps after the bowl leaves his hawn. Ah fuckin hate that. Cunts that dae it are the worst cunts in the world. The bowl goes wide right, curvin in at the last minute an comin tae a rest maybe a foot away fae the jack. He flashes that smarmy smile at me again as his specs slide doon his sweaty nose. He pushes them back up with his middle finger. Prick.

Mah turn noo. Ah pick up mah shiniest bowl. Ah love the way it feels in mah hawn. A good solid weight. Ah'd love tae cave daft Phil's heid in wi it. Ah click mah sovvie rings aff the underside ae the bowl while ah plan mah move. Ah've noticed err the years that this annoys cunts. So ah dae it before every shot. Ah hear Phil huffin an puffin. He's wantin me tae hurry up. Ah want tae take mah time here though, really savour beatin this bastard.

I roll mah bowl along the same path Phil used but mah swing is a hunner times better – mair finesse ye see. Mine curves in more sharply and comes tae a halt a midge's baw hair away fae the jack.

Perfection.

'Should probably call it a day noo, Phil, eh?' Ah look over at the soppy cunt. His jaw's hingin open.

2

I cannot believe how good Big Angie is at bowls. She's frighteningly good, to be honest. I watch her waddle off the green and back towards the bar. Okay, fair enough; she's better at bowls than me but at least I don't look like a bowl on stilts. Honestly, this woman is the most peculiarly shaped person I have ever seen. Skinny legs supporting her giant, bloated torso. They say that according to all known laws of aviation, there is no way a bee should be able to fly but I think the fact Big Angie is able to walk around is even more of a miracle. I'm not only offended by her appearance. Her decorum and behaviour around the club is, quite frankly, unacceptable. She's a horrible, overgrown ned. They really should do more stringent checks when someone applies to join the club. How hard could it be to find out if they live in a council house or not? That would be an easy way to keep out the riff raff.

Anyway, she needs to be removed from the club. I'm not the only who thinks so, oh no. Angie swans about the place like she owns it. Like everyone loves her. How could anyone love her? All she does is insult people, snap at them and make jokes about them. Folk are nice to her face, but behind her back? That's a different story. We all talk about her. Right now we've been postulating as to how the fuck she has so much money. She's dripping in gold jewellery and always wearing the latest Rangers tops. I've checked out the price of football tops and they certainly aren't cheap. She says her money came from a big bingo win but there's no way that idiot has the brain power to tell different numbers apart, never mind the manual dexterity in those fat fingers to check them off.

My theory is she bumped off her husband and claimed the life insurance money. I don't know if this is 100% true or not but I certainly wouldn't put it past her. So I start telling everyone in the bowling club that she isn't with her husband anymore because she killed him. Everyone nods in agreement as I start spreading the rumour that she's a killer.

'How do you know this though, Philip?' Dolly, my wife, asks me.

'Heard it down the pub,' I lie.

'Right, right, I see,' she bites her nails. She's even more scared of the big brute now, it's plain to see. With everyone believing the rumour about her, I ask the Club President, Gavin, if he fancies a dram or two in clubhouse, so I can seal the deal and get the daft cow out of the club for good.

'Well, Philip,' he says to me, 'removing her from the club would certainly be a popular decision.'

'I'm glad you agree, Gavin,' I reply, 'I just worry about what she's capable of, you know?'

'Aye, no wonder. Listen, I'll be terminating her membership with immediate effect,' he looks down into his whisky, swirling the last of the liquid around the glass before raising it to his mouth and letting it slide down his throat. He gets up from his seat and I do the same. We shake hands and he heads up the road. It's just me in the bar now. Well, me and the barman. The barman is called Jamie or James or something like that. I don't really care. He's Gavin's nephew, though, so I try my best to be pleasant to him. He's footering about with the till. Big fat bundles of twenties are stacking up nicely beside it. I give a little cough to get his attention.

'Aw sorry, sir,' the young guy says, 'another whisky?'

'No,' I reply tersely before remembering I have to be nice to him, 'eh, no bother I mean. Pint of Guinness… please.' I watch him as he goes to pour my pint. It's very therapeutic to watch a pint of Guinness being poured, but it's just pathetic white foam that dribbles out on this occasion.

'Need to change the barrel,' the barman says. He looks over at his open till. I can tell he doesn't want to leave it while he goes down to the cellar. 'You want something else instead?'

'I don't mind waiting. You go change the barrel and I'll make sure nobody dips your till,' I gesture round at the empty room. He laughs and goes down the stair. Silly boy. As soon as he's out of sight I help myself to a few crisp twenties from the till. I'll add that to my small nest egg I keep hidden from the wife. When he comes back up, he pours me a perfect pint.

'There you go,' he says plonking it down in front of me.

'Thanks,' I reply, 'how much is that?'

'Och, it's on the house since I kept you waiting.'

'Now that's customer service!' I take a sip and raise my glass to him.

'Nae bother, Mr. McNab. You're one of the good guys.'

Oh, you better fucking believe it.

3

Booze, bowls an bingo – in that order – that's wit ahm intae. Phil, oan the other hawn, he's intae being a fuckin snake. The cunt's only went an talked the Club President intae terminating mah membership. No even gettin a refund. See, he's been spreadin rumours aboot me, sayin ah killed mah man. Wee sleekit, weasel bastard. Phil, that is – no mah man. He wis just a wank.

Anyway, there's a big tourney in a fortnight's time, doon at Shettleston Bowlin Club, guaranteed they'll be wantin me back fur that – seeing as ahm the best an aw that. But until ah can go back tae the bowlin club, av goat mare time fur bingo. An ah hope they realise ahm still gawn tae Blackpool wi aw the bowlin biddies at the weekend, seein as ahm the wan who organised it. Couldnae leave they daft auld bastards tae run anyhin. They couldnae run a fuckin menage!

Ahm good at bingo. Ah know that sounds mental an you're probably sittin there like that 'How can ye be good at bingo?' but ah just um. Ahm probably better at bingo than ah um at bowls as a matter ae fact. Two year ago ah won the national, twinty grand ah walked away wae. Ah've spent nearly it aw right enough; New sovvie rings don't come cheap ye know, mah bowls were a pretty penny an ah've goat tae keep mah Broxi in the best ae gear as well. Ah took early retirement efter mah win an mah pension keeps me just aboot tickin over but folk still hink ahm loaded. So anyway, Monday night is bingo night fur me. Ahm hopin fur another big win soon. Ah like tae go by maself. Ah quite like mah ain company, just as well, ah suppose, seein as maist folk don't seem tae like me. Apart fae mah Broxi. Fuckin love that dug.

Ah buy mah books and saunter over tae mah usual seat. It's the same distance tae baith the bar and the bogs fae this seat. It's the best fuckin seat in the hoose an it's aw mine.

But no the night.

Ah recognise the occupant straight away; it's Phil's missus, Dolly, an she's parked her arse oan *MAH* seat. Dozy auld cow.

Ah sit doon facing her. Starin right intae they glaikit eyes.

'Aw, Angie,' she says, 'Didn't know you liked the bingo?'

'You know fine well that ah like the bingo, hen. Ah see ye here every week. Drawing yer fuckin eyes aff me. Wit ye dain in mah seat?'

She looks aboot tae see if anycunt's looking at us, like she disnae want anycunt tae see her hingin aboot wi me.

'Angie,' her voice is aw low an serious, 'can I ask you something?'

Ah copy her voice. Kinda takin the mickey. 'Wit?' ah ask.

'Did you really, you know, do it?'

'Dae wit?' There's a few cunts whisperin their disapproval at me an Dolly's conversation while the numbers are bein read oot but ah don't gie a fuck.

'You know, kill him, your husband.'

'Never mind that,' ah lean in close, mah nose nearly touchin hers, 'ah want tae know wit yer dain in mah seat?' This wee wifey is tryin mah patience. She's nearly as annoyin as her fuckin man. The game finishes before ah realise ah've no been playin. Fuckin stupit Dolly distractin me wi her pish.

'I'm sorry, Angie. It doesn't matter,' she says pickin up her bag, 'I'll leave you in peace. Forget I even said anything.' She shuffles oot the door an away. Mibbe ah wis a bit harsh oan her. She's merried tae a fuckin rocket efter aw, ah should've cut her some slack, her life's probably hard enough. Ah'll see her at the weekend fur the trip tae Blackpool. Mibbe ah'll have a wee word wi her then aboot that sorry excuse ae a man she calls her husband.

4

Wednesday night down my local. My sanctuary. I've told Dolly she's not to bother me when I'm here. She knows better than to pester me when I'm out with the boys – she learned that lesson many moons ago. The music's pumping. Dennis and Billy are talking football. Nothing bores me more than football. The official sport of the intellectually challenged. Me and Jim from the bowling club are discussing next week's big tournament.

'Fair amount ae prize money oan offer, ah've heard,' Jim says without taking his beady eyes off the barmaid. He rubs his bloated belly and lets out a big rift.

'Yeah?' I ask. This is news to me.

'Oh aye. It's being sponsored by Gavin's daughter. She runs her ain business. Some amount ae money she's flingin intae this. Especially in the wummin's competition,' his eyes drift down to the barmaid's arse, as do mine. She turns round and clocks us. We hastily avert our gazes.

'How much? Do you know?'

'Couple ae grand, ah think.'

'Fucking hell!' I can hardly contain my excitement. The thing with bowling clubs is that they tend to be ran by incompetent, decrepit idiots. This makes them very easy to steal from. Every year I pay for my car's MOT with money from the till in the bar. It's too easy. Nobody's even noticed. Not that they would suspect me; Mild-mannered Philip. Nice Philip. Boring Philip.

'No that we've goat any chance ae winnin it though, eh?' Jim says, 'No withoot Angie.'

He's right. Our women's team is notoriously shite with the exception of her.

'What's the prize money for men's competition?'

'Pfft,' Jim finishes the dregs of his pint, 'hee haw, mate. Hunner quid or somethin.'

'What's that all about?'

'She's a mad feminist, apparently. Aw aboot raisin the profile ae wummin in the game an aw that.'

I shake my head. Feminism – it makes me fucking sick.

'All these feminists do is moan about "equality". Where's the equality in that? Paying the women more than the men? Not on if you ask me.'

'Well, it disnae matter, dis it? The burds'll get humped anyway. They're aw pish.'

Jim has a point. But there's a way we could win. I might try and get that big lumbering brute of a woman back into the club. Then I hear some heavy footsteps. Jim has ordered two pints, both for him. The liquid in the glasses is vibrating and rippling like that bit in Jurassic Park. I turn round as the noise seems to be getting closer. I'm greeted with a familiar face...

5

See the fuckin noise ah make in these kitten heels, it drives me insane. Phil hears me approachin. Ah love that look ae fear in his eyes when he looks at me.

He looks me up an doon then nods tae the poor barmaid. She looks as if she's fed up wi his shite as she sits a whisky doon fur him. He hawns her a couple ae quid an turns back tae me, whisky in hand.

'Angie,' he says takin a sip.

'Bawbag,' I reply. Phil chokes oan his drink. I rub his back as if he's a wee boay an ah cin feel him squirmin at mah touch. That's the hing wi guys; they're jist overgrown wee boays. They never get any mare mature or any less daft. They're aw fuckin idiots. His cronies aw chuckle.

'Ah hear ye've been spreadin rumours aboot me?' Ah say tae the prick as he catches his breath.

'I wouldn't exactly call it a rumour, Angie,' there's that smarmy smile again. This cunt absolutely fills me wi rage. I can feel mah nostrils flare an mah tap lip starts tae curl back, like Broxi's does when she sees another dug. Withoot breakin eye contact wi Phil, ah bark my order at the wee lassie behind the bar. Ah can feel her starin at us. Phil flinches an the barmaid fumbles fur a gless fur mah Stella.

'It's lies, arsehole,' ah say, sittin doon oan the stool next tae Philip, 'aw lies. An you know it.' Ah hud a fag before ah came in the pub an ah can see he's a bit disgusted as mah breath washes over him. Good. He looks as if he's gonnae go intae another coughin fit but he manages tae suppress it.

'The other members have a right to know,' he takes a sip ae whisky, as if it'll gie him mare confidence. 'They have a right to know if a fellow member is a...'

'A wit?' ah enquire. Mah tap lip's curled back noo, but in a smile this time.

'A... a...' he lets oot a wee high pitched whine. He cannae even say the word.

'Aye, that's wit ah thought.' Ah get up an pat him oan the back once again. Ah down mah pint in wan and head towards the door. Ah cannae resist wan last wee dig at him so ah birley roon an say:

'If you're wantin me tae play in that tourney next week, aw ye need tae dae is ask,' then ah gie him a wink, jist to embarrass him in front ae his pals even mare.

6

How could I not just say the word? How could I not just say she's a killer? I mean, it's ***probably*** true. Maybe then the lads wouldn't be slagging me for taking that off her.

'Aye, Philip,' Jim says trying to hide his smirk behind his glass, 'ye looked like a real hard man there, mate.'

'Shut up,' I snap. Dennis and Billy have stopped talking about football.

'That your bit oan the side, eh?' Billy says to raucous laughter.

'Aye, very good,' I tighten my grip on my glass.

I can practically hear the cogs turning in Dennis's head as he tries to think of some witty remark to throw at me.

'She's a belter, Philip,' he says, 'that yer new burd?'

Silence. He's just ripped off Billy's joke. At least no one's laughing at this awful joke the second time round. Dennis looks around, hopeful for at least a chuckle from someone. I relax my grip on the glass as the ribbing seems to be over.

'Ah says is that your new burd, Philip?' he repeats even louder this time. I squeeze my glass so hard it breaks and whisky spills onto my chinos. I look as if I've wet myself. I swear to Christ, if these wankers say anything about this there'll be hell to pay.

I see their eyes drift down to my dripping wet crotch. Smiles spread across their stupid faces.

I'm up and away out of the pub. I've got what I wanted to be fair; Angie will play in the tournament, she'll probably win, she'll think she's got one over on me and I'll help myself to the winnings and put it towards a holiday or a new extension or something. I'm sure I can convince Gavin to let her play without reinstating her membership. Everyone's a winner.

I open the door to the living room. Dolly is sitting on the

couch watching some shit reality TV show. She looks at my soaking chinos and laughs.

'Have a wee accident?' she says.

I snap.

I've got her by the neck and pinned her up against the wall before she realises what's happening. I don't even need to say anything – the look of fear on her face tells me she's learned her lesson. I let go and head up to bed.

A slap here and a shove there, that's how you keep a woman in check – rule your household with an iron fist.

7

The bus is leavin fur Blackpool in hawf an oor an ahm the first wan here. It's another belter ae a day. It's only hawf seven in the mornin but awready it's swelterin hoat. Ah've goat mah favourite Rangers tap oan (the 02/03 away strip. Orange. Fuckin nailer) an ahm stawnin ootside the bowlin club. Cannae wait to see these auld bastards' faces when they see me. Hink ye kin get rid ae me? Ah jist keep coming back like the clap. Dolly is the first tae arrive. Phil draps her aff in his shitey-broon Volvo. Fur such a snob, he disnae hawf drive a shanner ae a motor. She gets oot clutchin her wee overnight bag, slams the door an disnae even say goodbye tae the prick in the driver's seat. Trouble in paradise, ah wonder. She adjusts the silk scarf tied roon her neck, pullin it up higher. Ah wonder wit the fuck she's dain wearin a scarf in this weather but that's the middle class fur ye ah suppose. Ah think nuthin ae it an say hiya.

'I'm really glad you're coming, Angie,' she says tae me. This isnae the wee shy nervous wummin fae the bingo the other night. She draps her bag at her feet and turns roon as her man toots his horn an drives away. She disnae wave – her fists are two wee tiny baws ae fury stuck doon at her side. She fuckin hates that cunt! Jist as much as ah dae, mibbe even mare.

Wan by wan the rest ae the bowlin biddies appear, aw nine ae thum. Ahm aw set fur a mad wan but these burds certainly don't look as if they urr. June, wan ae mah mare vocal critics, turns her nose up at me when ah offer her a wee nip ae vodka fae mah hip flask.

'Suit yerself,' ah say neckin hawf ae it. They aw look at me, disgusted. 'Aw fuckin cheer up. We're gawn tae Blackpool, no Auschwitz.'

'I'll have some of that,' Dolly says an she takes it right oot mah hawn. She takes a big dirty swig an gies me it back. Ahm a big fan ae this new an improved Dolly.

Efter wit feels like a lifetime oan the bus we finally make it tae Blackpool.

'Right, Dolly hen,' ah say, 'we'll dump oor bags at the hotel, get somethin tae eat, then find a pub. Wit dae ye say?'

'Oh aye,' she replies, 'sounds good to me.' Ah can see she's still mibbe a wee bit intoxicated fae the vodka.

We're walkin doon the main drag wi oor bellies full ae sorts ae greasy delights. Say wit ye want aboot the English, but ye cannae deny they know their way roon aboot a fuckin fryin pan. We're oan the hunt fur a decent pub, wan that'll hopefully be showin the Rangers game. There's hunners ae fuckin Irish pubs but nae decent proddy bars.

Then ah see it.

Union Jacks blowin in the wind beside Rid Hawns ae Ulster. It's fuckin beautiful. The Gallant Pioneer the place is called.

'Here we fuckin go, Dolly,' ah say as ah make a beeline straight fur the pub.

'Is there nowhere else we can go?' She says, ah cin tell she's no up fur this at aw. 'It's just that I've heard bad things about places like this.'

'Places like wit? Rangers pubs? It's jist a normal pub, hen.

It's jist like the bowlin club except there's nae Phil.'

'He doesn't really approve of this kind of place.' She adjusts that daft scarf round her neck again.

'Aw the mare reason tae go in then, eh?'

She smiles. 'Och, okay then.'

The music's pumpin and the Teddy Bears are wan up against Aberdeen. It's a glorious fuckin day. Ahm feeling generous so ah get the drinks in while Dolly gets us a seat. Ah push through the crowd at the bar, you'll no catch me waiting behind a group ae fuckin guys, no chance.

'Fackin 'ell, luv,' chirps some poncey wee English cunt as ah squeeze by him an lean oan the bar.

'Look, pal, if ah wanted tae hear an arsehole talk,' ah say lookin the boay up an doon, 'ah wid've farted.'

Ah get the drinks and head back tae Dolly. As ahm walkin taewards her, ah notice she seems tae huv a wee glow aboot her, like bein away fae hame an Phil is dain her a world ae good. Ah fire her gin an tonic doon in front ae her an sip mah pint as ah sit doon.

'Roasting in here,' she says, takin aff that daft scarf, 'isn't it, Angie?'

I clock a big rid mark roon her neck. Like somebody's tried tae throttle her. An ah've goat an idea who that somebody wis. She sees me lookin at her neck. She gies a wee shrug and tries tae hide it wi her hawn. Ah've seen that look afore. Ahm sure ah made that same face a few times maself.

'Wis it him?' ah ask. Nae point beatin aboot the bush.

'Och, it's not as bad as it looks, really,' her face contorts intae a weird hawf smile as she tries tae fight back tears. Ah raise a hawn tae silence her.

'Ah've been where you urr, Dolly hen,' ah take another sip ae mah pint, 'aw ahm gonnae say oan the matter is don't hing aboot. Get him tae fuck. Noo finish that an ah'll get us another couple.' She downs her G&T an hawns me the empty gless.

By nine bells, the two ae us are fucked. Steamin isnae even the word. 'Get the Davie Weir out,' Dolly shouts before collapsing in a fit ae laughter. A cheer goes up fae jist aboot everybody in the place an ah cin see Dolly's hut a wee riddy. Ah cannae help but smile. Ah've never really hid pals before so this is nice; me an Dolly huvin a laugh an a blether an a swallay. She's a good wummin; too good fur that prick, Phil.

Dolly pulls oot her phone an tries tae see who it is that's phonin her. 'Don't you dare fuckin answer that if it's him,' ah seethe.

'No, it's not. It's June,' she puts the phone ae her ear. 'Hullo, June. Oh yes, very drunk,' she hits the giggles wance again. 'Yeah, we'll join you for a few, certainly. I'm with Angie. Okay, see you soon, buh-bye.'

Ah'd rather stay here but ah can see Dolly wants tae join the rest ae her pals. 'Ah'll gie it a miss if it's awrite wi you, hen,' ah say. She tilts her heid tae the side and gies me a look. The kind ae look that a teacher wid gie a wean if it wis actin up.

'Don't be daft, Angie, you're coming with me. We'll have a rare time with everyone else back at the hotel. Just stay for a few. Please?'

Ah cannae say naw tae that face. She's like a wee puppy. Ah swear tae God that's the exact look mah Broxi gies me when she wants some ae mah dinner.

'Awrite,' ah agree, 'ah'll come fur wan. But that's it.'

Dolly smiles an pats mah leg. 'Let's go then.'

It's jist startin tae get dark as we head back tae the hotel. The streets are hoachin wi hen parties. A couple ae giant inflatable dicks blow across the road taewards us. Ah kick wan and send it flyin doon the street.

'Wouldn't mind doing that to a certain someone's willy,' Dolly laughs.

'Neither wid ah tae be fair,' ah say.

'Mind you, Philip's is a helluva lot smaller than that. I'd

struggle to find it!'

Ah can see the hotel in the distance noo an ah ahm startin tae feel quite sad. This hus been the best day ah've hud in a long time.

'Dae ye get oot much back hame, Dolly?' ah ask.

Dolly snorts. 'I wish,' she says, lookin doon at her feet.

'How no?'

She looks at me an ah look at the rid marks oan her neck.

'The bowling club is the only place he takes me. Do you know he took me there for our anniversary? Can you believe that?'

'Course ah can. Here, answer me this, Dolly.'

'Go on.'

'Ah bet Phil has a blue cock. Ahm ah right?'

She looks aw confused. 'What? Um no, it's em, normal coloured I suppose.'

'That's funny,' ah say, 'cos he's wan tight-fisted wanker.'

That wan tickles Dolly but once she stoaps laughin her face turns tae stone.

'Angie, I have to ask,' she says, 'it's about these rumours Philip's been spreading about you. Are they true?'

'Wit? That ah killed mah man?'

Dolly's eyes widen, ah cin tell she wants me tae say that the rumours are true.

'Aw ahm gonnae say, Dolly, is that that cunt won't be botherin me ever again.'

The two ae us walk intae the bar in the hotel. We're greeted by a cheer fae the bowlin biddies in the corner. They aw raise their wee glesses ae wine as we walk over. They're so fuckin twee it makes me sick. Ahm used tae them aw drawin their eyes aff me an lookin doon at me so bein greeted in this way makes me feel a bit uneasy but, ah hink tae maself, ah didnae hink much ae Dolly until ah goat tae know her so ah decide tae gie them a chance. Ah decide tae buy them aw a drink, show them that ahm really no the big bad wolf efter aw. Nine sweet white wines fur them, a gin an tonic fur Dolly an ah opt fur a hawf pint ae John Smith's fur maself. Don't want tae appear too un-ladylike, know wit ah mean?

'Listen,' June says, finishin aff her wine, 'I hear you're coming back to play in this tournament next week, Angie?'

'Aye, that's right. An ahm in it tae win it,' ah say raisin mah gless.

'That's good to hear. There's a lot of prize money on offer, I'm told.'

'Aw aye?' ah say, raisin mah eyebrows. 'How much we talkin?'

'Well, Gavin's daughter is sponsoring it-'

'The loaded wan?' I butt in. I cannae help masel.

'Yes. The prize for the women's competition is £2,000.'

'Fuck me! You bein serious, hen?'

'If we were to win. We'd be putting the money towards another trip. Instead of just coming to Blackpool for the day again, however, we'd be going Benidorm.'

Noo these auld burds are speaking mah language. Ah've always wanted tae go tae Benidorm. Folk say it's jist Blackpool but wi better weather and cheaper drink. Sounds like heaven oan fuckin Earth tae me. Ah've never hud anybody ae go wae though; Nae man, nae weans, nae pals an ah cannae exactly take mah fuckin dug tae Benidorm wi me, can ah? But if ah could win this tourney ah could be jettin aff intae the sun wi mah new pals.

'Oh, Angie,' Dolly gasps, 'That sounds brilliant, eh? God, I hope you win. I'd love a trip to Benidorm. Philip doesn't like places like that so I've never been.'

'Ah'll see wit ah can dae then, ladies,' ah say wi a wink. They aw raise their glesses tae me again.

The biddies aw start disappearin wan by wan an headin up tae their rooms. It's been a long day fur these wee wifies tae be fair. Ahm feeling a bit tired maself, mind you, but Dolly seems tae be in the mood fur gabbin.

Soon it's just me, her, June, an the auldest member ae the bowlin club, Frances. She's a big wummin, Frances, bit like maself, an her snorin's makin a fair racket as she sits wi her fat spillin over the sides ae her chair.

'Frances, hen, c'mon. It's time for bed,' June says, tryin tae rouse the sleepin beast fae her slumber. Ah get up tae get another drink fur me an Dolly. Ah get tae the bar then ah realise ahm bursting furra pish. Ah've drank some amount the day. A lesser wummin wid be oan her arse by noo – but no me. In the toilet there's only wan free cubicle. Wan seems tae be occupied an the other has a bit ae paper sayin 'out of order' oan it. As ah drap mah drawers and park mah arse oan the seat, ah hear the door of the cubicle next tae me open. Then somebody else comes intae the toilet. Fuck sake – ah get stage fright when there's somebody else in the toilet wi me.

'Aw hullo, June,' somebody says. Ah hink it's another one of the biddies, Amanda.

'Hi, Amanda, hen,' June says, confirmin mah suspicions. 'Good news about Angie coming back to play in the tournament, eh?'

'Oh yes, definitely. We may as well book our flights to Benidorm now, eh?'

Ahm feeling aw proud ae maself. Always knew ah wis the best at bowls in the club but it's always nice tae hear it fae somebody else. As nice as it is tae be spoke aboot like this, ah really need tae pish an if these cunts don't hurry up an get oot ahm gonnae explode.

'Ha! Absolutely,' June replies, aw theatrical an over the tap. 'Thankfully, Angie won't be there seeing as it'll be a *members only* trip. She's only here because we'd all have to pay extra for the bus if we said she couldn't come.' They start laughin.

Ah can feel maself shakin wi rage. Mah pish is literally boiling inside me.

'Aw thank God fur that, June,' Amanda says, 'the thought of seeing her in a bikini has been making me sick.'

Ah hear Amanda washin her hawns and biddin June goodnight. Ah consider stormin oot the cubicle an kickin fuck oot the two ae thum but instead ah wait until June leaves before I unleash a furious torrent ae pish that comes oot like a fuckin pressure washer. Ah feel a bit better efter mah pish an calm doon. Ah don't want them knowin that ah heard their wee conversation – ah've goat a plan.

Back through in the bar, ah find a pie-eyed Dolly sitten herself. Ah don't know if ahm upset, embarrassed or ragin wi the bowlin biddies fur talkin aboot me like that. Ah hink ahm mare annoyed at maself fur hinkin that they were anythin other than two-faced auld cows. But it's awrite – ah'll get thum back.

'Wan mare fur the road, hen?' ah say tae Dolly, giving her her umpteenth G&T of the day. She takes a sip then reclines back in her chair. 'Angie,' she says, 'and this is all hypothetical, okay. Just a wee fantasy. But, suppose I wanted to, y'know,' she makes a gesture as if she's cutting her throat open, 'somebody. How would I go about it?'

Ah raise an eyebrow an gie her a smile. 'This the same "somebody" who gave ye they marks roon yer neck?'

She gies a daft shrug an absent-mindedly stirs her drink wi the straw.

'Why ye askin me?'

She looks as if ah've jist gave her intae trouble.

'Oh, eh, no reason,' she splutters, almost knocking her drink over, 'it's just, y'know, what folk have been saying about you and what happened to your husband.'

Ah shake mah heid an roll mah eyes.

'Look,' ah say, 'if ah *wis* tae kill somebody. Ah'd dae it dead sneaky. Nae stabbin, or stranglin or anythin like that. Ye need tae be smart aboot it.'

'How else are you supposed to kill somebody? Like, poison them?'

'That could work, aye,' Dolly leans in to listen. 'But if yer usin an actual poison it's gonnae show up in forensics tests an aw that. Ye'll get caught.' She sits back an bites her nails, like a squirrel nibbling at whatever the fuck squirrels eat. Ah can tell she's hinkin hard aboot suhin. As much as ah wid like tae see her get ain back oan Phil, ah don't want her tae get the jail. She widnae last two minutes in there.

'Ye could make yer "hypothetical" victim in this scenario, assuming it's who ah hink it is, huv a wee accidental trip doon the stair. Auld codgers like him are prone tae takin wee tumbles int they?'

8

I nip over to the club to wait for Dolly. I've got her a bunch of her favourite flowers, just to say sorry for the little incident the other night. She's not due back for another hour or so, so I may as well go in for a bit. Gavin is sitting with his back to me at the bar as I walk in.

'Ahem,' I clear my throat.

'Aw, Philip,' he turns and says to me, 'how's it going?'

'Not bad, Gavin. Not too bad at all,' I sit down next to him

'Glad to hear it,' he gestures to the barman, 'another pint please, Jamie son.'

'Sorry,' I say, jingling my car keys, 'I'm driving. Just popped in while I'm waiting on Dolly.'

'Suit yourself,' he sighs. 'Miss the missus while she was away?'

'I did as a matter of fact. Never thought I'd say that. House is too quiet without her, to be honest.'

'Ach away,' he says, shaking his head, 'nothing better than some time to yourself. While the cat's away and all that, eh?'

'Aye, I suppose.'

'So, this tournament,' he looks at me with a smirk, 'Big

Angie is a cert to win the women's competition but I'm relying on you to win the men's competition. Can I count on you, Philip?'

'Course you can,' I say sternly.

'I know there's not a lot of money on offer for the winner of the men's competition, that's my daughter for you, but I trust that won't put you off giving it your all?'

I'll be walking away with both the men's and women's prize money at the end of the day so this doesn't faze me.

'Course not,' I say, 'It's all about pride for me.'

'You're some man, Philip,' he turns to look out the window as a bus pulls up, 'looks like your good lady has returned.'

'I better go and welcome her home then, eh?'

Dolly steps off the bus. I fetch the flowers from the car and I'm about to walk over to greet her with a cuddle and present her with them but then Angie steps off right behind her. Dolly looks at me with, what I believe to be, utter contempt then turns round and hugs Angie. I see Gavin laughing at the window as my wife embraces that fucking slob. I tighten my grip round the flowers then fling them into a bush. She's getting fuck all for fraternising with that woman.

'Aw here,' Angie shouts after Dolly as she walks towards the car, 'gies yer phone number, hen.'

Dolly, embarrassingly, obliges. They both shoot me dirty looks.

9

It's aboot six o'cloak by the time we get back tae Glesga. When ah open the door, there's a couple ae letters behind it an wan ae they bin bags that charities ask ye tae fill up wi auld claes. Broxi jumps aw err me like she's no seen me fur ten year. The wee guy next door wis meant tae come in an feed her while ah wis away an he seems tae huv fuckin furgot. She looks starvin. Ah pull a packet ae bacon oot the fridge an gie her a few slices. Poor dug's probably no ate fur the best part ae two days. Ah'll gie that wee prick a tankin when ah go an get mah spare key back aff him. That can wait til the morra though. The night ahm plasterin mah arse tae the couch an no movin fur nae cunt. Ah get mah jammies an mah housecoat oan, settle doon wi a bit ae Take Me Out oan the telly an phone maself a kebab.

As another sorry excuse ae a man comes doon the "Love Lift" tae whoops an cheers fae the desperate gaggle ae lassies, ah cannae help but imagine wit ah wid dae if ah wis oan this programme an Phil appeared.

'Ladies,' Paddy wid shout, 'are yah turned on or turned off?'

Sorry Paddy, but Phil here has made me turn mah light aff so hard ah've broke the fuckin hing.

10

Frosty. That's the only word I can use to describe the atmosphere between Dolly and I since we arrived home. She didn't say a word to me on the drive home and has only given me yes and no answers since we stepped through the front door. Suits me, to be fair.

Well, normally it would. But there seems to be something going on in Dolly's head. Like she's planning something. Her eyes don't look right either. She used to look at me with fear, like some poor dog looking up at its abusive owner. That's the way a woman should look at her husband; with a healthy mixture of fear and respect. But Dolly's eyes seem to be blazing since she stepped off that bus. I wonder what kind of nonsense Angie has been filling her head with. She's very impressionable, is my Dolly.

11

Ah've been waitin oan this bastardin kebab fur nearly an oor noo. Mah fuckin belly hinks mah throat's been cut.

'Won't be too much longer, hen,' ah say tae Broxi as ah pick up the phone ready tae gie that Imran cunt roon the corner a piece ae mah mind. Ah've ordered the dug her favourite – a tray ae donner meat. The vet made me put her oan a diet last year efter she goat awffy fat. That's the hing wi staffies; they just eat an eat an eat. It's as if they never get full. It's really mah ain fault though, ah jist cannae say naw tae that daft big face. But, since she's starvin, ah thought ah'd treat her. Spare ribs fae the Chinese used tae be her favourite but the vet said ah couldnae gie her them anymare, might hurt her apparently. Ah don't see how though, she's a fuckin purebred staffy. Crushin bones an that is wit she's bred fur. Ah took the vet's advice though, imagine huvin ae go in there wi yer dug's mooth in tatters, broke teeth an aw that an huvin the hoity toity cunt gawn, 'Oh, Ms. McCracken. I *did* warn you not to feed your dog bones, didn't I?' Fuck that.

12

'I'm going to the bowling club for a few pints,' I shout down the stair to Dolly as I button my shirt up in front of the mirror, 'Don't suppose you fancy coming?' For fifty-five I think I'm looking quite good. I smooth down a few wiry hairs in my moustache as I hear her soft footsteps coming up the stairs. She hardly makes a noise as she ghosts around the house in her slippers.

'Yeah,' she says, coming into the room and putting her arms around me, 'why not?'

This isn't like her at all. 'Why don't you wait down the stair while I get changed?' She says.

I raise an eyebrow in reply. She's up to something. I walk out the room and turn right to go down the stairs. I glance back and she's right behind me. My eyes immediately meet hers. She raises her leg and kicks me hard in the small of my back.

13

Still nae sign ae this fuckin kebab. 'The driver's just left the shop,' Imran said tae me oan the phone twenty minutes ago. Wonder if he means the wan in fuckin downtown Mumbai cos the kebab shoap ah ordered fae is only roon the corner. Ah go tae phone the cunt back but as soon as ah pick up the phone it starts ringin in mah hawn. It's Dolly.

'Dolly,' ah say, 'how's it gaun, hen?' She disnae answer me straight away. Ah cin hear her breathin though. Deep breaths, like she's tryin ae calm herself doon. 'Everythin awrite?'

'Angie, I need a hand,' she says wi a sigh. 'Philip's had a wee accident.'

Fuck. The conversation we hud in Blackpool comes rushin back tae me. Surely she's no went an done it? Ah better go an make sure she's no done anythin too daft. Ah hing up the phone withoot sayin goodbye. Ah stick mah jaiket oan tap ae ma housecoat an bolt oot the front door, still in mah slippers. The delivery driver's jist getting oot his motor as ah unlock mah gate.

'Delivery fur McCracken?' he says. Ah reach intae mah jaiket poakit, pull oot a tenner an fling it at the guy. 'Jist leave it ootside mah door, ah'll be back in a minute.'

'Wit aboot yer change?'

'Fuckin keep it.'

There's nae time ae waste. Ah dread tae think wit Dolly's went an done.

Ahm fucked by the time ah get tae hers. Ahm glad ye don't have tae be very athletic tae play bowls or bingo cos efter that run ah feel as if ahm gonnae die. Ah rattle her front door. The worst hing she could've done is hit the cunt ah hink, an she disnae huv the strength tae dae any real damage, even tae a skinny pathetic bastard like him.

Dolly opens the door efter the third chap. Her face has that same wee red flush tae it, like she had in Blackpool when she wis enjoyin herself. It's adrenaline or somethin that's goat her aw flustered this time though, ah hink. Her eyes drift doon tae mah left. I poke mah heid roon tae see wit she's lookin at.

She's only went an fuckin done it.

Phil lies aw crumpled up at the boattum ae the stair. He looks like a puppet that's been drapped fae a fair height. His legs an arms an that are aw at mad angles that shouldnae even be possible. His glesses are aw smashed tae fuck an mangled but somehow still clingin oan tae his face. Blood trickles doon his foreheid an runs intae his eyes. They're still open but there's nae sign ae life.

'Aw Jesus Christ, Dolly,' ah say lookin at the poor cunt oan the flair next tae me. 'Wit've ye done?'

'I gave him a wee shove down the stair. Made it look like a bad fall. If it's good enough for you,' she says, 'it's good enough for me.'

'Wit?'

She puts her hawns oan her hips. 'Well, ye know, I did it just like you said. I bumped him off. Same as you did to your man.'

'Dolly, hen, despite wit you've heard, ah've never killed anybody.' Ahm shoutin noo. Ah cannae help it.

Her face draps. She pulls me in an shuts the door behind me incase anybody hears me.

'What do you mean?'

'Wit the fuck dae ye hink ah mean?! Ah cannae believe this. Ah know ah act the hard wummin at times but ah couldnae kill anybody, fur fuck sake.'

'Everyone says that you killed your husband. The way you were talking in Blackpool made it sound as if you had done it before…' she looks visibly gutted that ahm no a murderer.

'That wis jist us bletherin ya daft bastard! That's wit pals dae! Ah goat a divorce. Ah goat a big guy fae the pub tae rough him up a bit so he'd leave me alane then he fucked off tae England. That's aw that happened. Nuthin excitin.' Ah push by her an head taewards the kitchen. Ah need a fuckin drink.

'So what are we going to do now?' she says, followin me.

Ah pour masel some ae wit ah assume is Phil's Glenmorangie an tan it in wan. That's fuckin better. Now ah cin start tae clarify the situation and work oot a plan. Ahm glad Philip's deid, right enough, but noo mah main concern hus tae be gettin rid ae the boady an makin sure Dolly disnae get caught.

'Right,' ah say pourin another whisky, 'first hings first – we need tae dae somethin wi the boady.'

'Hmmm,' she says, so coldly ah cannae believe it. She's just fuckin killed her man an she's considerin her options like she's fillin in the fuckin Sudoku in the paper. 'We could bury him out the back garden?'

'Aye nae bother,' wit a fuckin stupit suggestion. 'Then wit? The polis come sniffin aboot an see a patch ae grass that's been dug up? Roughly the same size as a guy? The guy they happen tae be lookin fur?'

'Yeah,' she says, scratchin her chin, 'good point.'

Ah jist laugh. Ah cannae help it. Look at the fuckin situation ah've goat maself intae. This wit ah get fur tryin ae make pals.

The two ae us stawn there fur a while tryin ae come up wi ideas when we hear some movement fae oot in the hall. We look at each other fur a good thirty seconds then head taewards the noise.

14

Fuckinnnnnng cow. Fucking AAAAAAAAH. Blood. Fucking crawling on the floor like a baby. I'll kill that fucking bitch if it's the last thing I do. FUCKING AAAAAAAH. Pain. Pain everywhere. There's nothing that doesn't hurt. Dolly. Fucking Dolly. Hate the bitch. Spit out some blood. Fuck. Dragging my broken body along the floor. More blood. Fuckinnnnng cow.

15

Phil's draggin himself doon the hall, leavin a smear ae blood behind him. His legs are totally fucked. His right leg's sittin at a ninety degree angle and hittin aff the wall as he tries tae get tae us.

'You,' he slurs, 'pair of evil bitchessss,' bubbles of blood appear in his mooth as he tries tae talk. He's pullin himself wi his left hawn an his right's tucked under his chest.

'Police,' ah think he's sayin. 'Jail,' he adds.

Ahm no gawn ae any jail. Ah done a wee stint in Cornton Vale mibbe twenty year ago fur breach ae the peace an it's full ae fuckin bams. It's no really a place fur the likes ae me.

'We need tae dae somethin,' ah say.

Dolly tuts. 'I was so sure he was dead,' she shakes her heid as if she's annoyed at herself.

'Obviously fuckin no!' I look around fur somethin ah can use tae put this cunt oot his misery. In the corner tae mah right is Phil's bowls. That'll do. He's a few feet away fae me noo. Ye wid hink he'd gie up but naw he just keeps comin, draggin his fucked up self taewards us. Ah lift a bowl oot the bag an turn tae face him.

He stoaps deid. His eyes wide open. Total fuckin fear.

'Do it, Angie, bash his fucking head in!'

Hearing Dolly swear throws me fur a moment. Swear words

just don't sound right comin oot her posh mooth.

'No,' Phil slurs, 'pleeeease.' The cunt's greetin.

'FUCKING DO IT!' Dolly screams.

Ah hawd the bowl wi baith hawns an bring it doon hard oan the tap ae Philip's heid. The noise turns mah fuckin stomach, it's just like the noise ae two bowls hittin each other but in a slightly different pitch an a wee crunch in amongst it. Blood spurts oot his nose or his mooth, ahm no sure, an goes aw over mah good slippers. The bowl's caved in his skull an it's fuckin stuck right in. His right leg twitches wance an that's it. He's deid. Well, he fuckin better be noo. Dolly claps her hawns an jumps up an doon like a wee lassie.

'Angie, that was amazing!' she squeals. This burd's went doolally.

'Calm yersel,' ah say, gawn back through tae the kitchen. Ah go tae pour another drink but mah hawns are shakin like fuck. Ah've just fuckin killed somebody efter aw.

'Let me get that,' says Dolly, takin the boattil aff me an pourin a measure oot fur each ae us.

'Wit happens noo?' ah say, no tae Dolly or the late Phil or anycunt really. Ahm no just an accomplice noo – ahm the fuckin killer. The abusive husband slayer.

'Who cares?' Dolly says, raisin her gless, 'cheers!'

She's goat a right tae be happy wi aw this right enough, she's finally goat rid ae Phil an he's definitely no comin back.

'Aye,' ah say raisin mah ain gless, 'cheers, hen.'

'Right,' she says, as if she's goat a plan. 'The body.'

'Aye, wit wur we sayin?'

'Well, we've already ruled out burying him. What else is there? Burning him? Dumping him in the Clyde?'

'Naw, naw, naw. Nae chance we can dae anythin like that. He'll get found.'

'Well what am I supposed to do, Angie? I can't just have him lying in the house. Stinking the place out.'

Ah pull mah phone oot tae check the time. Ah've goat

Broxi's smiling face as mah screensaver. It always cheers me up…

That's it.

Ah click mah fingers. 'Ah've goat it,' ah say. 'Right. Ah know wit we can dae wi the boady.'

Dolly gasps. Ah've never seen her so fuckin excited. 'Tell me the plan, Angie.'

'Ah'll get tae that. First we need an explanation as tae why he's missin.'

'Ah!' Dolly says, 'he told me he was going to the bowling club right before I, you know…' she does some kind a karate kick an then shrugs her shoulders. Ah cannae help but smile. She's mental.

'Right, that's good,' ah say, 'so see the morra morning you phone the polis an report him missin. Say he never came hame fae the bowlin club. You'll need tae act aw worried an devastated, can ye dae that?'

'Of course,' she says wi a wink. 'That's brilliant, Angie, honestly brilliant. Tell me about the body. What's the plan for that?'

'Well,' ah say, before drainin the last ae mah whisky, 'ah've goat a big hungry dug in the hoose that's no hud a proper meal fur a few days.'

Dolly looks like she's gonnae explode.

'I *LOVE* it,' she says.

16

By the time wi finish the boattil ae whisky, Match ae the Day's showin the shite games. It's pitch black ootside noo, finally, so we can get Phil ready for his big send aff. Efter much discussion, we opt tae transport his boady in a big suitcase. First we clean aff the bowl we used tae dae him in. Polish it right up an stick it back in its bag.

He fits in the suitcase wi room ae spare; he's a fuckin runt ae a guy efter aw. So we wheel him doon the road towards mine. Ah can hear Broxi scratchin at the door as ah put mah key in the lock. Mah kebab an her donner meat are still sittin by the front door. They'll be freezing noo so the dug can have mah kebab as well. That'll be a nice wee appetiser fur her before she gets tae her main. Dolly wheels Phil over the threshold so ah can pick up the poly bag wi the food in it. Broxi's sniffin at the suitcase an totally ignoring me as ah put the donner meat intae her bowl. She starts chewin at a corner an rips aff a bit ae fabric. Phil's finger pokes oot the hole.

'Right wait a minute, Broxi,' ah say grabbin her by the collar an pullin her away fae the suitcase. She's gonnae make some mess ae mah kitchen if ahm no careful. 'Dae us a favour Dolly, eh?' Ah say, 'gonnae grab a roll ae bin bags fae under the sink.'

Ah lay doon the bin bags oan the flair an tape them thegither so nae mess cin get tae mah good lino. Ah put some hawf way up mah cupboards as well, jist in case.

'Dolly, you undress him. We'll need to get rid ae his claes.'

'No bother, Angie,' Dolly replies an gets tae work. Ah go through intae the living room wi Broxi. A naked Phil isnae high oan mah list ae hings ah want tae see. While Dolly's dain that, ah try an think ae a plan fur Phil's claes. Any murders ah've seen in the news or whatever, the polis always find the cunt's shoes or jaiket in a park so there's nae point dumpin them. Burnin them's a terrible idea as well, this scheme's full ae nosy bastards; somebody wid see the fire. Then ah remember the charity bin bag. Ah'll wash his stuff then fire it aw in there. It'll get collected oan Monday morning. We'd be in the clear if his stuff wis ever found, there's nae way it could get traced back here. Tell ye wit, ahm fuckin good at this carry oan.

Dolly shouts through, 'That's him ready.'

'Good, stick his claes in the washin machine,' ah say, 'an while you're at it, bring in the boattil ae vodka oan the worktop an two glesses. Might as well make a wee night ae it, eh?'

Ah release Broxi tae dae her worst oan Phil an shut the door behind her. Ah don't really want tae watch that. The guy's been embrassed enough – ah did catch a wee glimpse ae his walloper efter aw.

17

The noises comin fae the kitchen were fuckin wild, ye could even hear it over the sound ae the washin machine. Snarlin, crunchin, squelchin you fuckin name it. We had tae turn the telly up full bung tae drown oot the noise. Wis enough tae make ye sick.

Efter aw the whisky we hud in Dolly's an the vodka in mine, we passed oot aboot two o'clock.

Ah get up aff the flair an shake Dolly awake. Ah let her have the couch, she deserved it. She must have a killer ae a hangover though, cos she's no fur movin. Fair enough.

Ah push the kitchen door open tae see the damage Broxi's done. The dug's fuckin went fur it big time. She's lyin oan her side in the middle ae the kitchen, wi a bone hingin oot her mooth an snorin like fuck. Her belly's so bloated she looks pregnant. Aw that's left ae Phil is a couple ae bones an his heid. The smell is horrific. Ah realise ah shouldnae huv expected the dug tae be able tae eat him aw. A heid is a lot easier tae get rid ae than an entire boady right enough. Ah'll keep the bones in the freezer fur her an ah'll wrap the heid up in a couple ae poly bags an stick it in the bin. Should be away at some landfill site before anycunt finds it, if they ever dae find it that is. This is an absolute canter. Ah stick Phil's claes in the dryer while ah square the place up a bit.

Ah put Phil's claes in the charity bin bag an leave it oan mah doorstep. There's a few other folk have theirs oot ready fur collection as well. Ah look aboot tae make sure nae cunt's watchin then swap mah bag wi wan fae across the road. Just in case.

18

Dolly reported Phil missin, the polis asked her a few questions an put a bit ae pressure oan her but she played the part ae the dotin wife perfectly. They came roon an asked aw the neighbours if we'd seen him. Ah told thum ah thought ahd seen um walkin by mah windae oan Saturday night, headin taewards the bowlin club. An that was that. The night before the tournament, the polis telt Dolly there was nothin mair they could dae. They said they'd searched everywhere an didnae huv any leads. They didnae really seem tae care. They hud other hings tae worry aboot; missin weans, drug dealers an aw that. They wurnae too bothered aboot lookin fur some guy who spent maist ae his time in the pub. Suited us. Ah asked Dolly if Phil hud any other family that might be upset tae find oot he wis missin. 'Well,' she said, 'he has two sons, who hate him. And an ex-wife who hates him even more than me, apparently.'

Phil's mates shared pictures ae him oan Facebook or some shite, but that wis the extent ae their concern. Ah started tae feel a bit sorry fur the cunt – he'd disappeared an naebody gave a fuck, no even the polis. Then ah remembered how much ae a wank he wis. Good fuckin riddance, ah say.

The mornin ae the tourney. Fuckin showtime. Mah bowls are polished up tae fuck man, they are fuckin *gleamin.* Polished aw mah sovvies up nice an bright anaw. Ahm lookin every inch the bowlin superstar that ah um. Ah've been oan edge a wee bit, ahm sure ye cin understawn why, so ah just aboot shite maself when there's a chap at mah door. Loud. Like the way polis chap yer door. Ah calm doon when ah look through the spy hole though, it's just Dolly.

'Awrite, hen,' ah say openin the door, 'moan in.'

'Angie,' she says aw excited, 'just *wait* 'til I tell you this.' She breezes by me an intae the livin room. Broxi jumps aw over her an she makes a right fuss over the dug. They've taken a right wee shine ae each other, they two. 'Look at this,' she pulls a broon envelope fae inside her cardigan an hawns it tae me. 'Found this in Philip's wardrobe when I was sorting through his stuff.'

'Fuck me,' inside the envelope is wads an wads ae twenty pound notes. Must be at least four grand in there. 'No fuckin way!' ah shout, 'Did he never tell you aboot aw this?'

'Never. I always thought he must have had a stash of money somewhere. But I never ever thought it would be as much as this.'

'Ah cannae believe this. Wit ye gonnae dae wi it then?'

Dolly smiles an cocks her heid. 'Don't you mean what are *we* going to do with it?'

'Och, away. You've earned that money, hen. That's aw yours.'

19

'Aw, Dolly,' Gavin says, runnin over tae greet us as we get oot the taxi, 'how you keeping, hen? I was gutted to hear about Philip. Hopefully he'll turn up soon, eh?'

'Yeah,' Dolly mutters, tryin tae avoid eye contact wi him an tryin no tae smile, 'hopefully.'

'Right, Angie,' he says, turnin ae me, 'You ready for this?'

'Too fuckin right ah um,' ah say tae the cunt, 'anyway, where's the bogs?'

'Eh, the toilets are in there,' he points tae the clubhoose. 'Second door on the right.'

'Cheers. Listen, Dolly, ah'll see ye oot there. Make sure ye get a good view.'

As ah walk intae the toilets tae get changed, there's June touchin up her lipstick in the mirror. She raises an eyebrow an gies me a nod as ah go intae a cubicle. Ahm startin tae think this wummin jist hings aboot toilets aw the time, seems tae be the only time ah encounter her these days.

'Terrible thing, eh, Angie?' she says tae me.

'Wit's that?' ah reply, buttonin up mah blouse.

'Dolly's man going missing.'

'Aye it definitely is,' ahm wonderin where the fuck she's gawn wi this an start tae panic.

'Anyway,' she's changin the subject. Thank fuck. 'We're all rooting for you today. I'm sure you'll be walking away with that prize money.'

'Ah sure will be, June. Don't you worry aboot that.' Ah slip oan mah special bowlin shoes an emerge fae the cubicle a new wummin.

'You look, um,' she hesitates an looks me up an doon, 'lovely, Angie.'

'Aw ah know, June,' ah scrape mah hair back intae a ponytail, 'ahm a fuckin honey.'

Me an June walk oot oan tae the green. Ah cannae believe the amount ae people here tae watch a fuckin game ae bowls, there's hunners ae cunts aw packed in here. Wit the fuck is gawn oan? Ah scan roon the crowd fur Dolly an gie her a wee wave. She puts her sunglesses oan her foreheid an waves back. There's a wee warm up game started between two guys fae Shettleston. Ah watch that fur a bit, neither ae them look up tae much. If ah could compete in baith the men's an wummin's competitions ah'd make a fuckin fortune.

Ah can hear a load ae commotion comin fae behind me so ah spin roon an get the fuckin fright ae mah life. A fuckin camera is right in mah face! Wan ae they big wans fur the telly. A few mare appear, microphones an aw that as well. Then Gavin comes oot wi his daughter, the two ae thum aw suited an booted.

'Ah, Angie,' Gavin says stoatin over wi his lassie, 'I'd like you to meet my daughter, Sophie.'

'Hi, Angie,' she puts her hand out. She's goat a right impressive presence this lassie, it's easy tae see she's goat a bit ae money just by lookin at her. I put mah hawn oot an shake hers.

'Nice tae meet ye, hen,' ah say, 'wits wi aw the cameras an that?'

'Oh, I called in a few favours with some friends at STV and convinced them to televise the game live. Amazing, eh?'

'It certainly is,' Gavin pipes up, 'and Angie here is our brightest hope of winning.'

'Aye, aye, very good. Listen, Gavin, climb oot mah arsehole fur a minute cos ah've goat some questions. Wit um ah competin in? Is it teams or singles or wit?'

'Well,' Sophie interjects, 'since it's on the telly and we have limited time, it's just singles. Four men and four women from each club. Straight knockout with shorter games. It's an unusual format but it makes it more exciting, don't you think? Anyway, good luck and I hope you do my dad's bowling club proud.' She totters away oan her high heels. Ah quite like this lassie.

'Feel free to have a wee warm up,' Gavin says, 'oh and, eh, you might get interviewed for the telly so don't, y'know, eh…'

'Spit it oot.'

'Don't give yourself, or the club for that matter, a showing up. Eh, Angie?' He pats me oan the back an fucks off.

Prick. Who dis he think he is?

Ah size up mah competition; a young lassie, maybe in her late twenties, two wummin aboot mah age, an wit looks like a fuckin walkin corpse. This auld timer must be in her nineties. Fair play tae her fur still gettin oot an aboot. The other wummin competin fur oor club, ah shouldnae say 'oor' club right enough, seein as ahm no technically a member, are June, Amanda an auld Frances. No exactly a stellar line up.

Before the first round is aboot tae kick aff, Sophie comes over an grabs me by the arm. She ushers me over tae some guy who's interviewin Gavin in front ae wan ae the cameras.

'...and we're hoping this will become an annual event and get more women and youngsters in particular, involved in the sport by showcasing it in this exciting format, Raman,' Gavin says to the guy.

'Thanks, Gavin,' Raman says, 'Now, Sophie. I understand this is one of Springboig's most talented bowlers you're with?'

'Yes, she certainly is,' Sophie says. 'This is Angie.'

'Awrite,' I nod directly doon the camera.

'Nice to meet you, Angie,' the presenter says tae me, 'are there any special tactics you're going to be deploying today?'

I look over Raman's shoulder at the decrepit auld wummin fae Shettleston as she tries wi aw her might tae lift her bowls oot her bag.

'No really, Raman,' ah say, 'ahm just gonnae go fur it as ah usually dae an hopefully ah'll fuckin hump whoever ahm up against.'

Before ah can continue wi mah telly debut, Sophie pulls me away. Ah can hear Raman apologisin fur mah 'bad language' an sayin this just shows how competitive this sport can be. Sophie's laughin an so um ah.

'Well done, Angie,' she says, 'that was brilliant. Not really suitable for Saturday afternoon telly but folk'll be talking about it and laughin. You should go and get ready. You're up first against the young girl.'

The guys fae Springboig aw get humped and it's an all-Shettleston final. Ah sweep aside everycunt, nae bother, an ahm in the final. June's made it tae the semi final but she's getting trounced aff the auld burd. This wummin is amazin, honestly, think the frail wee wifey act wis aw a big rouse cos she's a fuckin demon oan the green. Ahm lookin forward tae gawn up against her.

In the end, June gets beat withoot ever even havin a look in so it's me versus the walkin corpse.

She's better than anybody I've ever came up against, this wummin, but ahm still the stronger player. It's best ae three in the final an she won the first set. Only cause ah underestimated her right enough an played mah usual style which works like a charm against the fuckin numpties ahm normally up against. But no her. She exploits aw mah usual moves an ends up beatin me by a point. In the second game ah get wise tae her. Ah fuckin destroy her. Efter mah last shot, the crowd's oan their feet aw shoutin an clappin. This is amazin. Ah look intae the crowd fur Dolly an she's punchin the air an shoutin. Next tae her is June an Amanda. June gies me a thumbs up then she turns tae Amanda an high fives her. As the noise ae the crowd dies doon ahm sure ah can just aboot hear June say tae Amanda, 'Benidorm, here we come.'

Aye, that'll be fuckin shinin bright.

Near the end ae the last set, me an the auld timer are neck an neck. Her wee airms must be killin her though as her shots start tae faw a wee bit short. Wi mah last bowl, ah just need tae make sure it stoaps a few feet away fae the jack tae make sure she wins an they biddies don't get any ae the dough. Ah'll go long an pretend tae make a cunt ae it, her last bowl will faw short an she'll win. That's the plan. Fuck winnin the money an lettin June an Amanda an aw the rest ae they stuck-up snobby cows get a free fuckin holiday. Ah'll feel bad fur Dolly, right enough. She'd probably like gawn tae Benidorm wi aw them.

The crowd faws silent as ah line up fur mah last shot. Ah take a deep breath. Ah need tae make this look as authentic as possible. Ahm gonnae go wide right, then as it curves in, it should hit aff wan ae the corpse's bowls, knockin hers closer tae the jack an hopefully mine'll go oot ae bounds. When she takes her last shot, judging by how tired she's lookin, it won't go anywhere near the jack or any ae the other bowls in play. She'll win.

I roll mah final bowl. Ah don't get as much power behind as ah had planned though. Ah cin tell ah've fucked this big time milliseconds efter the bowl leaves mah hawn. It seems tae roll in slow motion alang the path ah had planned but when it curves in, it cuts right between the two bowls ah wis aimin fur, kisses the jack an stoaps. It's the fuckin perfect shot. Nae danger. The crowd's gawn fuckin mental noo. They're even chantin mah fuckin name. The corpse is gonnae have tae produce the goods noo or ahm gonnae fuckin win. They bitches will help themselves tae the prize money an fuck off tae Benidorm.

The corpse wipes the sweat aff her brow wi a wee hankie she produces fae her poakit an steps up. The crowd goes quiet again. Dolly waves at me fae the crowd, she's aw chuffed. At least she'll get tae enjoy the trip, even if ah won't. The corpse picks up her final bowl. She gies it a few swings back an forth then lets the hing fuckin FLY oot her hawn. It screams doon the green, smashes wan ae her ain bowls which then skelps mah last wan an sends it intae the ditch. It's the best move ah've ever seen in mah life. She's only went and beat me fair an square. The crowd goes mental once again as the corpse does a lap ae honour. God love her.

Ah look over at Jane an Amanda an silently mouth, 'Get it up ye,' then go an get changed.

Dolly comes intae the toilet as ahm washin mah hawns.

'Unlucky, Angie,' she looks gutted.

'Ach,' ah say, 'Listen, Dolly, ahm sorry ah didnae win the money. Ah know ye were lookin forward tae gawn away wi yer pals.'

'Ah well,' she's smilin noo, 'they may not be going to Benidorm anytime soon but we certainly are.'

'Wit? How um ah meant tae afford that? Ahm fuckin skint.' She goes intae her cardigan once again withoot sayin a word an flashes the envelope full ae Phil's money at me. 'Dolly, ya fuckin beauty!'

20

Two days later an the two ae us are sittin by the pool in some fancy pensioners only hotel in sunny Benidorm. 'Here, Dolly,' ah say, raisin mah mojito, 'tae Phil!' She clinks her gless against mine an we go back tae sunbathin.

Ah feel somethin blockin oot the sun efter a minute an ah open mah eyes tae see wit the script is – there wisnae a cloud in the sky a minute ago.

It's no a cloud disturbin mah sunbathin though – it's a big toned an tanned hunk. Wan ae the reps.

'Ladies,' the hunk says tae me in his daft English accent, 'we're having a little lawn bowls competition. You up for it?'

'Bowls?' ah laugh, 'Never played it in mah puff. No interested. Sorry.' Ah shut my eyes an lie back doon.

'There's drinks tokens to be won if that sweetens the deal?'

Ah sit up an look at Dolly an smile. 'Now you're fuckin talkin, pal.'

A FISTFUL OF COPPERS

'I can't go to school. She'll hit me again,' Carly whined. Her bottom lip quivered. She was talking about Chantelle at school. A big brute of a lassie who had been giving her grief. She slagged her for the fact she got her shoes from Brantano, for the fact her mum didn't have a car and for anything else that she could think of. She especially liked calling her "Clatty Carly". Chantelle was a right wee cow.

'Well, if she tries anythin the day while ahm there,' Carly's maw, Julie, said, 'there'll be three hits; me hittin her, her hittin the deck, an then the ambulance hittin ninety.'

Julie was heading straight to work after dropping Carly off and she checked her purse for bus fare. *Nae change. Bastard.* She rooted around in her hand bag – there must be some change in there. She emptied the bag and turned it upside down – nothing. Julie realised she was going to have to raid the wee jar full of coppers. *Drappin two quid's worth ae coppers intae the wee hing in front ae a bus full ae people – what a fuckin riddy,* she thought. She put the change into her purse and tried to zip it up but couldn't.

Walking through the fine drizzly rain to school, Carly was deathly quiet. The thought of what Chantelle might do to her today terrified her. She had visions of Chantelle grabbing her maw and tombstoning her into the ground before punching Carly so hard her head came flying clean off her shoulders and into orbit. Carly thought she was going to be sick.

'Hurry up, hen,' Julie shouted back at her daughter. As they approached the school gates, Julie watched Chantelle's maw drive away in her Range Rover. Julie felt her hand curl into a tight fist. Her nails dug into her palm. 'Snobby cow,' she muttered under her breath.

'Who is?' Carly asked. Julie hadn't realised she'd caught up with her.

'Eh, naebody, sweetheart.' Carly hid behind her mother as the playground came into view. Chantelle stood leaning against a wall. She spat on the ground. Carly grabbed the bottom of Julie's jacket.

'Please just let me stay off. Please, mum?' she begged.

'Ahm sorry, Carly doll. Ye cannae. Ah've got tae go tae work. Just go in there an play wi yer wee pals an ah'll wait here until the bell goes. Everythin'll be awrite.'

Carly reluctantly edged into the playground, hoping Chantelle wouldn't see her. She had no such luck. Chantelle blocked Carly's path. She circled her. Carly felt like a gazelle being stalked by a lion in those documentaries. Chantelle pushed her from behind and Carly went down face first into a puddle. Chantelle stamped an Ugg boot-clad foot down into the puddle, sending a mini tsunami crashing over Carly's face and walked away. Carly got to her feet and ran back to her maw.

Julie tried to contain her rage towards this wee horror that had just decked her daughter. She wanted to storm into the playground and drop-kick the wee bitch. She was about to do just that – then she had an idea. She dried her daughter's face with her jumper and took her hand.

'Here, hen,' she said to Carly. She emptied the coins from the purse into Carly's hand until she could hold no more.

'I don't want money, Mum, I want to go home,' Carly said, wiping tears away from her eyes.

'Yer no gawn hame. Yer gonnae gie that lassie a piece ae yer mind. Make a fist.'

'Like this?' Carly struggled to close her hand right over but it was a definite fist. Julie checked her watch; the bell was due to ring any second now.

'Aye, just like that. Now go an skelp her. She'll no be messin wi ye after this, pal.'

Carly walked over to Chantelle. She had returned to her spot leaning against the wall. She watched Carly striding towards her.

'Clatty Carly, Clatty Carly, ye gonnae run greetin to yer mammy again? Hahahaha.'

Carly let her hand swing back and forth like a pendulum as she came nose-to-nose with Chantelle. The rain was easing off now and the sun was trying its hardest to break through the thick carpet of cloud. Pockets of blue sky appeared here and there. Carly swung her hand back and dropped her shoulder. Her fist came round in a wide circle. Chantelle didn't see it coming until it was too late for her to react. Carly gritted her teeth and let her fist hurtle into Chantelle's jaw. The full weight of the one and two pence pieces crashed into the side of Chantelle's face like a meteorite. Carly kept driving her fist up the way, twisting it as it made impact. The shinier coins glinted in the sunlight as they sprung loose from Carly's hand.

SCUDBOOK

'Of course it's fucking fixed, how else do you think bookies make money?' Mhairi said to the seething punter in front of her.

'Och fuck off ya daft wee cow,' the old guy said to her, crumpling his betting slip into a wee ball and flinging it at her. The hot favourite in the 3:30 at Kempton had come dead last despite being tipped to win by many of the self-proclaimed "tipsters" who frequented the bookies.

'This guy givin you grief, hen?' The branch manager, Andrea, asked Mhairi. A formidable woman, was Andrea. Feared by the punters due to her no-nonsense approach to dealing with them when they gave her staff any bit of cheek.

'Naw, naw. Ahm just leavin,' said the old guy. Andrea and Mhairi were now the only people in the bookies.

'Right Mhairi, hen, I need to ask you somethin,' said Andrea, 'it's aboot that magazine that's appeared in the staff room."

'Wit magazine?' said Mhairi.

'The wan oan the staff room table,' Andrea looked around and lowered her voice, 'the dirty wan.'

The magazine had appeared seemingly overnight. Andrea was sure it hadn't been there when she closed up the night before and yet, that morning, there it was it all its glory. Naked women cavorted on the front of it under the title *Frank's Belters.* Their faces contorted into bizarre, wide-eyed expressions. Their hands gripping an assortment of phallic objects. The sheer obscenity of the magazine was heightened by the fact it was placed casually next to Malcolm's copy of 'Angler's Weekly'.

Of course Mhairi had seen it. It was the first thing she'd seen when she walked into the staff room before she started her shift. Naturally she'd taken a picture of the lewd magazine and shared it on Twitter. *Can't believe the creeps I work with*, she'd written as the caption. Her fellow part-time colleague, Shaun, commented, along with several laughing face emojis, *Nae danger. I start at 5, make sure it's still there when I get in, I want a swatch. Bet it's Malcolm's hahahah.*

'I'm asking everybody, is it yours?' Andrea asked Mhairi.

'Course it's no! You think I'm gonnae be sitting on my tea break reading a porno?' Mhairi said.

'Och I knew it widnae have been you, hen,' Andrea said, 'I'm just making sure. If nobody admits it's theirs, I'll need to get the area manager involved. It's bloody disgusting. I cannae have people bringing that kind of… vulgarity into my shop.'

When Shaun arrived later to start his shift, the magazine was still on the staff room table. Nobody had touched it for fear it may well have been 'contaminated,' as Mhairi had put it. Shaun had no such hesitation however. He picked it up and laughed as he flicked through the glossy pages.

'Fuckin hell, man,' he said, 'this is some proper hardcore shit.' Shaun's smile evaporated as he got near the middle.

Staring back at him was his own face.

There he was, smiling seductively, standing against a backdrop of football fixtures. Naked from the waist up. A small blue bookie pen tucked behind his ear.

Open-mouthed he turned the page. He was now unbuckling his belt as he leaned back against the Deal or No Deal machine. Shaun dropped the magazine. It landed face down. Mhairi watched the colour drain from Shaun's face.

'It's no that bad, surely?' she said, 'bet you've seen a lot worse.'

'There's p-p-pictures of me in there,' Shaun stuttered.

Mhairi picked up the magazine. She thought it looked a bit thicker than it was a few hours ago.

'No fuckin way. I need to see these,' she said. Mhairi erupted with laughter as she opened the magazine to find Shaun, spread across the centre pages, lying naked on the floor with only a handful of betting slips protecting his modesty.

Shaun couldn't believe what he was seeing. He had no recollection of the pictures of him being taken and no idea how they could have ended up in a porn magazine.

'Please don't tell anybody, Mhairi. I don't know how they've done this. It must be Photoshop or something, I don't know,' he said. Mhairi turned the page to see Shaun shoving a fistful of bookie pens up his arse.

'Hmmm, they look quite real to me,' Mhairi said, exploding with laughter again. 'I won't tell anybody, obviously, but you're telling me these pictures have just appeared magically in this magazine?'

'Fuck knows how this has happened but I want rid of it. Imagine if my pals seen this. Imagine if my da seen it!' Shaun was shaking now. His face had turned from chalk-white to a strange grey colour. He was freaking out big time.

'Right, calm doon,' said Mhairi. 'We'll bin it then I'll tell Andrea I've flung it out cause it was giving me the boak. Nobody will ever know.'

'Bin it?' said Shaun, 'I want the whole fucking hing shredded and set it on fire and then I want the fucking shredder burned as well.'

After Shaun ripped out the pages featuring him (all fourteen of them) and stuffed them into his pockets, the two of them went out the back of the shop. They took the two small metal bins from the staff room. They placed the pictures of Shaun in one and the rest of the magazine in the other. Shaun started a fire in each of the bins. His mysterious homoerotic photoshoot was gone forever.

Or so he thought.

The next morning the magazine was back, completely intact and undamaged, on the table in the staff room.

Andrea asked Malcolm about the magazine as the two of them opened up the shop that morning.

'Surely ah don't look like the kinda guy that reads porn mags, dae ah?' asked Malcolm, standing there in his dubiously stained jacket and milk bottle specs. Andrea looked him up and down.

'Em… no, course not, Malcolm. It's just that it must belong to someone who works here and I've already asked Mhairi and Shaun said it's not his either…' said Andrea. Silence filled the void between them. Malcolm felt hurt by the accusation that he was the owner of the filth in question. He picked up the magazine.

'Ah can assure ye, Andrea, that this isnae mine,' Malcolm said, picking up and flinging the magazine towards the bin. It missed and landed on the floor, flopping open to the middle pages.

The two of them stared in horror at the sheer amount of pasty Malcolm flesh that was now on show before them. He lay on his stomach on the navy blue carpet of the shop floor, wearing only his threadbare Gola boxers. He was looking over his shoulder at the camera as he filled in a football coupon. The glossiness of the magazine somehow accentuating his peely-walliness. There was a column of text next to the picture of Malcolm. It was an interview.

Malcolm scrambled over and picked the magazine up. He was shaking. Andrea was speechless.

'How,' was the only word Malcolm could force his mouth to make. Malcolm read the interview:

Malcolm Dempsey, everyone's favourite bookie, on life, love and being a virgin in his forties. 'Ahm savin maself for the right wummin – ahm no ready to take a gamble oan love just yet...'

Andrea snatched the magazine out of Malcolm's trembling, hands. She licked her index finger and turned the pages. She was mortified for Malcolm. He tried to grab the magazine back off her but she moved aside and kept it out of his reach.

'Please, Andrea. Don't tell anybody and for the love of God don't *show* anybody,' he said.

'I think this clears up who the magazine belongs to, eh Malcolm?' Andrea said.

'Look, ah don't know where that hing came fae or how they've managed get pictures of me like that.'

'I'll make you a deal. I won't tell anyone about your wee photoshoot in here,' Andrea waved the magazine about in front of Malcolm's face, 'or your… secret, and in return you can do me a couple of wee favours. Cannae say fairer than that, can we?'

Later that day, when Shaun arrived for his evening shift, Malcolm was scurrying around after Andrea. Making her tea, going to the shop for her and even doing some of her paperwork for her. Shaun watched him with confusion. Malcolm was a proud man who wouldn't lower himself to being a skivvy for someone, he had confided to Shaun, he detested.

'Mate,' Shaun said to Malcolm, pulling him aside as Andrea went to the toilet, 'wits happening here?'

Malcolm let out a deep sigh.

'If ah tell ye, ye cannae say tae anybody wit ahm aboot tae tell ye,' said Malcom.

Shaun had an inkling about what Malcolm was about to say.

'Mind that magazine?' Malcolm said.

'Was there pictures of you in it?' said Shaun

'How do you know? Did she show you them?' Malcolm nodded towards the toilet where Andrea was.

'Naw,' Shaun lowered his voice, 'there was pictures of me in it as well. But me and Mhairi set it oan fire, how can it be back?'

'Fuck knows, but we better get it aff her then, eh?

Andrea had taken to keeping the magazine in the safe where only she had access to it. She hadn't flicked through it. She had no desire to see erotic pictures of any of her colleagues – especially Malcom. She would just keep using it to manipulate him until she grew bored, she decided. And she was already getting bored. There was only so many cups of Malcolm's pathetic tea that she could drink.

A few weeks after the magazine had first appeared in the staff room, Andrea was sitting in the office one Wednesday night while Malcolm and Shaun served a steady flow of Champions League punters. The two men had decided to wait until the right moment to steal the magazine so Malcolm could try and destroy it. Shaun said he wouldn't be handling the magazine under any circumstances for fear that more pictures of him would appear in it.

Andrea was fiddling with her set of keys, trying to attach the new shutter key, when Shaun shouted on her to come out and deal with an irate customer. She slammed the keys down on the desk and marched through to face the guy. As she explained to the raging punter that own goals didn't count in first goal scorer bets, Malcolm took his chance and slipped through to the back office. He unlocked the safe, took out the magazine, locked the safe, placed the keys back silently on the desk and then stuffed the magazine into his rucksack in the staff room.

Andrea was too flustered from dealing with angry customers to notice the magazine was missing from the safe as she sorted out the cash that night. Malcolm got it home and sat in his bedroom leafing through it. The pictures of him were still there. He inspected them with the magnifying glass he used for fixing his model trains. They didn't look Photoshopped or computer generated or anything. The pictures were definitely of him – he could tell by the big mole on his arse. After quickly flicking through all the of pictures of himself, he came across pictures of Andrea. She was dressed as a dominatrix and the pictures showed her whipping Malcolm as he crawled on all fours like a dog. Malcolm giggled at the absurdity of the situation he found himself in. Here he was, in possession of a magazine filled with countless explicit images of him and his boss, pictures he was sure he would have remembered posing for, but didn't. He came to the conclusion the magazine was part of some elaborate wind-up. On the very last page of the magazine was a full-page advertisement which, he thought, seemed to confirm his suspicions. It said:

Did you find this magazine in your home or place of work?
No idea how it got there?
Even more surprised by the fact there are pictures of you and your colleagues, friends, family etc. in it?
Call Frank on 07728326665

Malcolm took a picture of the magazine using his phone and sent it to Shaun. *Well fucking phone the cunt then,* was Shaun's reply. Malcolm phoned the number from the advert. A robotic female voice greeted him after three rings.

'Hello. You have reached Frank. If you have found a pornographic magazine in your home or place of work, please press one.'

Malcolm pulled the phone away from his ear and pressed one.

'Thank you. If you would like to make a complaint about the magazine, please press one.'

Malcolm once again pulled the phone away from his ear but then decided he would wait to hear the other choices.

'If you would like to order an extra copy of the magazine, please press two. If you would like to speak directly with Frank, please hang up immediately.'

'Wit?' Malcolm said out loud to no one in particular. He listened for further options. The voice on the other end of the phone said nothing. Malcolm hit the END CALL button. As soon as he did this there was three knocks on his front door. 'Surely no,' he said out loud again. He went downstairs to answer it. He looked through the spy-hole. There stood a man who looked like the only name he could possibly have was Frank. He was the very embodiment of the name Frank; Short, rotund and smoking a cigar. Malcolm opened the door. Frank looked him up and down and removed the cigar from his mouth, blowing smoke into Malcolm's face.

'S'appenin mah man? Ahm Frank,' he said as he breezed past Malcolm and sauntered through into the living room. Malcolm was stunned. He immediately phoned Shaun.

'Mate, the guy Frank from the advert has just turned up at my hoose,' Malcolm whispered down the line, 'get here pronto.'

'Fuck fuck fuck. Right, I'll see if Mhari'll give me a lift over. I'll no be long,' said Shaun.

'Fuckin hurry up, the cunt looks mental,' Malcolm said, hanging up on Shaun.

Malcolm told Frank his two colleagues would be joining them. Frank said this was not a problem. Not a single word was exchanged while they waited on Shaun and Mhairi. Malcolm stared at Frank as he puffed on his cigar. The smoke hung in the room. Frank reached into the pocket of his stonewash denim jacket and produced a comb which he dragged through his long greasy hair. He slicked his hair back and it contoured perfectly to the shape of his skull.

As Frank tucked the comb back in his pocket, Malcolm's phone buzzed. *Outside mate*, the text from Shaun read.

'Why not just chap the fucking door?' Malcolm muttered under his breath. He opened the door and ushered Mhairi and Shaun into the living room to see Frank. The three of them stood in awkward silence. Frank looked them all up and down then gestured at Shaun with his cigar.

'That's some fuckin haircut, pal,' Frank said. 'Who done

that? The cooncil?'

Shaun gingerly rubbed the back of his head. He always got the back and sides of his hair shaved with a number zero and he was leaving the top to grow long. He was used to older guys in the bookies and down the pub giving him grief about his hair but this time the insult felt particularly cutting given that it came from the greaseball in the corner.

'Ahm Frank, by the way. Yeez gonnae sit doon or wit?' The three of them sat opposite Frank on Malcolm's flowery couch. Frank leaned forward in the armchair he was sitting in. 'Right, ahm assumin yeez are havin a bit ae bother wi a porn magazine?'

Mhairi, Shaun and Malcolm nodded in unison.

'Photies ae yerselves appearin in it?'

They nodded once again.

'Yeez want rid ae it?'

Another synchronized nod.

'Fur fuck sake can yeez no talk?' Frank laughed.

'Sorry, we're just a bit creeped out to be honest,' said Mhairi. 'Like, it just turned up in the staff room one morning.'

'Understandable,' Frank nodded. 'It can be a bit troublin, ah know that. A don't like this line ae work, but ahm here tae help. These magazines have got a habit ae turning up in work-places where there's a lack ae excitement or maybe where there's a boss who's being a bit ae a dick. Sometimes they just appear in hooses tae gie folk a wee scare. Ah mind wan appeared in this lesbian couple's flat wi pictures ae wan ae them having a bit a... ye know... fun wi the other burd's brother. No real pictures obviously, but real enough lookin that the burds ended up havin a barney cos ae it. Next hing ye know ahm at the door havin tae calm them doon an sort it oot.

'In any case though there's only wan way tae get rid ae these scudbooks,' Frank nodded at Malcolm, 'take it you've got it here? Go an get it fur me please mah man.'

Malcolm went up to his bedroom to fetch the magazine. Shaun and Mhairi sat staring at Frank as he slicked his hair back again. He put the comb back into his pocket. Frank took a quick puff of his cigar and blew smoke rings at Mhairi and Shaun.

'There ye go,' Malcolm said, handing the magazine to Frank and sitting back down.

'Right,' said Frank getting to his feet, 'first of all, have you tried burning the magazine?'

'Aye,' Shaun answered, 'me and her set it on fire but it turned up back in the staff room the next day.'

Frank let out a soft chuckle.

'I thought you would've been the wan,' Frank said, 'fair play, pal.'

'Wit d'ye mean?' said Shaun.

'It's just that tae get rid ae the magazine by burning it, the person setting it on fire has tae be a virgin,' Frank laughed again, 'ah was sure you widda been wan wi that haircut!'

'Fuck,' Malcolm said. Frank looked at him and flashed him a yellow-toothed smile.

'Ah-Ha!' Frank exclaimed. 'It's you then?' He opened the magazine to the page with Malcolm's interview and held it up for everyone to see. 'Aw aye, there he is, the virgin bookie! That's a belter!'

Malcolm's face turned red.

'Ye don't have to say anything, big chap. Here, just take this an dae the deed,' Frank said, handing Malcolm his still-lit cigar.

Mhairi and Shaun watched as Malcolm touched the cigar to the corner of the magazine. The three of them turned away as it went up in a bright blue light. There was a loud bang and then… nothing. The magazine was gone, the cigar was gone – and so was Frank.

'That was fucking mental,' Shaun exclaimed.

'You awrite?' Mhairi said, rubbing Malcolm's back.

‘Aye, hen, aye. Ahm fine. Look ahm gonnae get tae mah bed,’ Malcolm said.

‘Listen, we’re no gonnae tell anybody, Malcolm,’ Mhairi reassured him, ‘are we, Shaun?’

‘Naw, don’t be daft. Ahm no telling anycunt aboot anything that’s happened the night. Ahm sure ah must be trippin,’ Shaun said.

Malcolm showed his colleagues out to the front door without saying a word.

He went back through to the living room to turn off the lights. He felt totally drained after the evening’s events. Something on the table caught his eye. Lying there was a business card. He picked it up. It simply read:

Frank.

POSH CUNT

'Tony, what's on the cards for your dinner this evening?' Owen asked. This was the usual 4:45pm chat in the office.

'Well,' Tony replied, he always liked showcasing his culinary skills to his colleagues, 'this evening I'm making a tuna and avocado salad.' He sat back and waited for the plaudits from Owen.

'Very nice,' Owen nodded. 'What are you going to have with it?'

'Cous cous, I think.'

'Hmmm, expected something a bit better from a man of your calibre, to be honest.'

Tony was struck with panic. He was usually top dog when it came to fancy food. Owen looking down on him for having cous cous hurt him. He tried to backtrack.

'Eh, well, I'm not 100% settled on cous cous. I mean, I might go for something else like, um, ehhh,' he racked his brains.

'Quinoa?'

'Yeah, exactly! Quinoa. That's what I meant. Not cous cous. Definitely not cous cous.' Tony had no idea what quinoa was. He had a flashback of him and Owen laughing at the office junior for not knowing what kale was. He typed quinoa into his search engine as Owen's eyes returned to his own screen.

Quinoa, is a so-called "super grain" offering a wide range of health benefits. Gluten-free and easy to digest, the facts suggest it is as close to a perfect ingredient as you can get!

'Yeah,' Tony said, 'I'm trying to cut down on the old gluten so it'll be quinoa for me this evening.'

Tony wandered the aisles of Waitrose in a trance. They didn't have any quinoa left. If they didn't have any quinoa, then what the fuck was he supposed to have with his tuna and avocado salad? *Cous cous? No thanks, I'm not some sort of bloody peasant*, he thought. Tony didn't know what he was going to do. This was worse than the time they ran out of fennel. His evening was ruined. Then he saw one of the elusive shelf-stackers.

'Excuse me,' he said to the girl putting boxes of organic cereal onto the shelf, 'don't suppose you have any quinoa in the back?'

'I'll have a wee look for you,' she replied, 'back in two secs.'

She returned a moment later and there it was in her hands; the 500g bag of grainy goodness. His evening was saved.

'There you go,' she said with a smile, handing him the bag, 'one bag of kwin-oh-ah.'

'What did you just call it?' he sneered.

'Um, kwin-oh-ah?'

'Ha, it's actually pronounced *keen*-wah.'

'Aye awrite, whatever,' the girl rolled her eyes and walked away from Tony.

He shook his head and made his way to the tills.

Awful customer service. I'd be well within my rights to make a complaint about that awful, uneducated girl.

Later that night, stuffed full of quinoa, Tony sat watching *Question Time* with his wife, Kate.

'I mean,' he ventured to Kate, 'coming from a background like mine, I think Labour is the only party which seems to care about the working class. They are–'

Kate cut him off. She was giggling. 'What would *you* know about the struggle of the working class, Tony?'

'What's that supposed to mean? I *am* working class, aren't I?' he replied, shocked.

'Aye, if you say so,' Kate rolled her eyes.

Tony reflected on what she'd said for the rest of the night. He couldn't even sleep because of it.

I am working class. Just because I have a nice house, a nice car, a well-paying job and generally enjoy the finer things in life doesn't mean I'm not working class, surely?

The next morning, Tony met up with his mate, Greg, down the park for their twice-weekly run. Tony loved showing off to Greg. The two men were locked in a perpetual cycle of outdoing each other.

'Expecting my feet to be a wee bit sore after this morning, mate,' Greg said, leaning against his Mercedes as he performed some basic stretches.

'Oh yeah?' Tony replied. 'New shoes?' Tony copied Greg's stretches, leaning against his own car.

'Even better. Custom made, orthotic insoles. Have to break them in before I get the benefit out of them. Seventy quid.'

Tony raised an eyebrow and nodded. Inside he was seething with jealousy. He was going to have to try and find insoles that cost a hundred quid now. The two of them set out on their jog.

'Anyway,' Greg said, changing the subject. 'Last night's Question Time. Thoughts?' He made the shape of a gun with his hand and pretended to fire it at Tony.

'Well,' ventured Tony, 'some interesting points were certainly raised about the class system.'

'Too right. After that, I can't really see why anyone, especially people like us, would be inclined to vote for anyone other than the Tories.'

'Eh?' Tony said. He'd rather die than vote Tory.

'They're the party that looks out for the interests of the people with this,' Greg produced a wad of twenty pound notes from the pocket of his shorts. 'For instance; me and you.'

'Maybe you're right, actually.'

'*Maybe* I'm right? Of course I'm fucking right. What's the alternative? Some left-wing, nutjob, Green Party hippy bastard? No thanks, mate.'

Tony followed his da through the turnstile. Going to watch Partick Thistle had been their routine every other Saturday for years until Tony gave it up to spend his weekends golfing with Greg or visiting farmer's markets with Kate, hunting for the best organic produce the west end of Glasgow had to offer. After months, if not years, of pleading from his da, Tony had agreed to go to a game with him.

'It's good tae have ye back at the games wi me, son. It really is,' Tony's da patted him on the back as they sat down. 'OCH MOVE YER ARSE OSMAN YA LAZY SHOWER AE SHITE!'

Tony recoiled in horror at the vehement outburst from his da.

'You don't have to behave like a hooligan, dad.' Tony drew his eyes off his father.

Tony's da, looked him up and down. He was about to have a go at his son for being a killjoy but decided against it. His son was with him at the fitbaw and that was all that mattered, he supposed.

After Partick scored to go one nil up, a couple of young guys a few seats in front let off a flare.

'Oh for goodness sake,' Tony said, he started letting out a series of pathetic coughs. 'What a total disregard for other people. Hope they get kicked out.'

'Och, lighten up,' Tony's da said.

'No I will not, dad. I have asthma and those wee pricks with their pyrotechnics are making it play up.'

'Asthma? Since when the fuck have you had asthma?'

'I've had it for a few years now. I told you.'

'Talk pish, ye cannae just – AW FUR FUCK SAKE DOOLAN AH COULD'VE SCORED THAT!'

The half-time whistle blew and Tony and his da made their way down into the bowels of the stadium for a pish.

'I could murder a pie,' Tony's da said as he dried his hands. 'You wanting anything?'

'God no. You wouldn't catch me eating the swill they sell here. I don't even want to think about what they put in those pies,' replied Tony.

Tony's da had just about had enough of his shite. If Partick Thistle weren't winning, he'd probably be ready to take his son a square go.

Back in their seats, Tony had begun to loosen up and enjoy himself. Thistle went three goals up and all was right in the world. He even leapt in the air to celebrate the third goal, much to the disapproval of the two men in suits behind him. They tutted loudly to make sure Tony knew he had blocked their view.

'Fucking middle-class toffs behind us, eh dad?' Tony laughed.

Tony's da turned round slowly to look at his son. He couldn't believe what he was hearing.

'Fuckin pot kettle, son,' he said to Tony.

'What?'

'Well you're wan tae talk aboot folk being toffs.'

'Wit?' Tony changed his accent. Reverting back to how he spoke before he left home to go to university in Edinburgh. 'Naw ahm no. Ahm no a toff.'

'Ye fuckin are, pal. Ah hate tae be the wan tae break it tae ye,' Tony's da laughed.

Tony realised he was, in fact, a stuck-up, snobby bastard. The realisation hit him hard. The change had been so gradual, he hadn't seen it coming. The referee blew the whistle, signalling the end of the match. Tony and his da made their way out through the crowd.

'Sorry for being a bit hard oan ye, son,' Tony's da had noticed he had went deathly quiet since he laughed at him. 'Ye fancy a pint before we head up the road?'

'Actually I was just gonna grab an Uber and–' he saw his da was looking at him like a sad puppy. 'Och, okay then.'

'Pint ae Tennent's please, son,' said Tony's da to the barman, 'Eh, wit you wantin, Tony?'

'Ummmm,' Tony scanned the cocktail menu, 'I'll have a mojito, please.'

'You'll be voting Tory before ye know it if you carry on this way, son.' Tony's da and the barman shared a laugh at Tony's expense.

'Well, actually, if you took the time to actually look at their manifesto you would see that the Conservative party really are the best people to be in charge of the country.'

The music stopped suddenly. The quiet chatter of the punters died away. They were incredulous at what they'd just heard Tony say.

'Tell me,' said Tony's da, lowering his voice to a growl, 'that you didnae just say what ah think you just said?'

'I stand by it, dad,' Tony puffed out his chest. 'The Conservative party is the party for me.'

'You dirty, horrible, Tory bastard. You're nae son ae mine!' Tony's da grabbed his son by the lapels of his tweed blazer and marched him out the door. He flung Tony down on to the pavement outside. Tony looked up at his da, tears glistening in his eyes.

His da spat in his face.

'Posh cunt,' he said, walking back into the pub to applause.

PAT

Pat trudged up the road. A few years ago, the weight of the bag over his shoulder would have had him sweating and out of breath. Now though, the bag swung freely as it contained hardly anything. After only an hour and a half, he was already nearing the end of his round. In a way, Pat was glad; his back was fucked from carrying tons of letters and parcels around day after day and his knees were feeling the effects from years doing the rounds. Hardly anyone was sending letters anymore and private companies were delivering most of the parcels. Since Royal Mail announced they had acquired a fleet of drones six months ago, Pat had been dreading the day they were to be rolled out across the nation. Great swarms of them, delivering letters and parcels with far more efficiency than Pat ever could. As of tomorrow, he was fucked.

Pat walked into the depot, trying to stop his bottom lip from quivering.

'I'm sorry, mate,' Pat's manager, James, said, patting him on the back. 'That's you delivered your last letter. We go fully automated tomorrow morning.'

'Ah cannae believe this is actually happenin. You're really gonnae be replacin me wi a fuckin drone?'

'We're not replacing you, as such. I've told you this – all the posties are being kept on in the new drone maintenance department.'

'Aye, an ah've told you,' Pat thrust a finger into James' chest, 'that ahm no sitting in some dark, dingey workshop while they fucking things are oot in the fresh air. It's meant tae be the other way aboot fur fuck sake!'

James was getting fed up of Pat being a luddite.

'Pat, here's your options. Number one – you calm down, get your act together and move into drone maintenance. It's a good job, and with more and more of these drones going about, guys like you will always be kept in a job.'

'Aye, until they get other fuckin robots tae dae the maintenance? Then wit?'

'Well, that's highly unlikely to happen, Pat.'

'Just you wait an see. You'll be the next wan tae be replaced by these machines. Anyway, wit's mah other option?'

'To be honest, that's really your only option. Well, either that, or you quit.'

'Well, shove yer joab up yer arse then.'

James shrugged his shoulders and walked into the empty canteen. There was just no reasoning with guys like Pat.

Pat stormed out and slammed the door shut behind him.

Fuckin arseholes. Replacin me wi fuckin robots.

Outside, a group of a dozen or so drones hung in the air just above the depot. Their fans whirred softly. Pat picked up a stone and flung it in their direction. It struck a smaller drone on its metal body with a clang. It wobbled slightly off kilter then descended down to face Pat. A screen flipped up and James's smug face appeared.

'Please don't take your anger out on the drones, Pat.' The screen flipped back down and the drone re-joined the rest of its flock.

Pat put both hands in the air and extended the middle finger on each.

Dick.

Pat walked home. He unlocked his front door then kicked it open. He pulled off his boots and slumped into a chair. He was choking for a smoke. He opened up his tobacco tin – it was empty. He let out a long exaggerated moan, like a child about to throw a tantrum. He picked up his phone and text Spider, his weed dealer.

Need a tenner bag ASAP please brer

His phone buzzed with a reply seconds after hitting send.

There in 2 minutes. Just take the bag and put the money in its place.

'Wit is this clown playing at?' Pat said to his cat, Jess. Jess kneaded the rug with her paws before jumping up beside Pat. Pat's phone buzzed again, giving Jess a fright. She jumped off the chair and onto the couch.

Outside.

Pat went to the door. He looked through the spyhole – nobody there. He considered picking up the crowbar he kept next to the front door, just in case Spider was after tic money Pat had forgotten to pay or something. He decided against it. Spider was bigger than Pat, he'd probably kick his cunt in then split Pat's heid open with the crowbar. He opened the door and looked about. No sign of Spider's car. Then pat heard a whirring sound. The unmistakable sound of a drone.

'Ah don't fuckin believe this…'

The drone hovered down and came to rest at eye level. A screen flipped up on the top displaying a smiling Spider.

'Afternoon, Pat,' said Spider.

A small hatch opened on the underside of the drone revealing a tenner bag of weed. Pat puffed out his cheeks and shook his head. Pat eyed up the crowbar once again; he could take out the drone with one swing of it.

'Wits the matter? You wan ae these anti-drone cunts, aye?' Spider asked. 'Need to move wi the times, Pat. These drones are the future of drug dealing. They're gonnae make me an absolute fortune. I'm punting weed here in Paisley, eccies in Easterhoose and gear in Motherwell all while sitting on the pan doing a shite.'

Pat waved two crumpled fivers in front of the camera, deposited them into the machine and took his bag. 'Cheers,' he mumbled before going back inside and rolling a big fat joint.

Later on that night, Pat, caught in the grip of the munchies, walked round to the Chinese takeaway down the street. A bell chimed as he opened the door and Zhang greeted him from behind the corner.

'Pat! Long time, no see!' said Zhang. 'How've you been my friend?'

'Magic,' Pat replied with more than a hint of sarcasm. He studied the menu. The salt and chilli munchie box caught his eye. 'Aw here, Zhang. You still needin a delivery driver?'

'Delivery driver?' Zhang laughed. 'No chance. All about drone delivery now. Look! Here's one coming back now,' Zhang pointed to the door. The drone hovered outside for a moment before the door swung open. It floated in silently and sat on the counter. 'I just put the food in a bag, tie it to this bastard here, type in the address and away it goes. Amazing, eh, Pat?

'Forget it,' Pat slapped the counter and walked out. He stopped in at the off-licence on the way home and got twelve cans of Stella.

Pat woke up early the next morning with a monster of a hangover. He sprang out of bed thinking he was late for work but then the realisation set in that he didn't have a job anymore. He fell back onto the bed. He felt like a bag of smashed arseholes. Jess continued to sleep.

Kip for a few more hours then ah'll dive up tae the job centre.

Pat sat in the brightly lit waiting area of the job centre waiting to be called. Outside the window, a line of drones filed by. The sight of them did nothing to alleviate his hangover. A guy, no older than eighteen and with a face ravaged by spots, waved Pat over to join him at his desk.

'So, Mr, eh–,' Pat cut the young man off.

'Just Pat is fine, pal,' he said.

'Okay then, Pat. Says here you were a postman for twenty-five years. Ha! Postman Pat. Amazing.'

Pat had heard this one a million times before. He looked at the young guy with total and utter contempt.

'Ahem,' the guy cleared his throat, 'so why have you given

it up?'

'Ah wis forced oot. They replaced me wi a fuckin drone.'

'According to our file you quit?'

'Aye, well, they were gonnae sack me anyway and then they had the cheek, the fuckin cheek, tae ask me tae stay oan tae clean an fix they bastardin drones.'

'If you quit without good reason, Pat, you're not entitled to claim job seeker's allowance for thirteen weeks I'm afraid.'

'Thirteen weeks? You havin a fuckin laugh, ya plukey wee prick? How did yeez even come up with the figure ae thirteen weeks?'

'Now, please stay calm, Pat. We can still help you find work in that time and–,'

'Listen here, pal. Ahm a postie. Ah've always been a postie. Ah need a job as a postie or delivering somethin – anythin. But that's the hing; These drones have taken over. Ah cannae dae anythin else…'

Tears pooled in Pat's eyes. The young guy looked around the room, lowered his head and motioned for Pat to lean in close.

'I noticed you've got a bit of a limp. My dad was a postman, right,' said the guy, 'his back, knees, ankles, everything are fucked from years doing the rounds. Now he gets disability allowance, more money than he ever made as a postie.'

'Well, wit ye waitin for?' said Pat, 'gies the forms!'

Two weeks later, after burning through most of his meagre savings, Pat got a reply about his disability benefit application; rejected. Pat sat in the living room on a bed of stolen envelopes, totally naked apart from his Royal Mail hi-vis vest. He hadn't left the house for days. He could feel himself losing the plot. The routine he'd been in for years was gone now and he was struggling to adapt. He read, re-read and then read the letter again.

Turned down... Unsuccessful application... Seek employment immediately... Possible sanction...

He put the letter down and lay back on the envelope-covered floor. He took a deep, long draw on a five-skin belter of a joint. He couldn't believe just how bad his life had got in such a short period of time. It wasn't a brilliant life to begin with to be fair, but now he felt he'd truly hit rock bottom. No job, no money, no prospects and even the cat was being off with him now. Pat text Spider to see if he had anything stronger than weed. Two seconds later his phone buzzed with a reply.

Sending you a special delivery. Don't take it aw at once ;)

Pat, for the first time, sat eagerly awaiting the arrival of a drone. He watched as the black machine descended slowly over the flats across the road and floated over to his front door, its red lights blinking in the darkness. He rubbed his hands with glee. Pat wondered what delights Spider had enclosed for him.

Gear? Mandy? Eccies? Speed? Heroin. Fuck, hope it's no heroin. Or would that really be so bad...

Pat opened his front door and the drone flew in immediately.

'Please, do come in,' he said as he closed the door after it. The drone hovered motionlessly in the living room. Its fans made a few envelopes flutter away. It flipped its screen up and Spider's face appeared again.

'Jesus Christ, Pat,' he said. 'You awrite?'

The drone's camera made a gentle, whirring sound as it surveyed the scene in front of it. Pat stood, bollock naked; joint in one hand and the other hastily moving to protect his modesty.

'Ahm fine. Wit've ye got for me?' Pat asked, wearily.

'Show me the money first.'

Pat held the joint in his mouth and grabbed his last tenner from the mantelpiece.

'Is that aw you've got?' Spider asked.

'Aye. My livelihood was stolen aff me by our new mechanical overlords,' Pat said. 'Remember?'

Spider sighed, 'Fine. You're lucky I like you.' The hatch underneath the drone opened to reveal a bag of white powder and a single tab of acid. The grey alien face on the acid tab seemed to smile at Pat.

'Jeezo, I've no took acid since *France '98*. Wit's the powder?' asked Pat.

'It's called M-Kat. I'm sure a man in your current situation will appreciate its qualities. It'll cheer you up. The acid is for if you're needing a wee escape.'

'Never heard ae this M-Kat before. It'll dae, ah suppose…'

'Aw please contain your excitement, Pat,' Spider rolled his eyes.

Pat moved his hand from his crotch to reach for the goods.

'Woah! Ah don't need to see yer cock and baws, mate. A simple "thank you" would suffice,' Spider covered his eyes. The screen folded back down and the drone floated out into the hall. A moment later the drone reappeared in the doorway and the screen flipped back up.

'Eh, ye mind letting me oot?' Spider asked.

Pat was squatting on the floor now. He looked up. The white powder clung around the rims of his nostrils. He stuck a finger into the bag, picking up the remnants he hadn't already snorted and dabbed the powder into his anus. He was sure he'd saw someone do that in a film once.

'Tell me you've no just hoovered up a gram of M-Kat in wan go?'

Pat opened his mouth and stuck his tongue out. The smiling alien face on the acid tab was starting to bubble around the edges.

'Aw fur fuck sake, Pat! Let me oot, I don't want to see this.'

Pat opened the door, walked back to the living room and sat back down just as he began to feel the effects of the M-Kat hitting him. It felt magic.

He took one last draw of his joint and lay back on the envelopes. The acid tab had completely dissolved now. From what Pat remembered from the last time he had acid, he would be tripping within an hour. But for now, the M-Kat was rampaging through his body. It started off feeling amazing. All was well in the world.

For half an hour.

Then the paranoia kicked in.

Ah bet this hoose is fuckin HOACHIN WITH DRONES. Watchin me. Spyin oan me...

Jess the cat watched from the couch as Pat began to scratch at his face and murmur to himself. She tentatively left the living room and waited by the front door, hoping Pat would take the hint and let her out. Pat watched her pad across the carpet and out into the hall. He was sure he could hear the whirring sound of drones coming from somewhere in the house.

Where's she gawn?

Jess pawed at the front door. Pat sprang out from behind the living room door, giving her a fright. She pawed even more frantically to get out.

She knows somethin. Show me what it is, hen.

Pat opened the door and Jess bolted out into the rain. He grabbed his trusty crowbar to defend himself against the robotic hoards and followed her down the path, running as fast he could to keep up with her. His cock and balls slapped against his thighs as he ran. His hi-vis vest, his only stitch of clothing, flapped behind him in the wind. Jess disappeared behind the depot. Pat came to halt outside the depot as his bare feet landed in a puddle. The shock of the cold water seemed to allow a moment of clarity to wash over him. He looked around and wondered why the fuck he was standing naked in the middle of the car park of his old work while holding a crowbar. The clarity passed quickly, however, like the momentary calm that comes with being caught in the eye of the storm. Soon Pat was back knee-deep in his amphetamine-induced meltdown.

Then the acid began to take hold.

Pat looked at the flickering red lights hanging in the air above the depot. They belonged to the fleet of Royal Mail drones.

Their lights seemed to coalesce into one giant red orb. He had two choices now; run back to the house or get into the depot somehow. Pat panicked and ran to the doors of the depot. As he forced his crowbar into the tiny gap between the doors, the lights came on inside and a bleary-eyed James appeared.

'Pat?' James took in the sight of the scantily-clad, soaking guy staring at him through the glass. What's going on? You alright?'

'Just let me the fuck in, they're comin fur me.'

The doors opened with a soft whoosh and let Pat in. James held his head in his hands – he thought he'd seen the last of Pat.

'Why are you here so late at night, eh, James? Watchin me wi yer drones? Waitin for me?' Pat's eyes flickered all around the reception area of the depot. His tongue flicked in and out like a snake's.

'Not that it's any of your business, but I'm doing overtime,' said James. 'Pat, what do you want?'

James' head started expand like a balloon. Pat was freaking out. He stared at James in silence. The grinding of Pat's teeth was the only sound in the building.

'You should really have handed in your vest along with your bag and other uniform by now. In fact, it's still not too late to take that job maintaining the drones, if you fancy it? You clearly need a bit of help and I'd be happy to give–,'

Pat held up a hand to silence James. James' head was like a hot air balloon now, dwarfing his body.

'Ah'll come back as a postman. Take it or leave it,' Pat said.

James sighed. 'Look, mate. I didn't tell you this before because we knew how you would've reacted. But we've had complaints from residents. Several complaints saying you're rude, often reeking of drink and some people are claiming you've even stolen money from birthday cards. Pat, you need help. Are you on something?'

'No benefits anyway, that's for sure. You, Royal Mail, the cunts that stay round here an the fuckin government have all got it in for me. You're in cahoots an tryin tae ruin mah life ya cunts. Now, if you'll excuse me,' Pat brushed past James, 'Ah've got work tae dae.'

'Pat, you don't work here you madman! It's the middle of the night – go home.'

'Ah need tae deliver somethin,' Pat said, his hands twitching at his side. Delivering post was all he knew. Despite the fact he hated the job, he enjoyed the repetitiveness, the mundanity of it all. He needed his fix. He had to post something immediately. He entered the store room and found a bag, dozens of sheets of stamps and a pair of boots that were three sizes too big. He fired on the boots, put the stamps in the bag along with his crowbar and walked back round to his house after slapping James on the arse on his way out. He felt a bit calmer now he had work to do.

Pat got to work. He pulled out all the paper he had in his printer and put it down on the living room floor. On the paper he scrawled insults and some harsh truths to deliver to his neighbours;

Mr. Menzies, you're a senile auld BASTURT who reeks a pish.

Ms. Murphy, I've kicked your dug square in the baws more than once.

Mrs. Walsh, your wean is a bigger cunt than you. And I didnae think that was even possible.

Mr. Din, it's me who shites in your garden.

Miss. Thomson, I stole money out a birthday caird that was meant for your boy. I bought two porn magazines wi the money.

Zhang, the Dragon's Way is a fucking disgrace of a Chinese. Your prawn crackers are an abomination.

As the acid's grip began to tighten, Pat's grip on reality loosened. He was having a full on trip now. He felt happy and at one with the universe. The words he'd written seemed to slide down the paper as he stuffed them into envelopes. His bag grinned as he fed the expletive-laden hate mail into its gaping mouth.

'Postman Pat, Postman Pat, Postman Pat oot his nut oan M-Kat,' he sang to himself. A thought flashed into his mind; what actually is M-Kat? He typed M-Kat into Google.

M-Kat is a nickname given to the drug mephedrone.

Mephedrone. Mephe**DRONE. DRONE.**

'THAT BASTARD SPIDER HAS ME SNORTIN CRUSHED UP DRONES!' Pat screamed into his bag. The paranoia effects of the M-Kat were coming back with a bang and his acid trip was intensifying. He felt as if his skin was tingling all over. He looked down; patches of his skin were peeling off and falling to the floor revealing the muscle and bone underneath. They were all over his body. His arms, legs, torso, baws, everywhere. He looked in the mirror and started hyperventilating. He looked around desperately for something to cover the gaps where his skin had fallen off.

The stamps.

'These'll dae,' Pat peeled a stamp from its page and applied it to the open wound. Perfect. He continued doing this until all the patches were covered. He felt better now. Then a red light appeared at his living room window. He could just about make out the face of James on its tiny screen.

They're comin for me. The drones. They know I've snorted their weans. Aw fuck. James is their leader. King ae the Drones. Naw, naw, naw, naw. This cannae be happenin. Ah still need to deliver mah letters anaw. Aw fuck, fuck, fuck.

Pat grabbed his bag and bolted out the door.

'Pat!' James shouted through the drone as it followed the stamp-covered Pat. 'Are you alright?'

'Fuck off ya mechanical demon!' Pat screamed back. He vaulted his gate, took a sharp right and jumped over the gate of his neighbor, Mr. Menzies, to deliver his first letter. He stuffed the envelope through the old man's letter box and shouted 'Smelly auld CUNT,' in after it. Backtracking down the path now, Pat weaved and bobbed to avoid the low-flying drone trying to talk sense into him. What Pat saw when he looked at the drone, however, was a huge black bat with James' face. He was fucking shitting himself now.

Fuck this. Ah need to hide somewhere.

The leathery wings of the bat flapped as it followed Pat. He flung his bag of letters at the beast chasing him but it just bounced off its body. He swiped at it with his crowbar but missed with every wild, desperate lunge. He gave up and broke into a sprint. He took a series of twists and turns through the scheme and eventually the bat was gone.

Soaked with sweat and rain, Pat collapsed into a hedge. He closed his eyes and prayed that when he opened them the monstrosity would be nowhere to be seen. He opened his right eye a crack. Something red caught his eye across the road. It was a safe haven; It was a postbox. Pat checked the sky for bats. The coast was clear. He darted across the road and dove headfirst into the opening. His head made a sickening thud as it collided with the postbox's metal body and he fell to the pavement. Dazed and confused from the impact, Pat sat up and looked at the post box.

'Help me,' he said.

The hole in the postbox became a mouth. It smiled at Pat.

'Get in here, big boy,' it said in a husky, gravelly voice. Like the voice of a seventy-year-old, chain-smoking granny. 'Ah'll keep ye safe. Just climb intae mah gub.'

'Ah cannae. Ahm too fuckin big,' Pat sobbed. 'They're comin for me. The bats, the drones, everybody. They want me tae suffer for bein a bad postman.'

'That's no true, Pat. Ye were a good postie. Ye had yer flaws, aye, but who disnae? Just climb in here until they basturts leave ye alane, son.'

'Awrite then,' Pat wiped away his tears and stood up. He forced an arm into the postbox's mouth. Then another arm.

He got in up to his elbows then passed out.

A dog walker found him the next morning. Asleep with his arms lodged in the postbox. Covered head to toe in stamps. Drones circled overhead.

THE DUG

'Ah wish that fuckin dug wid shut up,' Margaret said to herself as she got ready for bed. Tyson, the Lhasa Apso, had been yapping non-stop for the three days he'd been staying with her. She was watching him for her son while he was on holiday. As if the dug had heard Margaret moaning about him, the barking coming from down the stair stopped.

The next morning, there was still no yapping. Margaret wondered if the dug had heard her complaining about his barking and taken the huff with her. The dug was fair getting on in years actually, she thought, maybe he'd died? Nah, Surely no…

Margaret slowly went downstairs, listening for any signs of life coming from the living room. Usually she could hear his nails clacking off the wooden floor as he pranced around, bursting for a pish.

But this time there was only silence.

She pushed open the door. It was met with a soft resistance. Whatever was behind the door made a gentle brushing sound as it was pushed along the floor.

Was that shite she could smell?

If Tyson had shat the floor again, Margaret swore she would be putting the dug in a box and posting him to her son in Tenerife. For such a wee dug, he had one rancid arse.

She poked her head round the door and saw Tyson wedged in between the door and side of the couch. Shite was caked into his hairy arse. She stared at him, willing his chest to rise and fall. It didn't. The dug was deid.

Aw fuck.

Margaret pulled her dressing gown over her mouth and nose to block out the smell. She picked up the phone and called her son. Under normal circumstances, she wouldn't have. A phone call to Tenerife? That would be about four pound a minute. But his dug had just died after all – he needed to know.

'Michael,' she said.

Michael laughed, his ma never phoned him unless some distant auntie or something who he'd never even heard of had passed away. 'Right,' he said, 'who's died this time?

'The dug.'

Michael gave a choked sob. 'I'll phone ye back,' he said.

The line went dead.

Margaret sat patiently waiting. A phone to her left and the deid dug to her right.

A few minutes later, the phone rang again.

'Sorry,' said Michael.

'It's awrite, son,' Margaret said. 'Listen, wit ahm ah gonnae dae wi him?'

'Right,' he sighed, 'you have to take him to the vet. They'll cremate him and give you his ashes. I'll give you the money when I'm back.'

Margaret looked to her right and wondered how the fuck she was supposed to transport Tyson's corpse halfway across Glasgow.

'Nae bother, son. Just you enjoy the rest ae yer holiday. Tell the weans their Granny misses them.'

'Will do. Cheers, ma. Bye.'

'Bye.'

Margaret got up and gave the cadaver a nudge with her foot. The dug was solid; rigor mortis had set in. She went up the stair and prepared herself for her quest to cremate Tyson.

Margaret wheeled her tartan shopping trolley into the living room. She just had to lift it the dug into it. But there was no chance she was going to touch the dug with her hands. So she grabbed her pink rubber gloves from the kitchen, a couple of towels and a black bin bag. She pulled on the gloves and stood over Tyson. There was no chance she was touching him, even with gloves on. So she went out the back and got a wee shovel. She slid it under his rigid body and slung a towel over him. She lifted him up and dropped him into the bin bag. He hit the ground with a sickening thud. She picked up the bag and tied it, the smell of shite still lingering in the air. She opened up her wee trolley and fired the dug in, head first.

She pulled the trolley out into the hall. She opened the front door. Motors zoomed by on the main road. She looked at the three steps she would have to bump the trolley down to get to the pavement.

She was getting pissed off now.

Fucking daft dug dying. Fucking idiot.

Margaret stepped out onto the top stair and bumped the trolley over the threshold.

'Hi, Margaret,' her pal said walking towards her. Margaret looked at the trolley. Tyson was making a very noticeable bulge.

'Aw, eh, hullo, Jane,' she replied. Jesus Christ, if anyone noticed what was in her trolley she'd be mortified. *Please don't stop and talk, please don't stop and talk...*

She kept walking.

Thank fuck.

It was a long straight road up to the bus stop now. Margaret tried to psyche herself up.

Heid doon and just keep wheeling this smelly wee bastard along. Don't stop. Nearly there. Right, I can see the bus stop. Aw fuck there's somebody there. What if they can smell what's in ma trolley? What if they ask what it is? What if they sneak a look? What if it's somebody I know? This is gonnae be what kills me. No the angina, no a stroke, no even a bad fall. It's gonnae be this; a deid bastarding lhasa fuckin apso.

Margaret sidled up next to the guy waiting at the bus stop.

She watched him out of the corner of her eye to see if he was looking at the trolley. He was. He fidgeted with his hands, putting them into the pockets on his jacket then took them out and placed them into the pockets of his denims. In out, in out, in out like he didn't know what to do with himself. He looked at the trolley then the road. He looked over his shoulder then back to the trolley.

The guy's phone buzzed in his back pocket. He pulled it out and read the text.

This is your final warning, Ally. If you don't get us that money by the night me and the lads will be round to see ye.

He looked at Margaret's trolley. Auld birds always have their purse in there, he thought.

Margaret locked eyes with the guy and gave a half-hearted smile.

He knows. He knows I've got a deid dug in ma trolley. Aw my god.

Margaret couldn't take any more of this stress. She was ready for just abandoning the trolley and running away. Well,walking away as fast her old, creaky bones would allow her.

The bus pulled up.

Right calm doon, Margaret. Yer nearly there. This must happen every day. Dugs die aw the time.

The bus doors opened to let her on. She tried to lift the trolley onto the bus but she could barely get it off the ground she was so weak with worry.

'Can ah get that fur ye, mrs?' Ally asked.

'Aw, wid ye mind, son?' Margaret said, admitting defeat. 'It weighs a ton.'

'Naw, don't be daft. Here, gies it.'

He hoisted it up with one hand.

'Fucking hell. Wit have ye got in here?' Ally laughed nervously. 'A deid body?'

'Naw! How?!' Margaret heard the panic in her own voice. She took a deep breath. She tried to think of something heavy that could possibly be in the trolley instead of a deid dug. 'Eh, a mean, it's eh, my son's... COMPUTER! Aye my son's computer. I'm taking it to get fixed.'

Ally's face lit up. *Jackpot.* A purse AND a computer. He could pay off his tic bill and still be up a few quid. He looked at the driver – he was looking at his watch. He looked down the bus – it was empty. He saw his chance and pushed Margaret out the way, bolting down the street with the trolley. Margaret couldn't help but smile as she watched this guy run away with a deid dug in an old woman's trolley under his arm. The bus driver opened the door to his cabin and was about to chase after the thief when Margaret told him just to leave it, the trolley didn't have anything in it anyway.

SAMMY'S MENTAL CHRISTMAS

It's Christmas, right, an ah've jist opened aw mah presents. Ahm the auldest grandwean so ah still get hunners ae shite even though ahm twenty-two noo. Wur huvin dinner at mah hoose an fuckin everycunt's here. Mah maw, obviously, mah Uncle Tommy, mah auntie Sharon, mah granny and granda an aboot a hunner fuckin weans. Well, maybe aboot ten ah hink. Aye, ahm sure it's ten. Tommy's goat six an Sharon's got four. Don't ask me aw their names though, man, ah've no goat a Scooby.

Mah bundle wis the biggest oot everycunt's, right, but there wis wan present ah didnae even ask fur an it's the best fuckin hing ah've ever owned in mah life. Mah uncle goat me a samurai sword. Big dullion so it is. This hing could slice a cunt in hawf nae bother. Mah auntie an mah maw are pure screamin at Tommy fur buyin me it.

'There's weans runnin aboot an you bring in a fuckin sword, Tommy? Are you that fuckin stupit?!' she's shouting at um. Ahm jist like that, 'Chill oot everycunt. Nuhin's gonnae happen. Ah know wit am dain.'

'Wit dae YOU know aboot samurai swords, Sammy?' mah maw asks me. Fair question right enough, al gie her that. Ah pick mah sword up aff the flare, nearly skewerin wan ae mah wee cousins in the process. The auld cunts are aw gawn mental noo. Apart fae mah granda an mah uncle. They're howlin.

'Calm doon,' ah say, 'no as if ah killed the wee cunt.'

'Take that hing up the stair an oot mah sight, Sammy,' mah granny says tae me. Mah granda looks as if he's chokin fur a shot ae it. Better no gie um a shot though. He'll probably kill mah fuckin granny. Some Christmas that wid be. Plus ah'd huv nae granny. Nae granny means one less bundle ae presents next year. Fuck that.

Ah put mah sword up the stair wi the rest ae ma stuff since it seems like nae cunt cin relax while ahm playin wi it. Ah go back doon the stair an mah granda hawns me a can ae Tennent's. It's fuckin barkin that stuff. See cos the can's metal, right, it like heats up as yer hawddin it an when ye get tae the last hawf yer lager's fuckin roastin. Gie me freezing cauld bucky err that shite anyday ae the week. Ah've goat a boattle in the freezer fur efter dinner. But it's Christmas, ye cannae be turnin doon drink ae any sort, only gimps dae that, so ah take the can aff mah granda an down it in wan.

'That's ma boay,' he says tae me, pattin me oan the back. Mah maw an mah granny urr sittin oan the couch wi their faces trippin them. They don't like it when ah huv a bevvy. Ah go a bit daft. Well, only a bit dafter than usual ah suppose.

There's a lot ae sittin aboot noo until dinner. Happens every year man. Ahm tryin ae be social, but aw ah cin hink aboot is mah sword up the stair. Ahm choking tae joost fuckin swing it aboot man, cut suhin in hawf. Like a melon urr a pineapple, that wid be good. But the only fruit in this hoose is tangerines fae mah stockin. Every year ah get fuckin tangerines. Ah hate them. Ah never eat them. Don't hink anycunt in this family has ever eaten any kind ae fruit.

Ah take mah uncle aside.

'Here,' ah say tae him, 'wanty go oot the back wi the sword?' He looks aboot tae see if mah maw and mah granny urr listenin ae us.

'An dae wit?' he whispers.

'We could throw tangerines in the air and try an hawf them in two wi the sword.'

He nods in approval at mah suggestion.

'Efter dinner,' he says.

I finish aff another can an so dis he. Cans ae beer look dead wee in his massive shovel hawns. He's a right big bastard, mah uncle.

Ah go tae get the sword but the Queen's jist came oan the

telly. As soon as her stupit face appears mah granny turns the telly aff. That means it's time fur dinner. Me, mah uncle an mah granda sit at the table while mah maw an mah Granny go an finish makin the dinner an mah auntie tries tae entertain the thousand weans kickin aboot. Ah've lost count ae how many cans ah've had so far. The Tennent's has went straight tae mah heid and ah cin tell ahm at least hawf cut.

It's a big dirty turkey fur dinner. Should see the size ae this hing man, it's bigger than me ah hink. Mah granny an mah maw baith have tae cerry it intae the livin room an the table feels like it's gonnae buckle under the weight ae this fucker. Mah maw gies mah granda a wee knife an he goes tae start carvin.

'Wait a minute,' ah say, an run up the stair.

Ah come back doon wi mah sword behind mah back.

'Here, Granda,' ah say an produce the sword wi a flourish, like a magician pullin oot a bouquet ae flowers.

'Aw fur goodness sake, Sammy,' mah maw says, aw annoyed an that.

'Well wits the point in huvin a sword like this if ye cannae use it?' Ah gie mah granda the sword an he starts carving up the turkey. It's gliding through the meat and making wafer thin slices. This is the best present mah uncle's ever goat me. Makes me feel a bit shite fur wit ah did tae him at mah da's funeral a few month ago though. He must've forgoat aw aboot that.

Hunners ae dinner an a few mare cans later an am sittin gouched oan the couch. Everycunt is apart fae the weans. They've been tannin sweeties aw day man an they're fuckin fleein. Wan ae thum bumps against the dinin table where mah sword is balancin an it faws aff and sticks bolt upright in the carpet nearly gawn right through the wee cunt's fit. The wean shites himself an staggers back intae the tree. It keels right oer and snaps in the middle, baubles and tinsel fly fuckin everywhere man an the fairy lights are gawn heavy rapid man it's like a fuckin rave urr suhin.

'RIGHT, SAMMY, THAT'S IT THAT HING IS GAWN RIGHT IN THE BIN!' Mah maw shouts.

Is it fuck gawn in the bin though, ah dive aff the couch and grab it afore she does.

'Moan, Uncle Tommy,' ah say, 'you grab the tangerines an ah'll get ye outside.'

'Couple ae cans fur the road?' he replies getting up aff the couch.

'Get some fur yersel and grab mah bucky fae the freezer, eh?'

While mah maw an that are aw fussin oer the wean, me an Uncle Tommy head oot wi the sword, the fruit an oor cerry oot.

'Yeez huv ruined Christmas, well done, I hope yeez are proud ae yersels' ah hear mah auntie Sharon shout efter us. Cow.

It's pissin doon ootside, right, the full scheme's deserted. Nae wee guys oot oan their new bikes or wee lassies showin aff their prams an dolls. Joost me, mah uncle an a big fuck off sword. This is the best Christmas ever man. We stagger roon ae the park, right, an mah uncle's fuckin downin the cans like naebody's business. Ah've cracked open the Bucky. It's freezing cauld but the alcohol an caffeine an aw that in it seems tae warm me right up. It's exactly wit ah wis needin man.

'Right,' mah uncle says playin wi a tangerine, 'ah'll fling them, you slice them.'

'Right, go fur it,' am hawdin the sword like a basebaw bat. The tangerine sails through the air towards me, it's quite dark an ah cin hardly see it. Ah manage tae hit it but it's mare ae a slap than a slice an it jist bounces aff the sword and lands in the mud in front ae me.

'Hahahaha,' mah uncle's laughin at us. Prick that he is.

'Your turn then, see if you cin dae any better.' See if this cunt manages tae slice this tangerine ah'll be fuckin ragin.

'Right, gies the sword.' He takes it aff me an gies me two tangerines. Ah take a few steps back.

'Ready, big man?' ah say.

'Aye, go.'

Ah pull mah arm back. Decent wee weight in these bad boys, ah think. A wee voice in mah heid tells me tae throw at his baws. So ah dae. Ah launch the tangerine at full pelt towards his bulge. He tries tae deflect it wi the sword but he's too slow. He doubles err as the tangerine makes contact wi his baws. The sword faws fae his hawn an intae the mud.

'AWWW, YA FUCKIN WEE WANK, SAMMY!' he bellows at me, clutchin his bits.

Ah cannae believe it man that was class. Ah've git wan mare tangerine tae throw. Ah could hit his big shiny dome wi it but ah better no—he'll fuckin kill me.

He stawns back up an grabs the sword aff the ground. He disnae say anyhin. He jist looks at me. Disnae take a genius tae work oot he's fuckin ragin. Ah can see his grip tighten roon the handle.

He looks like he's gonnae kill me.

He lumbers towards me. Ah back away but he's pickin up speed noo. Mah uncle's aboot tae try an kill me wi a fuckin samurai sword man an wit huv ah goat tae defend masel wi? A bottle ae bucky an a fuckin tangerine. Ahm no wastin good Bucky so ah aim fur his baws again wi the tangerine but the rage has turned him intae the fuckin Terminator man an he just flicks his wrist and slices the hing in two wi the sword. He disnae even seem tae care though, he just keeps his eyes oan me.

Ah run.

Ah run like fuck through the scheme, not a soul aboot tae help me. Ah aim ae get back tae hoose as quick as ah cin but then ah change mah mind. Wit if he scares the weans? Imagine seein yer uncle butcher yer big cousin wi a samurai sword, at Christmas ae aw times? That wid scar the poor cunts fur life. So ah just keep runnin laps roon the scheme, hoping that it'll tire him oot. Nae such luck. Ah cin hear his big fat feet slappin at the pavement as he comes fur me.

A polis motor screeches tae a halt in front ae me, their lights oan an aw that. The driver puts her windae doon an she's like that, 'Where you going in such a hurry, pal?' The polis see a young guy runnin wearin a trackie an carryin a boattle ae tonic an automatically hink am up tae nae good. Shockin.

'Ahm bein chased,' ah say, trying ae catch mah breath. Ah look oer mah shoulder an see mah uncle. He slows doon when he sees the blue lights. *No so brave noo urr ye, ya fat basturt?* The polis get oot the motor tae see wit ahm lookin at. Mah uncle's glued tae the spot. He's shittin himself.

Soon as the polis see the sword they've goat their wee yella tasers oot.

'Put down the weapon, sir,' the driver says. She's cool as fuck man. Wonder if she's single. Her an her pal, a guy who looks more like a typical polis (a wank), advance oan mah uncle. He's got his hawns in the air but he's still hawdin the sword.

'It's no wit it looks like,' he says. He's nearly greetin. 'It's his fault,' he points at me wi the sword, 'he flung a tangerine at mah baws.'

Ah take a swig ae mah Bucky. This is amazing man, it's like suhin oot a film!

'Put down the sword,' the poliswummin says again but mah uncle's no listenin. She inches forward. 'This is your last chance.'

Mah uncle takes a single step taewards us but the wee babe fires the taser at him. It latches oan ae his belly and he flops oan the deck like a big obese trout. The sword flies oot his hawn an the other polis is over at it rapid style. 'Ye cin have it if ye want, mate,' ah say ae him but he just looks at me as if ahm mental. 'Fair enough then,' ah say, finishing aff mah Bucky an headin hame, just in time fur Eastenders. Don't know wit mah uncle wis hinkin buyin me a fuckin samurai sword fur Christmas. Fuckin idiot.

TOURISTS

Maureen pressed the binoculars to her eyes and peered out between the blinds. With her phone in her other hand she phoned her pal, Annie.

'They're back. Three ae them this time,' she said.

'A see them, Maureen. A asked the rest ae the lassies at the bingo the other day if they'd seen them about but they said naw,' Annie said.

Across the road from Maureen's flat, Annie waved from her window. She scowled down at the three tourists taking pictures. They appeared to be a family. Mother, father and a grown-up son. The mother snapped pictures as the father and son smiled and pointed at graffiti on the wall of Annie's block of flats.

'Imagine,' said Maureen, 'flying aw the way from Japan to Easterhoose tae get yer picture took beside a menchie.'

The tourists looked up at Maureen's window and saw the binoculars peeking out at them. They smiled and waved.

'Shit, Maureen. They can see ye,' Annie whispered down the phone.

'A don't gie a fuck. They're in ma scheme and I'll spy oan them if a want,' Maureen didn't give the family a wave back. She just opened the blinds and scowled at them. A moment later a coach pulled up and the tourists got on and were whisked away.

'Hopefully that'll be the last we see ae them,' Annie said.

'Aye,' Maureen replied, 'They're freaking me out.'

The next morning, Daz was walking through the shopping centre. He turned into Greggs, saw there were no sausage rolls and swiftly exited. Walking further along he could hear some commotion coming from the pound shop.

'Get fucking oot!' A woman who worked there shouted, ushering out seven Japanese tourists. 'Yeez urnae welcome if yer just gonnae take fucking foties and no buy anyhin.'

The tourists smiled and snapped more pictures of the snarling shopkeeper. She let out a groan and went back to work. Daz had a wee laugh to himself. He checked the time, McDonald's breakfast was still on for another ten minutes. He could make it if he walked fast. He squeezed through the throng of tourists and smiled at them as they looked him up and down, nodding approvingly at his attire; grey joggies, white t-shirt and Adidas cap.

He walked down the escalator, pushing weans and auld cunts out the way – nothing was stopping Daz from getting his breakfast. He ran across the car park and into McDonald's. The queue was almost out the door. Frazzled-looking staff ran around behind the counter catering to the sea of punters. It was never as busy as this. Daz checked his watch – only two minutes until they stopped serving breakfast. He looked around to see if there was anyone he recognised so he could ask them to get him his McMuffin but all he could see was smiling Japanese faces.

Wit the fuck are aw these daft bastards dain in Easterhoose? He thought to himself.

It was 10:33am by the time Daz got to the front of the queue.

'Ye cannae get McMuffins efter hawf ten, mate,' a surly teenager told Daz. 'Want a cheeseburger instead?'

'Naw yer awrite, pal' Daz said, dejectedly. 'Ye cannae eat a cheeseburger when yer just oot ae bed. Ahm no an animal.'

Maureen's phone started ringing. It was Annie.

'Annie, wit is it? Are they back?' Maureen said, diving over to the window expecting to see more tourists.

'Naw, have you had yer dinner yet?' Annie asked.

'Naw, you?'

'Fancy gawn a wee stoat round to the chippy? I could murder a roll and fritter.'

The two women strolled down the road to the chippy. They stopped outside the glass door and gazed in in amazement.

Tourists.

The chippy was packed with them. From teenagers to people that must have been in their nineties at least. From outside, their voices were muffled but when the women opened the door they were met with a wall of sound. The tourists' voices filled the chip shop. Annie and Maureen fought their way to the front of the queue and were greeted by Stefano.

'Ladies! What can I get for you?' he said. 'Ah, hold on two secs.' An elderly tourist was pointing excitedly at the tomato-shaped sauce bottle on the counter and making a squeezing motion over his bag of chips.

'It's extra for sauce, my friend,' Stefano told him. The old man grinned and pulled out his wallet then waved it in front of Stefano. 'How much, please?' he asked.

'One pound,' Stefano held up a finger, 'per squirt.'

'You dirty robbing bastard,' Maureen said.

'You should see how much they're paying for the chips,' Stefano laughed.

The old man shook his head. 'I want it all, please. The whole thing, please.' He brandished a crisp twenty-pound note at Stefano who snapped it out of the man's hands like a frog catching a fly. The old man returned to his wife sitting at the table in the corner of the chippy. They both laughed and examined the novelty sauce bottle, taking pictures of each other holding it. Maureen and Annie both tutted and shook their heads.

'I'll have a sausage supper and she'll have a bag a chips, two fritters and a soft roll, son' Maureen said.

'No problem, ladies, I won't charge you as much as I'm

charging our guests here.' Stefano nodded towards the crowd of tourists taking pictures of fritters.

'Big chip!' One of them shouted enthusiastically at Stefano.

Maureen and Annie took their food and pushed through the tourists to get to the door. They had to wait patiently while a teenage girl posed for photos with a battered smoked sausage.

The sun came pouring in through Daz's bedroom window. High-pitched laughter came in after it along with the squeaking of trampoline springs. He got up to slam his room window shut, hoping the noise would silence whoever was laughing so hard at this ungodly hour. A face bobbed up into his field of vision, causing him to fall back onto his bed. He got back up and looked out the window in disbelief.

Tourists.

They had congregated in his garden, dressed not in their familiar shirts, chinos, blouses, cardigans or hill-walking gear but in Henleys t-shirts and Adidas joggie bottoms. Old men had on Burberry and Aquascutum caps instead of the fishing hats they seemed to favour. A woman took a video of her son and daughter bouncing on Daz's wee brother's trampoline. The group all looked up at Daz's window and waved.

'Konnichiwa!' said the bouncing siblings.

'No, no, no, no. It's "awrite, mate?" they say here,' said their father.

Daz shut his curtains and went back to bed.

Friday night meant one thing for Maureen and Annie; pub night. The two of them waited for the bus which would ferry them round to their favourite place in the world – The Centaur Bar.

The bus arrived and, as Maureen and Annie had been half expecting, was full of tourists. The driver waved them on. A young couple politely stood up and offered the women their seats. Maureen and Annie smiled and sat down.

'Domo arigato, pal,' Annie said to the tourists. Maureen turned to Annie in shock. The bus went silent.

'Wit the fuck did you just say?' Maureen asked. The couple who had given up their seats looked close to tears. They smiled and gibbered excitedly among the rest of the passengers. A woman bent down and hugged Annie.

Annie laughed, 'Right, hen. That's plenty.' She turned to Maureen. 'It means "thank you" by the way.'

'How dae *you* know that? I don't think you've ever even been ootside Easterhoose?' Maureen asked.

'I got a wee Japanese phrase book from the library.' Annie looked chuffed with herself.

The pub was hoaching with tourists. They were everywhere now, it seemed. They couldn't get enough of Easterhouse.

A middle-aged man in a suit staggered over to the bar.

'Pint ae Tennent's, please my man,' he said, trying his hardest to do an authentic Scottish accent. A guy with a beer belly so pronounced he could have been eight months pregnant with twins slapped him on the back.

'Fucking yes, Hachiro,' the fat guy said, 'spot on, brer.' Hachiro downed his pint in one and re-joined his friends.

'Here,' said a woman with a bin bag full of clothing. She approached a table full of hipster-looking Japanese tourists. She pulled out a bundle of t-shirts and sat them down in front of the hipsters. They were wide-eyed with anticipation.

'Look at these belters. Real, authentic, G-Star t-shirts. Aw the rage here in Easterhoose. Wit d'ye hink?'

The hipsters looked at each other, their mouths hanging open. Then, like ducks fighting over stale bread, they dived in and each grabbed a t-shirt.

'And that's no aw…' the woman said producing a bundle of white towels. 'These are real towels as used by guests at St. Andrews golf course.'

The woman opened up a towel. Written across it, in big blue lettering, was:

HOSPITAL PROPERTY

'Eh… that says St. Andrews Golf Course.'

The tourists rummaged in their bags, pulling out fifty-pound notes.

Maureen and Annie tutted at the woman as she walked by them towards the door.

'Wit you auld cunts tutting at?' The woman said as she stuffed her earnings into the pockets of her jacket. She gave Maureen and Annie a death stare and walked out of the pub. Unfazed, Maureen and Annie ordered two whiskies and a can of Irn-Bru and sat at the only free table. A young female tourist approached them. She was wearing an old Marseille football tracksuit, which she told Maureen and Annie in broken English, she had procured from a charity shop. She squatted down on the floor and made peace signs with her fingers as her boyfriend took a picture of her posing with the two women.

'Am away oot for a fag,' Maureen said with a sigh.

Outsidethere was a loud commotion coming from the spare ground across the road. Maureen looked up and squinted, trying to focus on what was happening. Floodlights had been erected on the previously empty plot. Scores of tourists crowded around in a massive circle. Camera crews, at least half a dozen of them, were filming whatever the crowd was watching. Over the heads of the crowd, Maureen watched as a brick was launched high into the air to rapturous applause. Maureen stuck her head back in the pub.

'Annie, come and see this,' she said, motioning for her pal to join her outside.

The crowd was growing now, both in size and volume. They were shouting at whatever was happening in front of them. The crowd parted with a chorus of *ooooooohs* as a fat youth was thrown to the ground. The excited voice of a Japanese commentator boomed around Easterhouse. The youth got to his feet and pushed back through the crowd shouting, 'Den-Toi ya fuckin wanks.'

'Is that... gang fighting they're watching?' Annie asked Maureen as she puffed on her fag.

'Looks like it,' Maureen said.

'These cunts are mental. Will we just go and have a wee swallay in the hoose?'

'That's the best idea you've had in years, hen.'

Daz was walking home from his mate's house, his blue poly bag containing his last two undrunk cans swung back and forth at his side. He felt deflated after being annihilated at FIFA once again. He looked across the road at the faces hanging around outside The Centaur and shuddered. He followed their line of sight to see what it was they were staring at. Around a hundred feet or so away from him was the aftermath of the gang fight. Most of the camera crews were packing away their equipment now as medics tended to the bloodied and limping losers of the fight. A suave-looking Japanese guy in a suit was interviewing a wee guy who Daz knew was called Jonny. The interviewer spoke to him in an excited voice, gesticulating wildly at the carnage behind and laughing while a woman in a dress translated for Jonny. The wee bam nodded and lifted up his red Lacoste hoodie to show where he was skelped with a metal pole. Daz heard the interviewer say, 'Brave young warrior,' and he couldn't help but laugh. Easterhouse was somehow becoming more and more mental. He shook his head and kept walking.

At the bus shelter just down by the McDonald's, Daz could see three women standing having what was clearly a heated debate. As Daz got closer, he saw that the heated debate was escalating into a fully-blown rammy. It appeared to be two old women and a neddy younger lassie.

'Fuckin tut at me again ya auld cow,' the young lassie shouted in one of the old women's faces. She grabbed each of the women's handbags, yanked them off their shoulders and bolted down the road.

Without even thinking Daz took off after her. He'd put on a bit of beef over the last few years, but his own misspent youth, often on the losing side of gang fights, meant he was still a decent runner. Within seconds he was right behind the thief.

'Gawn yersel, son!' shouted Annie. A van plastered in Japanese lettering drove alongside Daz and the woman, it slowed down to match their speed. The side door slid open and the man in the suit who was interviewing the boy after the gang fight stood next to a cameraman. He shouted and screamed as Daz swept away the women's feet from under her and she hit the deck. The commentator cheered and high-fived the cameraman. The van stopped and the man in the suit jumped out. Daz picked up the women's handbags as the thief got back to her feet and disappeared into a block of flats. Maureen and Annie hurried over as fast as their legs would carry them.

'Aw son, yer a gentleman,' Maureen said. Daz just smiled and he turned to carry on walking up the road. The man in the suit had other ideas though and he clasped a hand on his shoulder, pulled him back and thrust a microphone in Daz's face. He spoke in frantic tones and jumped up and down on the spot. Daz kept smiling and nodding but he was totally bemused as to what was happening. The man in the suit pointed to the camera. The translator jumped out from another van.

'You are live on Japanese TV!' she shouted.

A week later Daz, Maureen and Annie were wandering the streets of Tokyo in a daze. They were flown out after the video of Daz chasing the thief went viral. Daz was heralded as a hero and Maureen and Annie became stars in their own right for their sharp tongues. Annie immersed herself in the language and had managed to pick up a few choice phrases. Mostly swear words and insults.

They had two hours to themselves before they were due

to make yet another appearance on yet another weird game show. At the hectic Shibuya crossing, Maureen, Annie and Daz were approached by a gang of youths clad in Celtic and Rangers tops. They smiled and happily posed for a group photo with the oriental young team.

An old woman barged through the middle of the group, looked back and muttered something at them.

'What did she say?' Maureen asked Annie.

'She called us fucking tourists.'

THE UNIVERSE FACTORY

Tam got up from his desk. He needed a break from staring at the screen or he was going to scream. He navigated the maze of desks to the staff room. He walked over to the meal fabricator. The small silver machine scanned his ID badge and greeted him in a gruff Scottish accent. Tam heard everybody speaking in Scottish accents, thanks to the translator he had implanted in his brain, so he could understand his colleagues.

'Awrite, Tam?' The meal fabricator said, 'yer no scheduled fur yer break for another oor.'

'I know, I know. I just have a bit of a creative block just now,' Tam said, rubbing the back of his neck.

'Happens tae the best ae us, mah man. Anyway, wit ye havin? Fancy tryin somethin new? Ah've just downloaded an update that gies me access tae aw the food an drink fae the Bode's Galaxy?' The display panel of the machine lit up and displayed a gif of a winking man. 'Go on, Tam. How aboot a nice big bowl ae polyps?' The screen changed to show Tam exactly what a bowl of polyps looked like. He declined the machine's offer.

'Eh, naw. I'll just have a cup a coffee please,' Tam said.

'Fair enough,' said the machine and a Styrofoam cup full of hot brown liquid materialised on the tray for Tam to collect. 'Cheers,' Tam mumbled and walked away. The machine displayed a gif of a cartoon dog watching from a window as his owner drove away.

Back at his desk, Tam sipped the scalding hot coffee and burnt his tongue. 'Fuck thake,' he said under his breath.

'Everything okay, Tam?' asked Frigo the Rectoid, an eight-foot-tall, two-dimensional black rectangle. Tam's translator had given him a well to do Edinburgh accent.

'Aye fine, Frigo. Just struggling to come up wi ideas,' Tam said, letting out a sigh. He moved his mouse to deactivate the screensaver on his computer. The same computer he had used back on earth when he was an architect, only now it was running software that was infinitely more powerful than the simple drawing programs he had once used. Tam used to design buildings, now he designed parallel universes. The brightest, most creative minds in the universe ended up here, at the Universe Factory. A grey office building orbiting a black hole in the most remote, region of space. Humans generally weren't suited to the job due to their vanity. The first human universe creator became obsessed with watching the alternate versions of himself go about their lives. He ended up being sacked after a fortnight. Tam, however, had been in the job for seven years now and had been enjoying it up until now. He was running out of ideas.

A picture of Earth filled the screen of Tam's computer. He rotated it and zoomed in and out, hoping some inspiration would come to him. Tam usually had a wealth of ideas for other versions of Earth to insert into his parallel universes but today he had drawn a blank. *Adding in a third gender? Naw, already done that. Fish fly in the air and birds swim in the sea? Naw, that would be too weird. A world where humans never discovered electricity? Hmmm maybe. Naw, wait, disnae matter, tried that two year ago. Disaster. People's knees bend the other way? Nah, too mental. Why is this so fucking hard, man.* There was an infinite amount of possibilities and he couldn't think of a single decent one. He lifted his coffee to his mouth, but it was still too hot. He turned to Frigo to see what he was working on. Frigo was invisible when viewed from side-on.

'Frigo?' Tam said. Frigo turned to face him. The deep blackness of him had unsettled Tam from the moment he first lay eyes on him. It was even darker than the centre of the black hole outside the window. 'What you working on?' Tam asked.

'This,' Frigo floated a tiny hologram galaxy over to Tam's

side of the desk.

'Cool,' Tam waved his hands around the hologram, causing it to meander through the air. Even after seven years in space, he was still fascinated by alien technology.

'That's a new version of the Milky Way galaxy, where you're from. With a new version of Earth since you can't come up with anything half-decent,' Frigo boomed.

'What's different about it?' Tam asked.

'You aren't an ugly bastard in this version, hahaha!'

'Aw get it up ye,' Tam said. He batted the hologram away from him and back over to Frigo. The tiny galaxy was absorbed into his Frigo's body. He turned to the side again, disappearing from view, continuing to laugh at his own joke.

Tam lowered his head on to his desk. The coolness of the table calmed him. He sat like that for a couple of minutes and for those few moments he was back on Earth. He was sitting in his office in Partick; the low hum of printers in the background, the rhythmic clicking of mouses. These sounds always stimulated Tam back on Earth and hearing them again, if only in his imagination, caused ideas to pour into Tam's mind.

'Tam!' a shrill female voice brought Tam back to the Universe Factory in an instant. It was Clerisso, his boss. She was a small humanoid, no bigger than a pint glass, from a dwarf planet in the Andromeda galaxy. She buzzed around Tam's head, her tiny wings beating so fast they were almost invisible. 'I believe you have work to be doing? I don't seem to recall asking you to have a wee rest.'

'Sorry, Clerisso. It's just, eh, I'm a bit stressed out,' Tam said, the pitch of his voice fluctuating wildly. Clerisso had this effect on her employees. She was a formidable authoritarian.

'Well there's deadlines to be met, quotas to be filled etcetera, etcetera. These universes aren't going to create themselves, are they?' She zipped away back to her workstation, leaving a trail of pale purple light behind her.

He had an idea. He moved the cursor to the search tab and

typed in 'the Universe Factory'. The familiar grey building came into view. Scrolling through the list of options on his computer screen, Tam clicked on *Edit item* and a text box appeared. If he was struggling with his work in this universe, then why not create an alternate universe where another version of himself didn't have this stress? Knowing somewhere out there, across the dimensions, across time, he could be sitting at his desk, chilling without a care in the universe soothed his soul. Tam wasn't allowed to edit anything except Earth, so he had to be quick. Even from across the room could see Clerisso's beady little eyes glancing up at him every so often. If she caught him doing this he would be out on his arse. Shipped back to Earth with his memory wiped. *Maybe that wouldn't be such a bad thing ...*

Tam typed in 'automate parallel universe creation' and leaned back in his chair. He looked up at Clerisso. She had conjured up a 3D image of a sun and suspended it in the air. She waved her hands and the warm, orange colour of its surface faded to an icy blue.

He leaned forward quickly and hit the *ENTER* key.

Everything on Tam's screen disappeared. He turned to look at Clerisso, she was looking right at him. A pop-up message announced its arrival on the screen with an ominous sound like when a baddie appears in a kid's film. It read: *A fatal error has occurred. Universe production now in overdrive.*

Clerisso landed on Tam's right shoulder. 'WHAT THE FUCK DID YOU JUST DO, TAM?!' she shrieked in his ear.

'I – I – I – I just thought,' Tam stuttered. He turned to his left to look at Frigo.

Frigo was staring straight ahead, looking out the window. He turned to Tam.

'Fuuuuuuuuuck,' Frigo whispered, barely audible. Tam turned his gaze to the window as well. The black hole around which The Universe Factory orbited was spewing light forth from its centre. The light came out in beams, no thicker than spaghetti, tearing holes in the very fabric of space itself. From the staff room, Tam heard the meal fabricator laughing.

'Ah'll bet any money that wis fucking daft arse Tam,' the machine said.

'What's happening. Surely I didn't do that?' Tam said, looking at Clerisso then Frigo.

'Those beams of light are parallel universes leaking into this one. You've fucked it big time, mate,' Frigo said.

The strands of light ripped through The Universe Factory. Two of them ripped through Tam's computer monitor. Clerisso darted around trying to avoid them but it was futile, she was skewered by four of the beams at the same time and more light spilled out of her mouth.

'Get in,' Frigo said, enveloping Tam, absorbing him into his body. In an instant, the blinding light was replaced by absolute darkness. The dark smothered Tam with its embrace

When Tam woke up he was lying on the floor of the office. Several figures came into view as he opened his eyes. Something buzzed around his ears. He raised a hand to bat it away.

'Tam, I swear to fuck,' the voice, unmistakably, belonged to Clerisso. She was now less than in inch from his face and the cool breeze from the beat of her wings tickled his nose. 'You fall asleep on the job again and you'll be on the first flight back to that fucking shite-hole you call a planet. You understand?' She fluttered back over to her miniature sun, casting a glance back at Tam and muttering, 'daft cunt.'

'I'm sorry. I'm so sorry,' Tam said, climbing back into his seat. Everyone else in the office returned to their desks like nothing had happened. Like the universe hadn't just been torn apart because of his mistake. He turned to look at Frigo. He wondered what the fuck was happening.

'Wit happened there? How is everybody still alive?' Tam asked.

'We've entered that universe I made this morning. I made it so me and you weren't in it, just in case you fucked up and would you look at that; my decision has been vindicated. Don't try anything like that again, mate, eh?'

'Did you manage to bring anyone else?'

'No, just us. Everyone and everything else in our original universe has been destroyed. It's just a big white vacuum now.'

'Fuck,' Tam was shaking.

He picked up his coffee and drank it one long gulp. It was freezing cold now, but Tam didn't care. He went through to the staff room and slumped down into a chair. He thought about handing in his notice. He would have his memory wiped and be sent back to earth with a new identity. No one there was real though, he realised; they were all just copies. Tam could feel himself going into full-on meltdown mode. He looked over at the meal fabricator.

'Awrite, Tam? Skiving again are we?' the machine asked.

'Just having a wee existential crisis, mate,' Tam replied.

'Here,' the meal fabricator made a bowl of polyps appear for Tam. 'Get these doon ye.'

DAVIE

Davie was a big man. A very big man. And he loved tattoos. He loved them so much that he dedicated his life to stuffing his face and getting bigger and fatter so he could get even more, stretching his skin to breaking point. He reckoned his body had the same surface area as four king-size duvets. He was particularly proud of his gargantuan arse. He had kept it free of tattoos for years. Now, Davie believed it was finally big enough for work to begin on his latest masterpiece.

Davie printed off the picture of what he wanted inked upon his derriere; the pyramids of Egypt. There was no spiritual reason for this, he had no connection to Egypt or anything, he just liked the pyramids – he thought they looked cool. Davie was steaming when he printed the picture off though. He couldn't get tattooed while sober, it was far too sore. He didn't even realise he'd printed off the wrong picture…

He fell into the tattoo shop an hour later. Alec, Davie's favourite artist, smiled at the sight of this mammoth man lumbering into his shop. Alec had made a fortune off Davie over the years.

'Take a seat, big chap,' said Alec, pulling on a blue latex glove, 'what we doing today then?'

Davie fumbled around in his pockets for the picture. 'Here,' he said, thrusting the folded up piece of paper into Alec's hand. 'I want this oan mah arse.'

Alec unfolded the picture and gave a wee chuckle. 'Ye never fail to surprise me, Davie. Get yer bahookie oot then.'

Davie obliged and pulled down his grey joggie bottoms, revealing his cellulite-ridden buttocks. His arse was so big and so dimpled that it looked like a memory foam mattress which had been skelped with a hundred tennis balls. Alec got to work, meticulously portraying the landscape onto Davie's gluteus maximus. A landscape they were both very familiar with. Davie passed out a few moments after the needle made contact with his skin.

Alec wiped off the last of Davie's thick, cholesterol-laden blood and admired his work. 'Davie. Davie wake up. That's you done,' Alec said, giving Davie an open-palmed spank. Davie rose groggily from his slumber. His head thumping and his arse throbbing. He ambled over to the mirror with his joggies and knickers still round his ankles, cupping his cock and balls in one hand. He turned round so he could see his new tattoo. He could definitely make out a pyramid – but it wasn't of the Egyptian kind. Or the Mayan kind. Or even Aztec, or Inca. It was of the Scottish kind. It was, unmistakably, the Forge Shopping Centre. Davie screwed up his eyes. He thought he must have been in the midst of a vivid, Bucky-induced dream. He wasn't.

The greeny-blue glass of The Forge's pyramidal entrance stood out beautifully against the pale skin of Davie's right arsecheek. Just left of the crack sat a throng of trollies. To the right, an old woman, weighed down by her bags of messages, waited for a bus. A bin overflowed with McDonald's Happy Meal boxes and fag ends. The whole scene recreated in startling realism by Alec. Davie loved it.

THE VOID

Andy walked along the empty motorway. The freezing night air made him feel like he was breathing tiny daggers. The motorway was due to reopen in a few hours and it was his job to clear away the last of the traffic cones. He checked his watch. He couldn't believe he still had another four hours until his shift finished. Andy picked up cone after cone after cone, stacked them together in threes and then threw them onto the trailer. Single-handedly since his colleague, Piotr, had fallen asleep in the warmth of the van.

Andy counted the cones left to pick up – forty-two to go. His arms felt like they were being stretched as he carted another stack back to the van. He reckoned by the time he was finished he would have arms like an orangutan.

Two hours passed and Piotr was still asleep slumped over the steering wheel. Andy had turned the engine off half an hour ago in the hope the temperature inside the van would plummet and wake Piotr up. He still wasn't awake. Andy worried he might have given the poor guy hypothermia. Then he remembered Piotr was a lazy bastard and didn't feel so bad.

Another half hour passed. Andy stacked the last three cones together. He looked back at the long road he'd have to travel back with the cones. He realised he could've just pressed the horn on the steering wheel which would've woken Piotr up and they'd have been finished this arduous task hours ago. Piotr could've driven the van slowly and Andy could've just walked alongside it, flinging the cones on. Then he thought he didn't even have to wake the lazy bastard up. He could've just pushed him across into the passenger seat and driven the van himself. Driving forward a few yards, jumping out, gathering up the cones, fire them onto the trailer then back into the van and drive forward another wee bit. Andy couldn't drive, but how hard could it really be? Nah, it really wouldn't be worth the hassle if he crashed. Andy sighed and dragged the last of cones along the tarmac. He hypothesised that if he'd started with these cones at the end of the line, he would have had less distance to travel back to the van as he grew wearier.

Andy was the kind of guy who made things difficult for himself. He couldn't help it. He'd constantly find himself near the end of a task before realising there was a far simpler way to accomplish it. Arse from Elbow Andy – that's what his colleagues liked to call him. He hated his colleagues but what Andy really hated was the job itself. Lugging traffic cones around day after day, night after night, what a pitiful existence, he thought.

Andy stopped for a breather. He was half way back to the van and tiredness was kicking in big style. He doubled over with his hands on his knees and watched his breath come in out in beautiful white plumes. He decided that after tonight he wouldn't be Arse from Elbow Andy anymore. Enough was enough.

He took a few steps away from the cones and jumped on the spot, trying to loosen up his stiff joints for the final leg of his journey. He sized up the cones. Then something caught his eye and he stopped jumping. He even stopped breathing.

There was something written on the cone on top of the stack. Andy took a step forward to check what he was seeing. He rubbed his eyes, struck by disbelief.

Scrawled in black pen on the reflective band around the cone was his name – **ANDY**.

He took astep closer. Underneath the word **ANDY** was some smaller, almost illegible writing.

Andy's face contorted with confusion. It was a date – **24/11/2017**.

That was two days away. Andy slid this cone off the stack of three and placed it aside. There was something written on the cone underneath:

THIS IS THE DAY YOU'RE GOING TO DIE, ANDY.

His hands trembling, he picked this cone up and sat it next to the first one. The final cone said:

A MOST GRUESOME DEATH AWAITS YOU, ANDY. YOU WILL SOON BE CLAIMED BY THE VOID.

He looked around. Surely this was a wind up. Maybe Piotr was trying to scare him and he was sitting in the van pissing himself laughing.

Andy arranged the cones in order, from left to right. He stood back and took a picture of them on his phone. He looked at the photo – the flash had rendered the writing unreadable. Andy took this as a sign that this wasn't really happening. He had a wee chuckle to himself at the absurdity of this situation, stacked the cones together again and dragged them back to the van.

As he flung the last of cones onto the trailer, Andy clocked more writing on the rest of the cones.

Written on every single one of them was **ANDY**. He stepped away from the trailer and closed his eyes. He was sure that when he opened them again the writing would be away.

It wasn't. If anything it was written larger now. He looked into the van. Piotr hadn't moved. It definitely wasn't him. His eyes returned to the cones.

THE VOID BECKONS YOU, ANDY.

Fuck this, thought Andy. He jumped into the passenger seat of the van and woke Piotr up.

'How long was I asleep,' grunted a bleary eyed Piotr.

'It doesn't matter. I've collected all the cones,' Andy said buckling his seatbelt, 'let's go and open up the slip road and head back to the depot.'

Piotr yawned and nodded at the same time, put the van into gear and drove off.

A noise started to come from the trailer.

It sounded to Andy almost like a woman singing. He looked through the window at the wing mirror.

Black smoke curled out of the cones and around the side of

the trailer. Andy's mouth became very dry.

The noise intensified.

He rolled the window down to hear it more clearly – he knew it was coming from the traffic cones. Of course it was.

'Annnnnnn-daaaaaaay,' the ethereal voice of the cones floated in through the window. 'Come to the void, Andy.'

'WHAT DO YOU WANT!' Andy wailed, giving Piotr a fright and making him swerve into another lane.

'Fucking hell, mate,' he asked Andy, 'what is problem, huh?'

'It's those fucking cones,' Andy turned to Piotr, his eyes wide and wild, 'they want me to die.'

'You're fucked up, my friend.'

'You need to let me out,' Andy pulled frantically at the door handle but the door wouldn't open. 'LET ME THE FUCK OUT!'

Piotr slammed his foot down hard onto the brake.

'Okay, get out then,' he said calmly.

Andy got out the van and ran down the hard shoulder in the opposite direction. He didn't stop running until he got home.

Two days later, Andy sat in his bedroom, alone and terrified. He ignored his phone – his boss had been phoning him almost every hour. There was no way he was going back to work, not after what had happened. He was sure the lads at the depot would be having a field day discussing his meltdown. Fuck them, he thought, they hadn't seen what he had – the smoke, the weird voice and the writing on the cones.

As the clock inched ever closer to midnight, Andy started to relax. If he really was going to die today then there was only four minutes left for it to happen and there was nothing in his room that could harm him. He was safe.

Or so he thought.

Black smoke, the same black smoke he had seen circling the van the other night, crept into his room.

'Andy,' the voice said, 'the void is waiting for you.'

Andy sighed. It was game over – he really was going to die.

The smoke took the form of a hand and made its way towards him. It snaked up his body and clasped itself around Andy's neck. It squeezed the very life out of him. Andy's last thought before he passed out made him smile; he'd never have to hump around another traffic cone.

After what felt like either an eternity or a millisecond, Andy opened his eyes. He was standing in a factory. Not your typical factory however; all the machinery was white, the floor and the walls were white. Andy looked down to see what he was wearing; pristine white overalls.

'ATTENTION ALL NEW ARRIVALS,' came a familiar voice from a brilliant white speaker directly above Andy's head. 'WELCOME TO THE VOID.'

Andy looked around – he was the only person there.

'ANDY FLEMING, PLEASE MAKE YOUR WAY OVER TO THE MACHINE IN FRONT OF YOU.'

Andy did as the voice commanded and walked over to the massive white machine. A conveyor belt was attached to it which stretched out to the horizon. As soon as he plonked himself down onto the stool provided for him, the machine grumbled into life.

Along the conveyor belt came traffic cones. One at a time they passed by Andy.

'ANDY, PICK UP THE PEN IN FRONT OF YOU,' the voice boomed.

Andy picked up the black Sharpie pen in front of him.

'NOW WRITE SOME THREATENING THINGS ON THE CONES. THERE IS A GUIDEBOOK UNDERNEATH YOUR STOOL WITH ADVICE ON HOW TO BE THREATENING. THIS IS YOUR JOB IN THE VOID FOR THE FORSEEABLE FUTURE.'

'For fuck sake,' Andy muttered under his breath.

THE BUDGIE

Eddie sat in his usual seat at the bar, trying to catch the barman's eye. It was a Tuesday afternoon and the pub was near enough empty. The barman was trying his best not to engage Eddie in conversation as he put the glasses away. Once Eddie started talking to you there was no escape. He could talk for hours about any subject; darts, the weather, history, fitbaw, advertising, the economy – absolutely fucking anything. He was one of the regular punters Kyle was warned about at his interview.

'Here, pal,' Eddie said to Kyle. 'Did ye hear ah've got maself a wee burd?'

Finally, thought Kyle, a bit of decent gossip from the old cunt.

'Oh aye? What's her name?'

'Fury.'

'Fury?' Kyle asked, 'That's a weird name for a burd?'

'Nah it's a *good* name fur a burd. Picked it maself.' Eddie smirked as the penny dropped.

Kyle rolled his eyes and went back to his crate of glasses.

'Fury's a budgie,' Eddie announced. 'Ye didnae think ah'd really goat maself a wummin, did ye?'

'Naw, of course no.'

'Cos if ah did huv a burd, ah widnae be hinging aboot in a dump like this, wid ah?' Eddie laughed. 'I'd be oot wining an dining her. Oot the toon an that.'

'I should be so lucky,' Kyle muttered his breath. He wished he could just tell the daft old bastard to either shut up or to fuck off and die but he was far too polite.

'Ahm gonnae teach him how ae talk, so ah um.'

'Oh aye?' Kyle said, holding a glass up for inspection before giving it a wipe with his towel.

'Aye. None ae yer usual "who's a pretty boy?" pish though. Mah budgie's gonnae have good patter. Just like his owner, eh?'

'Aye, definitely,' Kyle laughed sardonically.

'Anyway,' Eddie said. 'Pint ae Guinness please, pal, an ah'll be on ma way. Need tae get back tae mah budgie. Ah've goat work tae dae.'

Eddie poked a finger through the bars of Fury's cage to stroke his soft, baby blue chest.

'You're a wee belter, eh?' Eddie said, opening the cage and placing a hand in. Fury hopped onto his finger straight away. He raised it to his face. Fury stared right into his eyes with his head cocked. Eddie smiled. He whistled the intro to the BBC News in the hope the bird would copy him. Fury gave a half-hearted cheep in reply.

'Ah well, we can work oan that wan,' Eddie said, rubbing Fury's head. He took Fury over to the window ledge where he kept the urn containing his wife's ashes. 'Moira, hen,' he said, patting the lid. 'This is Fury. He's mah new wee pal.'

The next morning, Eddie peered into Fury's cage to say hello. He was shocked to discover that Fury was hanging from his perch using a pair of distinctly human arms. His wings lay discarded on the newspaper at the bottom of the cage. Fury's new arms were skinny like those of a teenage boy who'd grown two feet taller over the summer. As thin as pencils. Fury attempted to do a chin up, failed and let out a little budgie sigh. He let go of his perch and dropped softly down next to his wings.

'Fury?!' Eddie said, his voice several octaves higher than usual. 'Wit's happened tae ye, wee man?'

The bird looked at Eddie and gave him a thumbs up. Eddie staggered backwards and fell onto his couch. Fury scaled the bars of his cage, opened the door and joined him.

'Ahm taking you tae the vet. This isnae right,' Eddie said.

Fury climbed onto his knee and gestured with his new perfectly formed hands that he'd like a pen and paper.

Eddie nodded. He grabbed a packet of yellow post-it notes from the kitchen along with a biro. He returned to the living room and placed them down next to Fury. Fury looked at the pen, almost the same size as him, with as much avian disgust as he could convey. He held his tiny little hands out as if to say, 'what the fuck am I meant to do with that, mate?' Eddie took what Fury had to say on board and went looking for a smaller pen. He found a wee red bookie pen in a drawer in his bedroom. He handed it to Fury who flashed him another thumbs up before accepting the pen.

NO VETS, Fury wrote.

Eddie nodded, his mouth agape.

I'M FINE.

Eddie nodded again. 'Wit dae we dae then?'

Fury turned the page over. JUST KEEP YOUR MOUTH SHUT. IT IS OKAY.

'Right, eh, nae bother.' Eddie went and put on his jacket on. He needed out the house away from this madness.

WHERE ARE YOU GOING?

'Tae the pub. Ah need a pint,' Eddie said, puffing out his cheeks.

TAKE ME.

'Naw, eh, I think you should stay here.'

FINE. WHERE IS THE REMOTE FOR THE TELLY?

Eddie sat silently at the bar, huddled over his pint. Kyle kept glancing over at him while he served the other punters. Everyone had noticed Eddie wasn't his usual self.

'Eddie,' said Kyle, 'you awrite, mate?'

'Fine,' Eddie replied. Kyle could see from his trembling hands as he raised the glass to his lips that Eddie was most definitely not fine.

He decided to try a different tactic. He was feeling a bit sorry for Eddie. 'How's the budgie getting oan?'

Eddie looked at him, gave a derisory laugh, then returned to staring into the dregs of his pint.

'Another pint? Wee vodka perhaps?'

Eddie shook his head. He pushed his glass slowly towards to Kyle, put his jacket on and left.

While walking home, he came up with a list of questions to ask Fury:

How did you grow arms?

How do you know how to write?

Are you going to grow anything else? Human legs, a human head etc.

What are you/we going to do?

He rehearsed all these questions on the ten-minute walk back to his flat. Depending on the bird's answers, he'd consider taking him back to the pet shop. In the lift, he repeated them over and over again, trying to sound calm. He didn't want to antagonise Fury after all, who knew what this budgie was capable of.

As Eddie walked into the living room Fury held up a post it note, on which he had written HELLO. Eddie gave a curt nod in reply. Fury returned to watching the telly.

'Listen,' Eddie said, sitting down next to Fury on the couch. 'Wit's the script here? How did ye grow they arms?'

Fury hit the mute button on the remote then picked up the bookie pen again. FUCK KNOWS, he wrote. His handwriting was smaller and neater than it was this morning, Eddie noticed. He must've been practicing.

'Right, okay. Fair enough. How dae ye know how tae write?'

BY READING THE NEWSPAPER AT THE BOTTOM OF MY CAGE.

'Ahhhh right. Very clever. By the way,' Eddie pointed to the cage, 'what'll ah dae wi that? Ah'd feel a bit shite locking ye up in it noo.'

I WANT TO KEEP IT. DON'T TOUCH MY OLD WINGS EITHER.

'Awrite, sound. Nae bother. So are ye, eh, gonnae grow anythin else? Human legs? Another heid? Anythin like that?'

NO, I DON'T THINK SO.

Eddie mulled over the bird's answers. He decided he seemed to be okay and not a prick.

'So wit happens noo? Wit dae we dae?'

Fury tapped the pen off his beak and scratched his head. Eddie could tell he was thinking carefully about how to answer this question. He was quite excited to hear his answer.

NOTHING.

'Nothin?' Eddie exclaimed. 'We could go tae the papers. Be oan the telly an that. We'd be fucking loaded! A budgie wi human arms that can write as well? You'd be a superstar!'

Fury let out an ear-piercing squawk.

DO NOT TELL ANYONE.

'Aw c'moan. At least think aboo–'

Another squawk.

PROMISE ME.

'Awrite, awrite,' Eddie removed his hands from his ears. 'Ah promise. No as if anybody wid believe me anyway, eh?'

I NEED MORE PAPER. I HAVE A LOT OF THINGS TO WRITE.

'Right, well, ah'll get ye some mare the morra. Ah'll get a few more pens from the bookies as well.'

THANK YOU, EDDIE.

'Nae bother, Fury.'

WHAT IS FOR DINNER?

Eddie found Fury on the kitchen worktop the next morning. He was lying on his back, bench-pressing a pen which had two lumps of blu-tac stuck on either side.

'Good morning, mah man,' said Eddie. 'You want a bit of toast or somethin?'

Fury gestured for the pen and paper. Eddie obliged and fetched them for him.

I'VE ALREADY EATEN.

'What did ye have?' Eddie poured himself a glass of orange juice and took a sip while Fury scribbled his answer down.

EGGS.

Eddie spat the juice everywhere. 'Eggs?! That's practically cannibalism!'

I'M TOO SKINNY. I NEED TO BULK UP. I NEED PROTEIN.

'Well, eat somethin that disnae come fae another bird, fur fuck sake. That's weird.'

OKAY.

'Drink milk or somethin. Ah'll make ye some fish an stuff like that fur yer dinner.'

THANK YOU, EDDIE.

'Nae bother, pal.' Eddie whistled a wee tune while he put some bread in the toaster. 'Here, Fury. Cin you talk?'

Fury shook his head.

'Whistle me a wee tune then, go on.'

PLEASE DON'T INSULT MY INTELLIGENCE, EDDIE.

Eddie thought he'd offended Fury. 'Naw, ah didnae mean it like that. Ahm no sayin you've tae whistle an dae tricks fur mah amusement. Ah wis jist wonderin. That's aw.' The toast popped out giving them both a fright.

IT'S FINE. DO YOU HAVE A COMPUTER?

'Naw, sorry, pal. How come?'

CAN YOU GET ME ONE? I WANT TO LOOK UP PICTURES OF BIRDS.

'Tell ye wit. Ahm headin doon the bookies. Cheltenham festival's oan. If ah win enough, ah'll buy ye a computer. Sound good?'

TAKE ME TO THE BOOKIES. I KNOW ALL ABOUT HORSE RACING.

'Wit? How dae you know aboot horses? Huv ye ever seen wan in real life?'

I TOLD YOU. THE NEWSPAPER AT THE BOTTOM OF MY CAGE. JUST PUT ME IN YOUR POCKET AND TAKE ME. I'LL TELL YOU WHAT HORSES TO PICK. WE'LL WIN BIG. I PROMISE.

'Aye?' Eddie smiled. 'Right. Ah'll take ye. Reckon ye cin pick a winner then, eh?'

DEFINITELY. LIFT ALL YOUR MONEY OUT THE BANK. PENSION, SAVINGS, EVERYTHING. WE'RE GOING TO MAKE A FORTUNE.

'We're on to a winner here, Moira, hen,' Eddie said, rubbing the urn for good luck on his way out the door.

Eddie lost everything at the bookies that day.

'Cannae *FUCKING* believe it,' he seethed, kicking his front door open. 'Every fucking penny ah had. Gone.' He put Fury into his cage before he throttled the wee bastard. He slammed the cage door shut and slid a pen and paper through the bars.

'Explain yerself. You telt me, you fuckin telt me, you knew aw aboot horses. Ye know fuck all! You've ruined me!'

Fury shrugged his miniature shoulders before picking up the pen.

IT'S YOUR FAULT FOR LISTENING TO ME.

'You fuckin said you knew wit ye were dain ya wee wank!'

Fury squawked as loud as he could.

I'M A FUCKING BUDGIE, MATE.

'You're gawn back tae the pet shoap. Right noo!' he checked his watch. The shop shut in ten minutes. 'Aw ya basturt! It'll be shut by the time ah get there. Right, first thing the morra morning, you're oot ae here.'

GOOD.

Eddie stormed through to his room, grabbed the £20 note he kept under his mattress for emergencies and went to the pub. At £2.40 a pint, he worked out he could get 8 pints.

Enough to numb the pain of being persuaded to hand over his entire bank balance to the bookies by a budgie.

Kyle noticed Eddie was in a bad mood as soon as he walked into the pub, his face like thunder. 'Big Davie was in here earlier,' Kyle said to Eddie. 'Said he seen you doon the bookies the day. Lost a few quid on the auld geegees, eh?'

'Mare than a few quid, pal.'

'Och, happens tae best ae us, Eddie. Finish that pint an ah'll get ye another wan. Oan the hoose.' Kyle didn't like seeing Eddie like this. Although he spoke a load of shite, he always made his shift go quicker. Plus, seeing him so down and annoyed the past two days was putting him on a bit of a downer.

'It's that fuckin budgie,' Eddie lamented.

'Aw aye? Havin trouble teachin it to talk?'

'Naw it's no that.'

'Well wit is it then? Is it whistling too much or something? My auntie had a budgie that would sit up aw night and whistle.'

'Ach,' Eddie took a sip of Guinness, 'ye widnae believe me if ah told ye, son.'

'Try me.'

Eddie motioned for Kyle to come closer. He leaned over the bar and brought his head down level with Eddie's.

'Would you believe me if ah told ye it wis the budgie's fault ah lost aw that money at the bookies?'

Here we go, thought Kyle. Same old Eddie spouting the same old shite.

'And,' Eddie continued, 'would you believe me if ah told ye that this budgie ae mine can write?'

'No gonnae lie, Eddie. Probably no.'

'That's no even the most mental thing about the whole situation.'

'Oh really?' said Kyle, feigning interest.

'Right, don't laugh when ah tell ye this, awrite?'

Kyle pretended to zip his mouth closed.

Eddie sighed. 'The budgie's grew arms.'

'Arms?' Kyle said, raising his eyebrows.

'Aye, arms. An keep yer fuckin voice doon, eh? Ah don't want tae folk tae know aboot this.'

'Tell ye wit. I'll believe it if I can see the thing for myself. Ye got a picture?'

Eddie looked dejected. 'Ah don't have a picture, naw.'

'Enjoy yer pint,' Kyle said, patting Eddie on the shoulder and going to talk to the other punters. He didn't even notice Eddie slipping out of the pub, wiping away a tear from his eye.

Eddie had had five of his planned eight pints and was feeling a bit inebriated. The cool night air did nothing to sober him up before he arrived home to face Fury.

Eddie could hear music playing from inside his flat as he stepped out of the lift. Opening the front door slowly, he poked his head in to see what was happening. Along with the music he could hear a lot squawking, chirping, cooing and cheeping. He crept down the hall and looked in the living room. A group of magpies picked through the various nicknacks Eddie had lying on his coffee table. A robin sat with its face pressed up against the telly, engrossed in the music videos that were playing. A flock of seagulls sat neatly in a row on the couch. On the window ledge sat Fury, deep in conversation with a scabby looking pigeon. Fury rolled up a small piece of newspaper and snorted a fat grey line of powder. Eddie looked at the scene in front of him, stunned. Then he noticed the urn lying on its side.

'IS THAT MAH MOIRA'S ASHES?!' Eddie roared. He immediately regretted doing this. The birds, startled, flapped their wings and made their way to the open window, shitting everywhere and stirring up a cloud of his deceased wife's remains.

'Jesus Christ, Fury! Did ah say it wis awrite fur ye ae huv pals in?'

Fury gave a dismissive wave and rubbed his beak.

'You're a fucking arsehole, ye know that?'

Fury wrote FUCK UP in the thin layer of ashes on the window ledge. Then he stuck his tiny little middle finger up at Eddie. Eddie grabbed him and slung him into the cage. The bars vibrated as he slammed the door shut. He closed the window over and went to bed, sobbing. This had been comfortably the worst day of his life and he couldn't wait for it to be over. The first thing he was doing in the morning was grabbing Fury's cage and marching to the pet shop to return the fucker.

'Ah'd like tae return this bast- ah mean budgie, please,' Eddie said to the guy behind the counter. The guy peered over his glasses and into the cage. Fury sat with his back to both of them, his arms crossed. The guy gave a solemn nod. He got up from behind the counter and flipped the sign on the door round so it read CLOSED.

'C'mon through the back with me,' he said to Eddie. Eddie followed him, carrying the cage.

'What seems to be the problem?' the guy asked, lifting Fury out.

'Well, he cost me my entire life savings and snorted my wife's ashes,' Eddie fumed, setting the cage down. 'And his wings fell aff an he grew human fuckin arms.'

'I see, I see,' The guy inspected Fury's arms. 'You're looking bigger, have you been lifting weights?'

Fury nodded.

The guy laughed and turned to Eddie, expecting to see him laughing as well. He wasn't. 'Oh, please forgive my bad manners. I'm Robert by the way,' he extended a hand for Eddie to shake. Eddie declined. 'This budgie can be a bit of handful, eh? Talks a fair amount of nonsense as well.'

'Aye. No half. The cunt told me he knew aw aboot horse racing. He knows fuck all! Just gies mah money back and ah'll be on mah way.'

'He really just needs a firm hand. You sure don't want to

keep him for another week or so? See if you two can get on any better? You've already had him longer than most people manage.'

'Not a fucking chance. Just gies mah 15 quid,' Eddie thrust his open palm in front of the guy's face. 'You're lucky ahm no askin ye fur wit that hing cost me in the bookies anaw.'

'We don't do refunds, I'm afraid, sir. Can I interest you in an exchange?'

Eddie took a swipe at Fury's cage, knocking it off the table, and walked out.

'Might I suggest, sir,' Robert shouted after him, 'that you don't take betting advice from budgies in the future.'

Fury made a wanker gesture as he watched Eddie leave.

ACKNOWLEDGEMENTS

There are so many people who have played a massive part in getting these stories into your hands. First of all, I want to thank Laura and Heather at 404 Ink for taking a punt on me and publishing this book. You two are amazing.

My editor, Robbie Guillory for turning the misshapen abomination that was my original manuscript into this actual real book and making me a better writer along the way.

I also want to thank everyone on Twitter who read and shared the early drafts of some of these stories – cheers, troops.

Ricky Monahan Brown and Beth Cochrane of Interrobang, Sam Small and Mick Clocherty at The High Flight and Ross McCleary of Inky Fingers for being the first people to really support and shout about my work as well as allowing me to spew my nonsense at your excellent spoken word nights.

My amazing girlfriend, Vanessa, for putting up with me as I stressed over every single little thing in the process of writing this book – I love you.

My wee brother, Jay, for being a constant source of inspiration with the mental things he says.

And finally, my Maw – I definitely get it from you. x

ABOUT CHRIS MCQUEER

Chris McQueer is a 20-something year old writer and sales assistant from Glasgow. He has been writing for around a year and a half and in that time has had short stories published in magazines such as Gutter, The High Flight, The Football Pink and in the first issue of 404 Ink.

After leaving school at 16, Chris found himself working under the hallowed title of 'Sandwich Artist' in Subway where he was the source of constant complaints as he couldn't cut footlong sandwiches equally in half. He has also had spells working as a labourer, a crime scene cleaner, a social media customer service advisor, a barber, and also has a failed attempt at starting his own business under his belt. Now he works in a sports shop where he is regarded as the greatest seller of trainers the world has ever seen.

Chris kept his writing a secret from his friends and family for several months before his girlfriend, Vanessa, encouraged him to share his work through Twitter (@ChrisMcQueer_). Since then he has gone from strength to strength and has earned a reputation as 'That Guy Oan Twitter Who Writes Short Stories'. He currently lives at home with his mum, younger brother and Timmy the dug.